# THE WOMAN WHO BEAT THE ODDS

## THE WOMAN WHO: BOOK FOUR

### C.K. CRIGGER

**WOLFPACK PUBLISHING**
— EST 2013 —

**The Woman Who Beat the Odds**

Paperback Edition
Copyright © 2022 C.K. Crigger

Wolfpack Publishing
5130 S. Fort Apache Road, 215-380
Las Vegas, NV 89148

wolfpackpublishing.com

Paperback ISBN 978-1-63977-877-5
eBook ISBN 978-1-63977-878-2

Library of Congress Control Number: 2022944810

# THE WOMAN WHO BEAT THE ODDS

# CHAPTER 1

T.T. THURSTON STOOD BEHIND THE COUNTER IN HIS mercantile store, an uneasy feeling creeping along his bones. He didn't like the way the three fellers standing over by the gun display huddled together, looking over their shoulders and speaking too low for him to hear. If he had to be blunt, he hadn't liked their looks from the moment the cowbell at the door pinged to let him know someone had entered the store.

They'd tried opening the cabinet once, but hadn't succeeded. He kept it locked for good reason. With a cockeyed look at him, they gave up, but in his opinion, still seemed shifty. And he ought to know, having been in this business a good long time. Been robbed a few times, had thwarted robberies a couple times more. He had some idea of what to look for when it came to people with nefarious intentions. Made him glad he'd followed Mrs. Billings' advice when she suggested he put his guns in a locked display case. That was after he complained to her about somebody walking off with a used Hopkins & Allen double-action .32. The pistol hadn't been particularly valuable, but the theft still irked him. He hated thieves.

He liked Mrs. Billings, though. Respected her, too. She'd arrived at the back door early that particular morning, in time to listen to his tirade when he discovered the .32 missing. She'd been delivering her more-or-less weekly supply of butter made of her good Guernsey cow's rich milk, and a few dozen fresh eggs. Those white Langshan chickens of hers and the Orpingtons her late husband had raised were both good laying breeds. Brown eggs. Folks seemed to think the brown eggs put more roses in their children's cheeks.

A consideration neither here nor there at the moment with these men in the store, but it brought Mrs. Billings—Mrs. Deputy January Billings—to mind. He wished she were here right now. Here as Deputy Billings, he meant, not as egg and butter supplier Mrs. Billings.

T.T. touched the shotgun under the cash register counter, decided to leave it lay, and started toward the men. "Help you?" he called out.

One of them turned to face him. "This here Mauser Broomhandle in the case caught my eye. Don't see many of them around. Kind of pricey."

"They are an expensive gun," T.T. agreed. "Imported from Germany. Had somebody put in an order for it, and now he's trying to make up his mind to buy." A fib. He had no such buyer in sight. He just didn't want to open the case for these men. One man maybe he would've, but not for the three.

"Sure would like to try me one of those." The man

smiled, showing tobacco stained teeth up top with a propensity to stick out kind of like an upside-down beaver's. "Knew somebody who had one. He was pretty good with it."

"Pretty good?" One of the other men spoke up. "Too blamed good, you ask me."

T.T. knew somebody with one of the German-made pistols, too, but he wasn't going to say so on account of it might just be the same person. Mr. Eli Pasco was a well-known former bounty hunter living on a ranch not far from town, whose preferred weapon was a Mauser Broomhandle. If these shady appearing characters referred to Pasco, it justified every bit of his present caution and more.

It wasn't often total strangers rode into town. And when they did, they didn't usually arrive all at once in groups. This wasn't like the old days, when men routinely wore a gun on their hips. Come the new century, folks here liked to say they were modern and civilized, even aside from the troubles that had plagued them in the last year or so.

But T.T. took note of these three, all armed, one man with not one, but two revolvers at his side, plus a large knife. A regular *bandito* looking feller. That uneasy feeling was causing T.T. to itch. The sooner they were out of his store, out of his town, the better he'd like it.

"So," he said, putting on his friendly storekeeper face, "what can I get for you boys? Where you headed? Need any coats or gloves? Cold out today."

"Spitting snow," the bandito said.

The talkative one grinned. "Nah, nothing like that. Turns out I'm short of chew, sir. If you'd be so good as to get me a couple plugs of Beech-Nut. It's fresh, ain't it? I like my tobaccy fresh."

"Fresh." T.T. nodded. "You bet."

"And I'm short on ammunition," the feller with two guns said. "I'll take a box of .44 cartridges."

"Rimfire or center fire? Got 'em up front." T.T. headed back to the counter, relieved to get the ominous trio moving away from the guns, and ring up the sales. The third man kept his head down and turned away, which, if he'd only known it, only raised T.T.'s curiosity even higher.

*Why?*

The very question he asked himself. Answered himself, too. *Because I have a feeling.*

So much, in fact, he took special note of every detail possible, including following them out and watching them ride off down the street. He thought they might've already had a hard ride to get here.

When they disappeared from his sight, T.T. finally drew an easy breath. Mrs. Bergstrom came in just then to buy three eggs and have him weigh out some brown sugar. Seems she was baking a cake and in a hurry to get it in the oven before the afternoon was over. T.T. put the strangers to the back of his mind while he tended her needs. Business picked up later due to the usual closing rush, but as the storekeeper walked homeward, he was reminded of the men when he spotted the horse one of the unsettling strangers had been riding.

The horse stood at the rail in front of the Barefoot Saloon, and through the open saloon door T.T. saw the fellow, the one with the teeth, leaning against the bar holding forth with three or four local men. No sign of his companions. T.T. couldn't help but wonder where they'd gotten to. Down at Fat Mary's...ahem...boarding house, probably.

So. He scowled. They were still hanging around town. Yet another "why?" came to mind.

Without his conscious volition, T.T.'s feet took him to the office and jail the town marshal and the sheriff shared. Shared because the town only had funds for one building. Not that the walk did him, or his feet, a particle of good. He'd closed the mercantile at 6:15 p.m. exactly, just as he did every evening. Acting Sheriff Dabney had gone home just as exactly at 6 p.m. Which suited T.T. just fine seeing as Dabney wasn't who he wanted to talk to. But the town marshal, with whom he did want to speak, was nowhere to be found.

T.T. muttered something that would've shocked his wife, and wrapped his coat collar tighter around his neck against a flurry of snow, come early this fall. A wasted trip, but by dang, he would've liked to discuss those men with Marshal Southbrook. The marshal, he figured, being better than nothing although Mrs. Deputy Sheriff Billings would've been his real choice. She would've understood his misgivings. He still had trouble with the decision the county commissioners had made not to accept her as sheriff after Hank Schlinger quit, preferring to put a man like Dabney in the position over a female.

He spat into the road. Dabney was a chicken-hearted know-nothing, do-nothing excuse for authority. Still worried, T.T. went home, ate his dinner, and listened with half an ear while his wife grumbled because he was late getting home and her creamy sausage gravy had turned to glue.

* * *

WHILE T.T. MIGHT'VE BEEN LATE HOME the evening before, he was right on time getting to the store the next morning. Which meant 6 a.m. on the dot, he being a man who kept regular hours.

He wasn't real surprised when he spotted footprints, clear as a bell in the overnight inch or so of freshly fallen snow, leading to the mercantile's back door. Maybe not even surprised when he found the lock jimmied and the door standing half-open so's any Tom, Dick, or Harry could walk right in. He was a little surprised to find only one set of prints when there might've been three. Which didn't stop him from being madder than a groom left at the altar and swearing up a storm.

Without stopping to think the person who made the tracks must still be inside since there were none going the opposite direction, he didn't pause as he plunged on into the store. As he figured, the wet footprints led straight toward the gun display case, but before he got more than half a dozen steps, something slammed into the side of his head and he went down like a steer at the slaughter.

He was still unconscious an hour later when a line formed outside the front and someone thought to go to his home and ask if he was ill. Shaken, his wife Edna produced a key to the front door. It didn't occur to anyone to simply go to the back entry, though most everyone knew that's where T.T. always entered. Anyway, T.T. awakened to find his wife patting his cheeks and sobbing over him. A lump on his head the size of two of Mrs. Billings' largest chicken eggs put together—or so it felt—hurt like Hades. As he wasn't shy about letting Edna know.

Another thing that hurt was the theft of the Mauser Broomhandle C96 semi-automatic pistol, an extra 7.635 x 25mm clip, and two boxes of the ammunition to fit it.

Though somebody had called for both Acting Sheriff Dabney and Marshal Adam Southbrook, a madder than hops T.T. gestured to Tim Thurston Jr, his son and clerk—arriving late to work as usual—and gave him orders to fetch Mrs. Billings. He ignored the kid's plea that it was a long cold ride out to her place.

Dabney arrived on the scene where, no surprise to anyone, he fluttered about like a discombobulated rooster, all noise and of no use. Southbrook, with more sense of purpose, listened to T.T.'s mumbled explanation and description of the three men, and set out to search the town.

Doc LeBret, more practically, showed up in record time. Kneeling beside his still woozy patient, he felt T.T.'s head with surprisingly gentle fingers. "No dents," he informed the relieved bunch of onlookers. "Good thing Thurston has a hard head. Take more than a bump to put him down."

T. T. was not amused, especially since he'd just spent the last hour knocked out cold on the floor of his shop. Bump? Heck of a bump, in his opinion. Gingerly, he touched the swelling.

Doc bandaged the storekeeper's head, offering headache powders that didn't do a blessed thing either for T.T.'s headache or his short temper.

Nobody noticed yet another stranger who stepped off the morning train with a smile on his face and a duffle bag for luggage. He walked downtown from the depot, stopping at a cafe that sat catty-corner across the street from the mercantile, where he seemed to ponder the activity at the store. A good-looking fellow of early middle-age, his broad, cheerful smile grew even wider as he ordered breakfast.

# CHAPTER 2

JANUARY BILLINGS OPENED THE DOOR TO LET HER DOG Pen, short for Penelope, outside. It had snowed during the night, an inch or more. Showed no sign of melting anytime soon, either. Having stepped onto the stoop without a jacket, January gave a violent shiver. Over at the barn, a feather of smoke drifted from the stovepipe rising above the roof, a sign her hired man, Johnny Johnson, was up and about doing the morning chores.

Her good neighbor Bo Cobb and she shared Johnny's labors between them, but the Billings ranch didn't have a bunkhouse, so Johnny had a cozy room fixed up in the barn for the nights he stayed over. It wasn't as if he could sleep in the house, after all, what with January being a young widow and he an even younger man about to turn nineteen.

She gave a snort as a recurring thought shot through her mind. As if anybody would know if hanky panky went on out here on the ranch, whether in the house or in the barn. Not that it ever would, still, she had to take care. It might be silly but she needed to be above reproach if she ever wanted to run for sheriff.

On the other hand, she wasn't sure she did.

January chuckled as she watched her dog shovel her nose through the snow and scoot it along. Her heart filled, watching the old dog play like a puppy. A metal triangle hung from the back stoop eaves. The cold bit into her fingers as she picked up the clanger and gave the triangle a few whaps. Johnny appeared and waved, acknowledging her signal that breakfast was on the table.

Over the flapjacks and eggs, eggs always being in plentiful supply around the ranch, they discussed the day's work.

"We could use more molasses to make up Etta's mash," Johnny said, Etta being a mare that had foaled late and was still nursing. "For both her and your Mollie horse. The poor old girl had a rough trip finding her way home."

"That's true." Mollie got lost last spring after she ran away from gunfire. She'd been with Eli Pasco at the time, and he hadn't had time to stop and search for her, although he'd gone back later. Lord only knows where the old mare had been. January had been so overcome she'd cried when she went to the barn a couple weeks ago and found Mollie there, munching hay as if she'd never been gone. How she'd got there was anyone's guess.

"If we have bad weather, we might have trouble getting to town," Johnny was saying. "One of us better make a trip soon."

He looked hopeful he'd be the one.

January smiled. "I'll go today. Go ahead and put

molasses on the list, but don't make up too much of the feed at a time. Etta's filly needs weaned and I don't want Mollie getting fat. I'm taking most of the other horses off that mix now since they're not working as hard. Except for the Shires, of course. They'll be out clearing roads." She hired the team out to the county for road work. It helped with the ranch's bottom line.

Johnny nodded.

"It's too cold to work on the new house today," January added. "But I've got eggs and butter for T.T."

The house January mentioned was the one she and Shay had begun shortly before Shay was murdered. More than a year ago, now. She still worked on the house sporadically, although sometimes she wondered why. Why go through the motions? This house, Shay's old house, was plenty big and fine enough for her. It's just that it was farther from town than the new one and inconvenient should anything come up. The sheriff's job, for instance.

Johnny's lower lip stuck out, an indication he thought sure that since she had business at the mercantile, he'd be left to mind the ranch.

But today, January surprised him. "Don't pout, Mr. Johnson. It doesn't become you. We'll both visit the metropolis. You can drive the buckboard. I'm riding. Hoot needs the exercise."

"How about Pen?"

The dog looked up at hearing her name, but January shook her head. "Not today. We'll have dinner in town and the cafe won't let her in. I don't want her getting in any fights with the strays."

"No. She'd be the one Dabney'd throw in doggie jail. Or he'd take a gun to her."

"Huh. He'd play hell."

Johnny laughed, his mood restored although January hadn't been joking. But then, neither had he.

Too much had happened in January's life for her to blithely go unarmed. Not even just into town to deliver a load of butter and eggs to T.T. Thurston. Carpentry being one of her fortes, she'd built a rack with a quick release mechanism under the buckboard's seat. Since Johnny, who'd already been wounded once while in her employ, still most often went around without his rifle, he was aware of the shotgun hidden there. No one else knew, though. January's sincere wish was to never have need to use it. She just preferred being prepared.

Once they left the yard with Johnny driving the buckboard, January reined Hoot, the silvery gray gelding that had belonged to her husband, up close beside him and said, "I'll meet you at the bridge. With this snow, I want to make sure the new house is closed up tight."

Johnny nodded. "See you there. I won't be far behind."

January clucked to Hoot, gave Johnny a wave, and rode on ahead. Hoot tossed his head, wanting to run, although, unsure of the footing, she held him back.

It didn't take them long to reach the bridge. The bridge she'd built with her own two hands over the stream at Kindred Crossing as a sort of community gift. It lay on land her grandfather, one of the first settlers in the country, had homesteaded. The same grandfather who'd gone insane and carved a big letter S in her cheek with his knife when she'd been a child. She'd come to terms with the scar nowadays, thanks to Shay Billings, but the habit to turn her face to the "good" side when meeting people was pretty well ingrained.

Her new house rose above where the old barn used to be, set a couple hundred yards from the bridge. A house with a stone foundation, created from rocks cleared from the land around it. The outer shell was complete, with a roof and windows and doors, although she thought she might put in another window or two. The interior was mostly still a blank canvas, except where she planned the kitchen and a bedroom. An indoor privy—bathroom, that is—was on her list, as well, if she could find anyone with knowledge of plumbing to hire. Could be she'd have to learn the basics herself.

But as she drew Hoot to a halt in front of the house, she discovered the door hung ajar. Dismayed, though certain she'd secured it yesterday, she dismounted and approached cautiously. It took only seconds to find evidence the house had been entered. Used. And abused. Snow had gotten inside, piling onto the raw plank flooring.

"Son of a..." January sucked in air, stifling her words. It was cold in the room, although earlier it must've been warm because the hearth in the front room had a residue of ashes and soot where a fire had been left unattended and allowed to burn out. Evidence of a meal cooked and eaten littered the kitchen area where a kitchen stove was already connected to a stovepipe. Also a gnawed bacon rind, bits of burned cornbread, and greasy drips from something unsavory, all sure to entice a rodent invasion. Somebody had even spat tobacco juice on the raw wood of the floor, not once, but many times. The air reeked of it. Between that and the danger of warping where the planks had gotten wet from the snow, she suspected she might need to replace some of the floor.

The final straw came when she found whoever had stayed there had thought to do some shooting, using a knot in the fine pine paneling she'd installed around the fireplace as a target. Until a bullet ricocheted off the stone beneath the wood and evidently changed his mind. She found the bullet where it had burrowed into the wall across the room.

Outside, Johnny called "whoa" to the horse pulling the buckboard. He jumped down and stepped inside. "What the heck?" His nose wrinkled as he surveyed the damage. "Somebody has a lot of nerve."

January could barely breathe as a hot flush of anger threatened to consume her. "They'll rue the day if I catch them."

"They?"

"As in more than one. Look over there." She pointed to the area around the fireplace. "You can see where they set their saddles to serve as headrests for their bedrolls. I see disturbances in the dust for at least two, maybe three people."

"Hey now!" Johnny whistled and eyed his boss with admiration. "You're a good detective, boss."

It had taken her months to get him to call her by her first name, but he still preferred the title of boss.

She sighed. "A detective who needs to buy a couple good sturdy padlocks. Hope T.T. has some in stock."

Johnny snorted. "He will. He has everything crowded into that store."

But they were to discover that while T.T. had locks aplenty, he lacked one thing—the Mauser

Broomhandle C96 semi-automatic previously in his gun display case.

They were only a mile outside of town when they met Thurston Jr. on his way to the ranch and saved him a trip in the cold.

\* \* \*

No MATTER that T.T. had spent an hour this morning unconscious on the floor of his mercantile. He was behind the counter now, tending to customer orders and running the cash drawer just like always. The only thing different is that his wife insisted on placing a stool there for him to sit on.

He wouldn't admit it for the world, but he was truly grateful to her. The dizzy spells, along with his aching head, were driving him to distraction. He tried to hide them by clutching the counter for support when he felt himself tilting sideways off the stool. Edna, of course, noticed, although she said nothing. Too used to his ways to think he'd give up his position before the workday was done. Especially since so many people had seen him laid out on the floor. He figured it was the supreme embarrassment.

Edna tied up a parcel for Mrs. Coons, and came over to stand beside him and pat his hand. "Can I get you anything, dear? Coffee? Tea? A cup of water? The doctor said you need to drink plenty of fluids."

T.T. forced a grin—unless it was a grimace. "Whiskey'd hit the spot."

Edna frowned. "I don't think Doctor LeBret meant whiskey."

"No, but I do."

She went off to fetch him a cup of something, and when she returned he thought for just a moment maybe she really had brought him the desired alcohol. Alas, when he lifted the cup to his lips, he discovered some kind of anemic tea. He hated tea. It didn't do a thing for his aching head, either. It seemed Edna was bound to add to his punishment.

T.T.'s spirits lifted when January Billings, bundled against the cold in a bright woolen cap, a heavy coat, and knitted mittens strode briskly into the store through the back.

"Mr. Thurston," she said, "Timothy says you've been attacked and robbed. What is Dabney doing about it? Or did Marshal Southbrook find the men?" She eyed him and frowned. "You don't look well. You're white as a snowman and I can see the bump on your head from here. Shouldn't you be home and, most likely, resting in bed?"

T.T., aware of his wife nodding her head at January as if to say she agreed and that it wasn't *her* fault, answered for himself. "Naturally I'm here. It's my store, ain't it? Even if a thief did get some licks in."

His gaze went from Mrs. Billings to his son, who'd entered behind her. "How'd you get here so fast? Did Tim fly?" He was the only person in town who called the younger Thurston by his shortened name.

January, as she was meant to do, chuckled. "Wouldn't that be something? But no. Johnny Johnson and I were already on our way to town with a load of butter and eggs. We met Timothy just outside of town."

T.T. feigned good cheer. "Ah. Right on time. I'm powerful low on both those items. Folks'll want to stock up if we're in for more bad weather." He attempted to stand, staggered instead, and grabbed for the counter. "Give me a minute. I'll add up what I owe you."

Removing her mittens and pretending not to notice his unsteady stance, she shrugged. "That's all right. It can wait. I repeat, what's Dabney doing about the robbery and assault?"

Scowling, T.T. shook his head, causing him to lose balance again. Edna got to him just in time to keep him from going down. After a moment, he said, "Southbrook talked to folks and found some witnesses who saw those men leave town not long after I usually get to the store. But about Dabney, who knows? If I had to guess, I figure you'll find him over at the jail drinking coffee and complaining that he can't be in two places at once. The main place being right where he is and doing nothing. He told me hours ago he figured whoever hit and robbed me was long gone and probably out of his jurisdiction by now."

January huffed out a sigh and raised her brows. "I need to know exactly when and what happened. Timothy mentioned you talking about three men who'd been in the store yesterday afternoon and who raised some suspicions. Tell me about them."

It was probably a good thing a bit of time had passed between then and now, T.T. thought. It had given him a chance to get his memories of the suspected thieves down on paper. He and January had had a conversation early one morning when she brought in supplies, and she'd told him things that helped when it came to accurate descriptions and even hints of motivation.

He rummaged under the counter where he'd stuffed the pad with his notes. "Here." He thrust it at her and cocked his thumb at his son. "Go help Johnson unload the buckboard. Keep count of everything. I'm gonna owe Mrs. Billings some money."

"Yessir."

She looked up from her perusal of his scrawl. "I've got a list. I figure I'll owe you. By the by, you aren't the only one with trouble, Mr. Thurston."

"I'm not?"

"Umm." She was reading from his notes again. "Someone—more than one—got into the house I'm building and did some damage." Her mouth twisted. "Going by your experience, I'd lay money on it being the same bunch of men. I guess it's a good thing I wasn't there working by myself. I'd rather not wear a gun when I'm crawling up and down ladders and whatnot, but could be I'll need to."

T.T. had plenty to say about the danger of shooting herself in the leg, but as January was involved with his notes, he went silent until she looked up.

"I appreciate this, sir." A little smile twitched at her lips and lifted the scar on her cheek. "What did Dabney have to say when he read them?"

The forceful blast of air from his snort stirred the roll of wrapping paper at the counter's edge. "Him. I don't know as the man can even read. I wrote these up later. He just listened with half an ear at my descriptions and said, 'What am I supposed to do? Go up to every man in town and check 'em on your say so?' Didn't mention about following any kind of trail out of town, even after Southbrook came back with what he'd discovered. Which wasn't a whole lot of anything."

She blinked. "Did you tell him yes, that it's part of his job?"

He shook his head. "Nah. Didn't figure it was any use. That's when I sent Tim to find you. So. What do you think?"

"I think it's a fine example of note-taking and there's a lot to keep in mind. But for now, the object of the theft is my first consideration. That, and what you overheard one of the men say."

T.T.'s eyes, still a little blurry from the thump on his head, sharpened. "Which part?"

"About knowing someone who had a Broomhandle and was pretty good with it. Even more, what the other one said. About being too good. Whatever 'too good' actually means."

He nodded. He'd been sure she'd pick up on that. "What will you do now?"

She shrugged her coat closer around her. "Ride out and talk with the man we both know who owns a Broomhandle. And who is good, very good, with it."

"I figured." T.T. gave a sigh. "What about Dabney? You going to clear it with him?"

At this, she laughed. "Think it'd make any difference? But I suppose I should."

# CHAPTER 3

JANUARY, SPOTTING JOHNNY FINGER A FANCY RED AND black striped shirt over in the men's wear section of the store, asked T.T. to slip it into her order. The kid worked hard for her, and she suspected he'd be doing even more if she had to replace Dabney. What's more, if she recalled right, there was a dance at the schoolhouse on Saturday night and Johnny would want to impress the Langley girl with some new duds.

Not that he needed the shirt, January thought, smiling. Evie was head over heels anyway.

After instructing Johnny about the molasses and the locks and a few other items on her shopping list, January walked over to the sheriff's office.

She was of two minds about the situation with T.T. How much should she confide to Dabney? Was there any point in telling him about the invasion of her half-built house? Should she tell him she planned to talk to the local owner of a gun like the one stolen from the mercantile? She doubted he'd even realize the man she referred to was Eli Pasco.

As it turned out, she needn't have worried. Dabney was nowhere to be found. She found only Marshal Adam Southbrook in residence, bent over some paperwork on his side of the single room.

Sucking on a long twisp of his mustache as if trying to hold back a smirk, he informed her Dabney was out for the day. "Soon as I learned those fellers T.T. told us about had left town and passed it on to Dabney, he decided to come down sick. Said he thought he was catching a bad cold, maybe even pneumonia, and went home for his wife to make him a poultice."

"A poultice?" Involuntarily, January swallowed down the wrong pipe and coughed. She blamed it on the bubble of laughter rising in her throat.

The marshal let his own laugh loose. "Yup."

"In other words, he didn't want to get on a horse and go looking for trouble. Well, if he decides his pneumonia is better, tell him..." she hesitated, "tell him—"

"I won't tell him anything," the marshal said. "Little weasel don't want to know about anything that requires effort anyhow, especially anything that might take him out of town." He paused. "I got a notion you're lookin' into what happened over at the mercantile this morning."

"At Mr. Thurston's request."

The marshal nodded. "I figured. Smart. Everybody'll be better off if Dabney keeps his nose out. If you need help, Mrs. Billings, let me know."

"I will." Heading for the door, January stopped midstride. "Why don't you run for sheriff, Mr. Southbrook?"

"Too old. Too broke-down. Too tired." Southbrook winked.

Granted, she thought, he was pushing sixty, and he

did have a gimpy leg due to a horse wreck. But too tired? She wasn't so sure.

Returning to the mercantile, January sent Johnny back to the ranch with orders to use the new locks on her house at the bridge when he went by, and to please stay at the ranch until she got home. She mounted Hoot then, and set out toward Eli Pasco's place.

Misgivings assailed her about seeing Eli again. The last time had been in the spring at Sheriff Hank Schlinger's wedding when she'd coerced him into a dance. She'd thought maybe— But no.

Nevertheless, her heart beat a little faster when she guided Hoot into his ranch yard and stopped at the house.

Pasco had done a lot of work around the place since the first time she saw it. Painted, mended, dug, planted. Built a new outhouse and made it whimsical with flower boxes and a porch. Maybe she'd have to copy his design when she moved to the bridge. Depended on if she found a trained plumber.

Eli had attended to the barn, as well, and he'd erected a series of good rail corrals. A cat, she thought it the same one the Winklers had abandoned when they sold out, sat in the sunshine with two kittens cavorting around her, chasing their mama's whipping tail.

She dismounted, brushed creases from the split riding skirt she'd donned for the trip to town, and mounted the porch steps to knock on the door. And though she waited, and anticipated, the door remained closed.

Of course. He wouldn't be sitting around inside. He'd be out checking his livestock after last night's early cold and snow. As she should be doing, except this thing with T.T. had come up and to indulge him with a little investigating was the least she could do.

Determined to speak with Pasco now, she turned and followed a beaten path to the barn, thence on to the corrals. She found Windswept lazing in one by himself. A couple mares were separated from him in another, and a black goat stood atop the manure pile keeping watch over them all. January couldn't help her giggle. A goat. Imagine that!

There was no sign of Henry, the horse Eli had ridden during their search for Windswept and Zora Winkler, but she spotted tracks leading off toward the river and the area where Eli had mentioned he planned to run a small herd of cattle. She whistled to bring Hoot to her and they followed the tracks, passing under towering pines where the sigh of their branches made a soft accompaniment to the songs of birds.

Before long, she spied Pasco in the distance, fixing a fence rubbed down by cattle on their way to water. Henry's head hung over Eli's shoulder, observing. January knew, for all the trouble they went through to get Windswept back after he was stolen, his speed would never make up for Henry's steady companionship.

Eli looked up when Henry and Hoot's whickered exchange of greetings announced her arrival. Even at a distance she saw something cross his face. What? Was she an unwelcome visitor?

But then, her visit had to do with a robbery and assault. Nothing personal. Not between January Billings and Eli Pasco.

Eli leaned on his posthole diggers and watched her

come. She stopped beside him, Hoot shaking his head up and down as if to say "howdy."

"Mrs. Billings," Eli said, cool as could be.

"Good day, Mr. Pasco," she said in return.

At the dance last spring, he'd called her January. She'd called him Eli, the tip of her tongue lingering on the L sound.

"It's been a while." His dark eyes studied her.

"Yes. I hope you had a good racing season this past summer. Did Windswept pan out on the circuit as you expected? I heard some good reports."

Small talk, never easy for her.

A muscle in his jaw flexed. "Pretty much paid our way. Got some mares scheduled for breeding in the spring." He paused a beat. "To what do I owe the honor of your visit?"

Now she was here, she hardly knew what to say. Resorting to blunt speech, as if they were strangers and their shared adventure never happened, she plunged ahead. "Thurston's mercantile was robbed this morning, and T.T. attacked. He was struck from behind and knocked unconscious. Items were taken."

Eli went still. "That's a shame. I'm sorry to hear he got hurt." A single brow lifted. "But what does that have to do with me?"

"Probably nothing." She was certain it did. Not politic to say so, though. Or not at this point. "One thing was stolen which brought you to mind."

"Me?" Eyes narrowing, he stared at her. "You think I'm a thief? In case you've forgotten, Mrs. Billings, I work the other side of the law. I catch thieves and bring them to the law. Used to, I mean. I didn't become one of them."

They both knew bounty hunters often pushed the line between legal and not, especially when the runaway was wanted dead or alive. Of the two, the dead were easier to handle.

"I'm sorry. I didn't mean to imply otherwise." Inwardly, January swore at her clumsy tongue. "Of course I don't think you're a thief. I should've said, one of the suspected thieves said something that might—just *might*—have been a reference to you."

He plunged the diggers into the soft soil. Once, twice, then said, "What would that be? A reference to me? In what way?"

The questions were what she'd been waiting for. "You may know Mr. Thurston had taken a special order for a gun like yours. The Mauser Broomhandle is rather distinctive. It intrigues a lot of men. This time, the would-be buyer backed out when the gun arrived, so it's been on display and for sale in the mercantile. Yesterday, three men entered the store and spent a good deal of time eyeing the gun and whispering among themselves. One mentioned knowing someone who had that particular model. Thurston also heard another say something about that man being good with it. 'Too blamed good' were the exact words. Or so I'm told."

Eli breathed in deeply. "And you think he meant me? Why?"

"*Thurston* thought he meant you, perhaps in a reference to your previous profession. And you are known to be proficient in its use." She added the last part rather dryly.

"Huh." The diggers shushed into the hole again. "You know Thurston is half-deaf."

"Yes. But he's also an accomplished lip-reader. He

has to be, dealing with customers day in and day out."
He'd pulled a gun on her once, early one morning when
she entered the store from behind him. He hadn't been
expecting anyone and being hard of hearing, she'd startled him. Too bad he hadn't been as wary this morning.

Eli measured the depth of the posthole with a notch
cut into the handle, and satisfied, set the diggers aside.
"I'm busy, Mrs. Billings. I'm also out of the profession. I
don't see this situation has anything to do with me. The
county has a sheriff. If there are questions, why isn't he
the one asking me for answers?"

Anger flared. Was Eli being difficult because she was
the one asking? "He should be, of course. He seems to
have opted out of his duties. Nobody trusts Dabney so
Mr. Thurston asked me to look into it. He took note of
some of these men's characteristics, in case you might
be concerned."

"I'm not." He picked up a cedar post and stood it in
the hole.

January took a deep breath and carried on. She
was here, asking questions and begging for help, on
behalf of her friend T.T. she told herself. It wasn't
personal. "One of them, according to T.T., has ugly
tobacco-stained teeth protruding so his jaw juts out
and is misaligned. He can barely close his mouth,
according to T.T. Another wore two guns, hung
bandolier style. He didn't get a real good look at the
third man, because he kept his head down and turned
away. He did say the fellow was small, dark, and didn't
talk much."

At this, Eli picked up the shovel and began filling in
the hole around the post, tamping as he went. His
expression, she saw, had switched from anger to some

kind of acknowledgment. She believed the descriptions had struck a chord.

"Damn," he muttered, almost inaudible.

She waited, her hand resting on Hoot's neck.

The post was set before Eli looked up. "All right. I'll finish fixing this fence and ride on into town and talk to Thurston. You did say the men left town?"

"Yes. Or at least, no one has seen them since last night."

"Then I expect it's a waste of my time. I'll be along, Mrs. Billings, when I'm done here."

It was dismissal, plain and simple. And frigid as a day in December.

Angry again, January flung herself into the saddle and spun Hoot, clucking to him to hasten away. She hadn't had the chance to mention the muddle made of her house which, when pondered upon as she had on the way out here, could very well be connected with the mercantile robbery. But then, from the looks of things, Eli Pasco wouldn't have cared anyway.

* * *

ALL ELI HAD KNOWN to do when he looked up and saw her coming was to assume a layer of unconcern. Deceptive, as he'd felt an inner heat set fire to his bones and blood. Or so it seemed. He'd been working hard when she appeared. His breath had been short and though the day was cold, he'd been sweating. He thought at first he may've been seeing things. It took Henry greeting January's gray gelding to convince him she was even real. And though his heart gave a jerk, he couldn't say if it meant joy or...or apprehension.

Some of both, he guessed. Hadn't he just spent the last several months convincing himself he'd forgotten all about her?

And now here she was. January Billings, bold as brass and settled on doing a job.

As if the spring had never happened.

"Mrs. Billings," he'd greeted her at a pause in his work, and "Good day, Mr. Pasco," she replied. Like strangers. Both of them.

Even the news about T.T. Thurston's misfortune, while regrettable, hadn't shaken him from his intent to remain uninvolved. Not until Thurston's descriptions of the suspects were revealed. Then it seemed he had no choice but to at least talk with Thurston.

But not to January. Not yet.

He'd meant to replace the whole section of fence while he was here working, but settled now for a temporary patch. If the thieves were truly gone, he could come back and finish the job the way he'd intended. It they were still around, the fence would hold until he found the time.

If he had to break down and tell January what he suspected about these thieves—well, he'd rather not. But the situation had suddenly become like an infection getting into his blood. He had to discover the truth and eradicate the poison.

When he figured enough time had passed for January to have returned to town ahead of him, Eli mounted Henry and followed. After talking with Thurston, he'd have a drink at the Barefoot saloon before he returned home. See if there were any whispers about the incident. If the men Thurston had described to January were who he thought they were,

Dabney might have to call for help from other law enforcement. He wouldn't need to handle the situation by himself.

And more importantly, neither would January.

Upon arriving in town, Eli found Thurston, due no doubt to his wife's intervention, had agreed to close the store early. A sure sign, some might say, he'd been hurt worse than he admitted. Eli entered the mercantile seconds before she came to lock the door, and then she didn't want to allow him to stay. Thurston's insistence prevailed, but she remained watchful.

"Come into the office, Mr. Pasco," T.T. said. "Edna, is the coffee still hot? Looks like Mr. Pasco could use a cup to take the chill off."

Arms akimbo in a show of displeasure, Mrs. Thurston scowled. "It's time for your headache powders, Mr. Thurston. You should be home in bed."

"Yes, dear. But me and Mr. Pasco have need of a discussion. I'll be home directly. You go on ahead. But coffee first, if you don't mind."

It seemed clear that she did mind. Her glare seared Eli. "Do not keep him long, you hear me? He needs to be where I can take care of him."

T.T. tried to object, but Eli smiled. "Yes, ma'am."

The coffee was only tepid. Maybe a sign they'd best keep their conversation short. Another thing about the coffee Eli soon discovered; the offer had been a ruse— and an opportunity for T.T. to pour in a shot of good Jack Daniels Tennessee whiskey to add some flavor.

"Ah," T.T. said, swigging a mouthful, "that's what I've been needing all day."

Eli grinned and pushed his cup toward the store-keeper. "I don't blame you. Have this cup, too. I can always get a drink in the saloon before supper." He'd planned on visiting the saloon anyhow, as January had told him about one of the men stopping in there.

Eyes glinting, T.T. didn't argue.

In the end, Thurston didn't have a whole lot more to say than what January had told him. A couple snatches of conversation that T.T. said raised his hackles. Something about doing like they'd done in Republic, a mention that had made all three laugh, one in a high-pitched voice. Oh, the descriptions were more complete, too. Which, he had to admit, didn't make Eli feel any better. The beaver-toothed man could be no other than Desi Holloway, which meant the man with the two guns must be Paul Krakowski—known as Krak. The two had ridden together for years. And served time together, down in Walla Walla.

As for the third member of the group... Yeah. Him.

Eli had to ask. "About the third person. What about that one? You haven't mentioned him."

T.T. shrugged. "That's because he didn't have much to say. Kind of kept himself in the background." He thought a moment. "Matter of fact, I didn't actually hear him say anything. Just that laugh. And I couldn't..." He gulped, as if willing himself to admit what most folks already knew. "When he did talk, I couldn't tell what he was saying. He kept his head down so I couldn't see his face, let alone his lips. I know he mumbled something a couple times. I just don't know what."

Eli figured it had cost the storekeeper his pride to confess he had trouble with his hearing. "Anything else you noticed about him?" he asked. "The way he was dressed? If he was armed?"

"Yeah, he had a gun, all right. Wore it on his left

hip." T.T. shrugged. "As for the rest, well, he was short. I think I said that already. Kind of skinny. Seemed like his clothes were too big for his frame. Ah. Wait. I remember something else. His hat."

"His hat?"

"Yeah. He didn't just settle it on his head. He tied it down, like he was going out in a windstorm." T.T. demonstrated with his hands.

Eli drew a breath. "Thurston, could this person have been a woman dressed up like a man?"

T.T.'s eyes bugged. "A woman?" He paused as if thinking. "Well, yeah."

Eli had a sick feeling he knew just who she was, too. Ruby Pasco, his father's former wife. She'd come back to haunt him.

He didn't let on to T.T. about his suspicions. No sense in stirring up controversy if it wasn't called for. Then, just to make sure he didn't make an enemy of Mrs. Thurston, he helped T.T. lock up and had him mount Henry, giving the storekeeper a ride home.

Snow spat out of the dark sky as he made his way back to the center of town where lights reflected off the snow. This last bit of information didn't change his plans any. He still wanted to see if anyone had talked to Desi Holloway or even Krak Krakowski, although the latter wasn't noted for being gregarious. But Desi, well, with a few drinks in him he could be depended on to shoot off his mouth in the saloon.

In the morning something even less pleasurable awaited him. Like it or not, he had to talk to January Billings. He couldn't make up his mind if he looked forward to seeing her again or just the opposite.

# CHAPTER 4

BACK IN TOWN, JANUARY HADN'T WAITED FOR ELI TO show up. She spoke with the marshal, taking no more than five minutes, letting him know who Pasco suspected two of the men to be. Southbrook said he'd look through any wanted papers that had come in, both to him and to the sheriff's office.

Then it was on to the mercantile where she let T.T. know to expect Eli soon. But only when Mrs. Thurston wasn't looking. T.T.'s wife had let everyone know she thought they should let the robbery slide. She didn't want anyone coming back to exact revenge on T.T. Or their son, when he took over the store.

January didn't agree with the woman. Not at all. But when you came right down to it, she'd done all she could. Lacking proper clues and proper authority, it didn't seem her responsibility to step in. Well, no more than she had already. At least T.T. seemed soothed, thinking action was being undertaken. Guilt burdened her at the lie.

Afterward, she rode home alone through the gathering darkness. Pen greeted her with a dog's usual enthusiasm, tail wagging and little excited yips. Also, she found Johnny had cleaned up after he cooked his supper, and even provided enough leftovers for her. She hadn't felt up to stirring the fire in the stove and cooking.

Johnny, not only a good employee and a good friend, would be her choice for a deputy if she ever were the sheriff. Either deputy or manager for her ranch. His choice.

Not, she assured herself, that she planned on running for sheriff. Ever. She'd had enough of being dragged into either her own or other people's fights, no matter how righteous they might be. Avenging her husband's death had been as far as she had ever thought to carry the load. She'd learned her lesson in the spring when she'd almost been murdered not once, but several times. A madman—no two madmen, twins —had set upon her and only by a miracle had she come out alive.

*No more.*

And yet, the idea had been planted.

In the morning, she'd barely had time to cook breakfast for Johnny and send him on his way to the Cobb ranch to spend the day working for Bo, when a knock on the door announced a visitor. At first she thought it must be Johnny returning for something, overcome to the point of forgetfulness by the gift of the red shirt, but it wasn't.

Pen had gotten up and rushed ahead of her. The dog gave a little welcoming "woof," her tail swooshing through the air strongly enough to create a breeze.

January opened the door and came face-to-face with

Eli Pasco. Eyes widening, she was unaware of her scar
turning color until she felt the heat. And Eli noticed.
She knew he did by the way his gaze flicked to her
cheek and as quickly away. He reached down to scratch
behind Pen's ears.

"What's gone wrong?" she demanded. "Has there
been another robbery? Another assault?"

"No. Or not that I know of. Sorry," he said. "I didn't
mean to startle you."

She let out a breath. Why then, was he here?

Looking beyond him, she noticed he'd thrown a
lightweight canvas tarp over his saddle. The tarp
covered most of Henry's back and allowed the horse to
cool down slowly. An indication this—whatever this
was—might take more than a couple minutes.

"Come in." January opened the door wider and,
feeling the chill, motioned Eli into the house. Questions
drove helter-skelter through her mind, but she voiced
none of them. Let him begin. He must be here for
serious reasons, not because he missed her. Or to apolo-
gize for his coldness yesterday. She wasn't much
surprised to learn she was right on only one count, the
first.

Spinning on her heel, she led the way to the kitchen
and indicated a chair. Certainly politer than he'd been.
"Coffee?"

He nodded and sat. "Please."

She placed a big pottery mug in front of him and
saw his nose twitch. The room still smelled of coffee,
fried ham, and flapjacks with a topping of apple syrup.
The apples were from the orchard Shay had started.
She sold many a box of them to neighbors for a little
extra pocket money.

"You're here early, no doubt without your breakfast." She moved toward the stove. "Are you hungry?"

He was. She knew he was, even though he shook his head. "Don't bother. I'm fine."

"No bother." Ignoring his denial, she stirred up the embers and pulled the skillets back onto the stove plates to heat. She was glad to have something to do that kept her hands busy and her back turned to him.

They spoke of the weather until she set a plate of food on the table in front of him, a knife and fork clattering down beside it.

"All right, tell me what's happened? Have those thieves been back? Is T.T. all right? The mercantile?"

"Looked fine when I rode out," Eli assured her hastily. "It's something Thurston said yesterday when I was talking to him and I thought you should know about it. After you left town, he remembered more about one of them. Well, all of them, actually. More than he told you." He cut a couple reasonably-sized bites of ham and poked one in his mouth. He slipped the other to the dog.

Her mouth tightened. "Good. I hoped he would. And I hope he'll tell Southbrook. Or even Dabney. Southbrook is probably the better choice, but T.T. knows that."

"He will, but I think he'd rather tell you."

She plopped down in her chair and picked up her coffee. "I'm not the sheriff. It's not my place to mix in with the troubles in town. I should've refused to even listen to T.T. yesterday, let alone bring your name into it. You were right to hesitate. I'm sorry."

"When a friend asks for help, it's hard to ignore them." He smiled wryly at her.

Which friendship? The one between her and T.T. Thurston, or did he mean himself and her? Or were they friends at all? She sighed, sat back and crossed her ankles, just like a real lady. "So what has happened between then and now? I take it something has."

"Apparently Dabney is sick in bed and nursing his pneumonia with his wife's poultices. Doc LeBret has *not* been called in." He grinned briefly. "But Southbrook found paper on two men who sound like the thieves. A Desi Holloway and Paul Krakowski. They only got out of prison a month ago and are already on the newest wanted list being circulated." Grin fading, he finished his meal and pushed the plate aside. "It's the third member of their little band that concerns me."

"The small person. T.T. didn't have much to say about him."

"No. That one kept apart as if to remain unidentifiable. But Thurston remembered a couple things. Oddities."

January sat up straight. "Such as?"

This time it was Eli who sighed. "Like the way he tied his hat onto his head as if afraid it might pop off. Like a strangely high-pitched laugh. Or the fact something was out of place with the fit of his clothes."

It took January only a moment to figure out the hints. "Is he saying the third person is a woman?"

Eli made an undefinable sound, maybe agreement.

Her eyes narrowed. "Any idea who this woman might be? There aren't many notable outlaw women in this part of the country. Not ones who actually ride with a gang. Most female criminals are found in cities."

But they both knew of at least one who went where

she wanted and did as she pleased. The same one who had gotten away in the spring.

They looked at each other. After a while, January said, "Do you think it's possible? Would she come back here?"

"She's a vengeful woman, January. I think you know that. And she fancies a grudge against me."

Oh, yes. She did. And one against January, as well. "Not to mention she's as crooked as a dog's hind leg." Then she looked at her dog lying beside her chair. "Sorry, Pen. Didn't mean to insult you."

The dog's tail thumped.

"There is another thing." Eli's gaze fixed on the dog. "Ruby seldom travels with this small of a gang. Only two men? And neither one with money, looks, or class. That's not to her usual taste. Especially the money part. She does like to live high on the hog."

"So you're saying there are more of these ex-convicts hanging around and we just haven't seen them? Or maybe these two are gathered here waiting for more to come wandering in?" She stood and paced around the room. Once. Twice. Then stopped to glare at him. "So what else can they be waiting for? What do they want?"

Eli shook his head. Having finished his breakfast, he stood, too, ready to leave now he'd delivered his news and warning.

"Or who?" January said, fierce and angry as she followed him out. "If she is after you or me, why rob the mercantile and savage T.T.?"

"Everything is a game or a competition for her. She likes the challenge. And she likes to win. You already know she possesses a cruel streak as wide as that bridge you built."

Oh, January had figured the cruel streak within an hour of first meeting Ruby. Even the foofaraw over the Mauser Broomhandle told a tale of sorts. It might be a warning to Eli, announcing that Ruby Pasco was back and playing her usual game. Ruby wasn't done with Eli. She still wanted revenge on the man who'd spurned her.

"Watch your back," January told him as he whipped the tarp from Henry. The horse didn't seem bothered in the least by the thing flapping in his face though Pen barked as a layer of snow flew over her.

"Always," he said, mounting and looking down at her. But he hadn't always, and it had almost gotten him killed once that she knew of. Or no. More than once.

"You, too," he added. "She's unpredictable, you know."

*Unpredictable, untrustworthy and just about every other un a person with a dictionary handy could think of,* January thought. But she nodded.

How long would it be this time before she saw him again? Turning back into the house as he heeled Henry into a fast walk, she put the question out of her mind.

\* \* \*

ELI GAVE Henry his head as they took the trail back to The Falls. The wind had picked up, whipping the inch or so of fresh snow in a cloud around them where it clung to Eli's hat and denim-clad legs. Henry's long winter coat turned white over his rump.

Once in town, relieved to get out of the weather, Eli stopped at the marshal's office, intent on passing on what he and January had discussed. But their discussion wasn't his main concern. Not now. That changed when he reached town.

His new purpose lay in what he considered an extraordinary circumstance for a settlement of this size and at this time of year. Something odd enough to draw his attention, which might've been due to the conversation between him and January. The part about Ruby being here with only two men clustered around her.

It had happened as he passed the depot at the edge of town, where the noon train had been stopped. He'd seen four men get off, each carrying either a duffle or saddle-bags, an indication they probably weren't locals.

Eli didn't claim to know everyone around The Falls. He hadn't lived here long, nor within that time had he associated with folks a whole lot. He'd been gone from the ranch most of the summer and early fall taking Windswept to the races and rounding up breeding appointments. Easy money, what with Windswept in great demand. But still—

Eyeing the men, at first it seemed they didn't know each other. He was almost past them before the notion struck him they were only giving the impression they didn't. Could be they were ignoring each other a little too studiously. Besides, there was one who struck him as all too familiar.

Then his eye caught the movement of someone standing in the shadow of the little white- painted train depot. The four men who'd gotten off the train were drifting that way, even though the path into town led in the other direction. *A meeting?*

If he'd been a rooster, his hackles would've raised.

As far as what Southbrook thought of his report, well, he wasn't quite sure. The marshal listened closely and thanked him, saying he'd be on the lookout for strangers.

Eli rode for the ranch after their talk, urging Henry into a lope as soon they passed the outskirts of town. He needed to get home and get the new posts in the ground before it froze for the winter.

Later, although he worked up a sweat despite the chill in the air, he couldn't quite put the scene at the depot out of his mind. The more he thought about the incident, the surer he became that there'd been something about the way the figure in the station's shadow moved. Something familiar and with a certain grace.

Tamping dirt at the base of a post with unusual force, Eli looked over his shoulder. If he was right about the shadow man, he'd have to keep checking the hills on a regular basis if he didn't want shot dead. The trouble was, if he was right and the shadow he'd seen belonged to Arden Holzer, a careful watch might not do him any good. The man was known to possess a long-range buffalo gun that had no trouble reaching say, from the hillside north of him, to the flat where he was building his fence.

He'd be dead before the report of the gun cracked the stillness, and no one the wiser.

No, there was only one thing to do. He had to get back into town without anyone seeing him—and he meant *anyone*—and discover if Holzer was the man he'd seen. Check whether these strangers belonged with him. See if the small man in the robbery of T.T.'s mercantile was indeed Ruby Pasco as he suspected. And then?

He hadn't made up his mind yet.

But first he needed to get this fence in.

He worked on through the afternoon until dark, his muscles tense and stiff as the wire he strung from the posts.

# CHAPTER 5

As tired as she'd been, sleep eluded January when she went to bed. Which meant when the pounding on her door began sometime during the night, she'd been asleep only a couple hours. At first, she tried to ignore the racket. Covering her ears with a feather pillow proved of no use whatsoever, as Pen woke up, startled into barking loudly enough to shatter eardrums more adapted to the quiet.

She groaned. This demand for attention could only mean trouble.

January, well aware that whoever was outside hadn't come on a social call, threw back the blankets and scrambled out of her warm bed. Heart thudding, she reached for the old coat she hung on the back of a chair for when nature called during the night and wrapped it around her.

*Who is dead?* The thought pulsed through her brain like a train headlight traveling a rough track.

Ever cautious, she didn't light a lamp. With her eyes accustomed to the dark and the rime of snow still on the ground magnifying the light coming through the windows, she could see well enough. She did grab up the .38 Colt revolver that had belonged to her dad from the bedside table and carried it with her as she padded barefoot across the front room to the door.

Even then she didn't throw back the inner latch, in use since a young woman had sneaked into her house one night and tried to kill her. Didn't open the door right away, either. She stood to the side in case the person outside decided to shoot through the door and called out over Pen's howls. "Who is it? What do you want?"

The pounding stopped. "Missus Billings? Is that you?"

After a second, January recognized the voice. She eased open the door just wide enough for the man outside to stumble in. "Who were you expecting?" she grumbled. "The Thanksgiving turkey? Of course it's me."

"Huh?" her visitor said. He lowered his hand, still raised from his assault on her door.

She moved aside to light a lamp.

The short fellow standing there, his nose glowing red from the cold and his left hand semi-permanently formed into a fist from years of clenching the reins of a bridle, allowed his mouth to gape open. He was not anyone she'd normally expect to find at her house at this hour. Or any time, really.

"What's happened? Why are you here? Has someone been killed?" Her questions poured out in a rush.

He gulped. "No, ma'am, nobody killed. Not when I left town leastwise."

The band of nerves around January's belly loosened. "Then what are you doing here, Sam? It's the middle of the night. Are you in trouble?"

Sam—she didn't know his last name; didn't know if he had a last name—shook his grizzled head. He'd pulled a knitted cap off as he inched a few steps farther into the room. His graying hair, what there was of it, stood up in tufts. "Squirt sent me," he said.

*Squirt*. A relief, she thought. Or was it? At least it hadn't been Marshal Southbrook. Or T.T. Or Eli Pasco. On the other hand, it wasn't like Squirt, also no last name that she knew of, to have sent his helper at the town livery stable out in the wee hours just to wake her from slumber.

"Why Squirt?"

He'd been eyeing her askance, as if wondering what kind of woman wore a man's union suit to bed, then if roused, put on an old outdoor coat. He paid her scar no mind, having seen it before.

A trace of amusement curled her lips into a half-smile. Poor old fellow had probably expected to have the treat of seeing a woman in a frilly nightgown with a peignoir over the top. Instead, January Billings greeted him with a gun in her hand and wearing a barn coat.

He still hadn't gotten his mouth to working on any kind of explanation. Sometimes it took him a while to loosen up. Besides, he was probably half-frozen.

Ruing her lost sleep, January sighed. "Come on through to the kitchen, Sam. I'll stir up the fire and fix us a pot of coffee. I imagine you're cold through and through."

"Yes, ma'am, I be. Thankee, ma'am."

He followed her to the kitchen, Pen padding along

at his heels. Sam managed to give the dog a pat with his non-balled up hand.

With the fire going and coffee on the stove, January pulled out a chair across from Sam and sat. Amused, she followed his gaze as he gaped around the tidy place and drew a finger over the smooth oiled finish of her table. A table she'd built.

"This is fine, ain't it? Pretty wood," he said and lifted his bulbous nose to sniff like a hound dog. "Smells good in here, too. Clean."

"Thank you, Sam. This is a good house." She kept it that way, too. Growing impatient, she stirred. "Tell me why you're here. You said Squirt sent you. Why Squirt? Does it have to do with one of the horses that came from this ranch?"

*At two in the morning?*

"Uh, no, ma'am. It's on account of Mrs. Carter's old mare had a touch of colic—we take care of her, ya know —and Squirt and me stayed up late getting some mineral oil down her."

What did Mrs. Carter's horse have to do with her? January's brow puckered as Sam continued his tale.

"Squirt says he's gonna start dosing her with vine-gar. He swears vinegar'll keep her healthy another few years." He beamed. "The mare got to feeling better after the oil worked, and Squirt went outside to clear his sinuses and have a smoke. He don't never smoke in the barn."

January wasn't any too sure but what she'd heard more than she wanted to know. Most particularly since they still hadn't reached the point of his visit. "I'm glad to hear the mare is better."

"Yeah. Anyways, after a while Squirt comes back

into the stable. Sneaked in like a cat through the side door and he was powerful upset. 'Sam,' he says to me, 'you gotta go get Dabney. Root him out his bed whether he likes it or not and bring him here. And Sam, don't let nobody see you. Either you or him.' So I asks him, 'why is that,' and he says, 'cuz somebody knocked South-brook on the head just now, and dragged him off into the bushes over on the north side of the corral.'"

January's eyes opened wide. "What?" It came out kind of squeaky and breathless.

"Yeah. That's what I said, and he tole me he figured it was the same bunch what whacked T.T." Sam's head bobbed like a yo-yo on a string. "So I do as he says, not showing myself on Main street at all and pretty soon I get to Dabney's house. It's dark around there. Dabney's got a lot of trees—"

January remembered them from a time she'd gone to Dabney's house to talk with his young daughter and nodded impatiently.

"—and I start to walk up but then I seen a feller standing under one of the trees drawing on a seegar and I stopped. And then I seen another feller watching the back door. Ma'am, somebody is keeping an eye on Dabney to see he don't come out of that house."

She felt a little weak-kneed, to tell the truth. What in the world was going on?

"What did you do?" she asked.

Sam hunched his shoulders. "I come on back to the barn and told Squirt. By that time, Squirt had dragged Southbrook into the barn and had him layin' down on the cot. Out cold, though, and I could see Squirt is scared he ain't gonna pull through. That's when he told me to saddle that old spotted horse and come get you.

He says you'd best get there before daylight and come into town real quiet-like."

With that he stopped. After a moment, something else occurred to him. "That coffee ready yet?"

It was.

Deciding she wasn't going anywhere on an empty stomach, January whipped together a bit of breakfast for her, Pen, and Sam, got herself dressed and loaded up with firearms and ammunition.

Leaving a note on the table for Johnny, knowing he'd be worried when he arrived in the morning and found her gone, she left instructions for the care of the ranch and begged him to stay until she returned.

With that, she saddled Hoot and, leaving Pen in the house howling in despair at being abandoned, they were off, riding through the dark and cold toward town. She found it a little eerie, and even more so when they reached The Falls and Sam guided her in a roundabout fashion to the side of the barn. They took both horses in through the small door usually reserved for people. In case anyone was keeping watch, she didn't want them spying two horses who'd recently been ridden hard. And Hoot, with his silver color and fine breeding was a little too well-known and distinguishable to be overlooked. If Ruby was with the group who'd landed in town, she'd spot him in a heartbeat.

Squirt, looking as if he might've been asleep, came out to meet them, an expression of relief on his face. "I was skeert you might not come," he said, greeting January.

His nod at Sam served as a 'well done,' whereupon Sam scurried off to have a couple hours sleep.

She didn't pull any punches. "I didn't want to."

"I didn't know what else to do. I figured you was the closest to a lawman we got here what with Southbrook out of commission and Dabney penned up in his house."

She shook her head. "How is Marshal Southbrook? Have you gotten hold of Doc LeBret?"

"Not yet. I figured if I went to the doc's office in the middle of the night them outlaws might take notice. Come daylight, I can waltz on over to fetch him. I'll double over a few times and cough like I got *pewmony* while I'm at it, and make sure folks hear me say Sam is even sicker. Ought to keep people away from us for a while."

January couldn't help chuckling. "Why, Squirt! Who'd have thought you wanted to become a thespian? And at your age, too. Good thinking! Your plan will work a treat." She trusted so, anyway.

Squirt blushed like a fourteen-year-old.

She soured then. "Did you think about Eli Pasco? He might help."

"Yes, ma'am, but I wasn't sure about Sam fetching him. Figured Pasco might be a little quick on the draw, with what folks are saying."

"What are they saying?"

"Some think he may be associated with some woman outlaw and that she might be with these yahoos. That he's a bounty hunter and he's made too much money bringing in outlaws to bother with making sure they're alive to come to trial."

"You met him, talked with him. What do you think?"

Squirt sighed. "I think he's an even-handed honest man and that somebody wants to make sure he don't get a fair shake. But that's just me."

*Me, too*, January thought.

"Where is Marshal Southbrook?" she asked. "Maybe I can take a look at him. See if there's anything I can do."

Relief smoothed some of the wrinkles on Squirt's weathered face. Even his handlebar mustache, which had been drooping, appeared to perk upward. "This way." He led her to the small room right at the front of the stable where he lived, though Sam bedded down in whatever stall he found empty most nights. If they were all full, the hay loft served.

Right now, the marshal filled the single cot, blankets covering him to his chin. Meanwhile, a single blanket tossed aside showed where Squirt had been dozing as he sat on a chair placed close beside the marshal.

January went to kneel at Southbrook's side. The man breathed heavily, but as she felt for a pulse in his neck, she discovered it to be strong and steady.

She turned to Squirt. "Has he been awake at all?"

The wrangler answered in a whisper. "Roused a little once. Asked for water, which I give to him, and he said his head hurt. Then he went back like this."

With a touch as gentle as a feather, January felt over Southbrook's head and neck before looking back at Squirt. "I don't feel any depressions in his skull, but there's a big lump, placed almost exactly where T.T. was hit."

"Them depressions he ain't got," Squirt said hesitantly, "is that good or bad?"

Puzzled for a moment, January replied, "It's good he doesn't have any. It means his skull isn't broken. But he still needs to see Doc as soon as possible."

Rising to her feet, January led the way out of the room and went over to a small window that looked out into the street. "Sam said something about strangers in town. Where are their horses?" She hoped to maybe tell something about them from their animals or saddles. People often left their saddlebags with the hostler.

"That's the thing, Miz Billings, they ain't got horses."

"They don't? The people who attacked T.T. did."

"Yeah, but those two left town and nobody's seen 'em since."

January's heartbeat took a leap forward. She bet she knew where they'd holed up. And she and Sam had ridden right on past them. "So more strangers came in after them? How many?"

Squirt nodded vigorously, barely visible in a barn aisle lit by a single lantern. "Four or five men that I know of. Could be more."

"Four or five? How do you expect me to..." Her voice died away as he gaped at her. "Well, I guess I'd better walk around town. See what I can see." She'd really rather not. Four or five men against one woman? Those were terrible odds and they raised a whole lot of alarm in her.

She blew out a breath. "Do you know if they're staying at the hotel, Squirt?"

"One of them. I talked to the clerk. He says it's a feller named Arden Holzer. Kind of a pansy name, if you ask me. Don't know about the others. But the clerk says this Holzer rented four more rooms. He don't know if anybody is in them or if Holzer just wanted peace and quiet."

Not very helpful. January slipped out the side door they'd come in through, suddenly wishing she'd brought Pen with her. Pen was good at warning her of strangers. But at the time, it seemed better to leave the dog on guard at the house, where Johnny would take care of her when he got there in the morning.

She looked up at the sky. In a few hours, she amended, noting a lightening of the darkness. Better if she made her rounds here right away, before the town woke up. If she was lucky, the outlaws were not early risers. Not if they went around thumping men on the head in the wee hours of the night.

January started off, footsteps silent and cautious. She kept to the shadows, flitting from doorway to darkened doorway and slinking past openings between buildings. Once she spotted motion and stood stockstill, only to laugh at herself when the movement turned into a raccoon waddling toward the river. But it wasn't really funny.

Not a soul showed himself until she came to the Barefoot Saloon. The saloon door stood open a crack and her hand was on the handle when she heard people speaking in low tones just inside. Although the saloon normally closed by midnight—or so she'd been told—when peeking through the inch-wide space, she could see the back of a tall man and another shorter one. Beyond them, Bud Knowles, proprietor as well as bartender, rested elbows on the bar and leaned his head on his hands, eyes closed as if asleep.

She couldn't hear what the speaker was saying; single words here and there at best.

"*Ruby,*" one said. She heard him distinctly. Not exactly a surprise, still the name jumped out at her.

The shorter man addressed the taller one as *sir*, in a tone of respect. Apparently this *sir* was the man in charge. That was all she gleaned. The door, open only a little, was too thick for anything else. Worse, she was unable to see either of the men well enough to identify them.

That's when she felt a warm breath on the back of her neck, and a hand come around to clamp itself over her mouth. Whirled out of the doorway and into the darkness at the side of the building, she struggled fruitlessly.

Never mind the whisper telling her to hold still.

It took what seemed a very long time before her brain recognized the whisperer. *Eli.*

# CHAPTER 6

JANUARY'S BOOT-HEEL CAUGHT ELI A HEFTY WHACK IN THE
shin. A flash of pain came close to making him lose his
grip on her waist where he could feel her gun belt. He
held her against his body, afraid if he let go she'd get to
her gun and shoot him dead before she realized he
wasn't trying to hurt her.

To the contrary. He wanted to get her away from the
saloon before Arden Holzer, whom he'd spotted and
recognized right away, finished conferring with his man
and discovered her trying to listen in. From what he
knew of Holzer, the man had no compunction about
killing a woman, especially if a woman like Ruby Pasco
urged him to it. Unfortunately, January's scar made her
instantly recognizable. Eli was certain Ruby wouldn't
have neglected to tell Holzer about it. The woman's
vanity always led her to disparage every other female,
and the scar made January an easy target.

He was never so glad in his life as when January
finally quit fighting him. Still within the circle of his

arm, loosened now, she spun around. Her eyes widened in realization.

"What are you doing? Trying to scare me to death?" She hissed the words through clenched teeth, as mad as he ever hoped to see her.

"No. Trying to keep you from getting killed." He was kind of mad himself, his leg smarting where she'd slammed her boot against it. He guessed he ought to be grateful she didn't wear spurs.

"Come on." Taking her hand, he led her farther into the side alley, until they came out behind the saloon. "And be quiet."

She yanked her hand loose, almost falling over a heap of empty bottles in the process. One tilted, tipping into another with a soft clank. "What are you doing here?" she demanded, her whisper fierce.

"I might ask you the same. Last I heard, you said since you weren't the sheriff, you weren't mixing in the town's troubles."

She made a throwaway gesture. "And so I wouldn't be, but along about two a.m. a knock on my door brought me to a different conclusion. Mister, I wish with all my heart I was home in bed with my dog at my side."

Eli couldn't help smiling. For a woman with her record of taking the law into her own hands and bringing some of the country's worst criminals to justice, she had a funny way of breaking from her stated intention to remain in the background. And in stating her sleeping arrangements.

His smile faded when he heard someone shouting from the front of the building. "I'm telling you, man, I heard people talking. Look in back. Hurry." Footsteps hastened toward them.

"C'mon," he breathed, and pulling her behind him, took long strides toward the other end of the alley.

"No. We'll be boxed in," she said. "Here."

Now she was the one pulling and he resisting. Until she squatted down at the side of the saloon's loading dock, built high enough to make unloading beer kegs easier on Knowles's back, but not so high he had to stretch. She dived under the set of steps that led up to the platform, yanking on his arm until he joined her beneath the structure. January turned her head into Eli's chest and hid her face in case the pale gleam of her skin showed in the darkness.

They hadn't time to edge further under the dock. Beating the man who ran down the alley by the breadth of a heartbeat, Eli saw he held a shotgun ready to fire. The outlaw made two complete circuits, peering into doorways, testing locks, and checking the few alley-facing windows some of the businesses enjoyed. What he didn't do was look for openings under the three or four unloading docks.

In all honesty, Eli admitted to himself, he probably wouldn't have either, never knowing about or taking the hollow spaces beneath them as a place of concealment.

"How did you know this was here?" he whispered to her when the shotgun-bearing outlaw had gone to the head of the alley to report to Holzer.

"I deliver things to Thurston's Mercantile," she said, just as softly. "He has a dock just like this and I noticed it there. I think they were all built by the same person."

It was tight quarters, Eli noted. Not that he was complaining, but if he had to pull his gun in the confined space, there might be some bumping of bodies. On the other hand, she'd been the one to draw him in with her.

At any rate, she said nothing about it and neither did he. Not that they had the opportunity as after conferring with Holzer, the yahoo with the shotgun took up station at the end of the alley. They settled in to wait him out. Once or twice, Knowles walked out on the dock where they heard him muttering angrily to himself about the men taking over his saloon.

It was nearly daylight before they were able to emerge from the shelter. By then a few townsfolk had gotten out on the street. Even from their hiding place Eli and January heard people talking. One fellow in particular endured a loud fit of coughing. The scent of coffee on the boil proved an agony to ignore. Horses and wagons traversed the street and at last Holzer's man went away.

"Time to move." Eli spoke in a normal tone. Careless now of the scrape of his boots on the dirt, he stretched protesting legs full length, grunting as a cramp shot along his calf. "If I can."

"Finally." January sounded sleepy. In fact, from the weight of her as she'd leaned against him, Eli thought she may have dropped off for a little while. Lucky her, being small enough for the space not to crush her like it had him.

At last, he had a chance to ask what was going on. Why had he found her sneaking around the Barefoot Saloon while attempting to remain unseen? And she to question him as to why he'd come to town, showing up at exactly the right moment.

He steered her to the street and stood waiting as a group of women from the bordello down along the river walked past. Not at all appealing to anyone but men as lonely as the few cowboys, weary from an overnight stay, accompanying them. The women, in the light of day, appeared tired and worn as their chatter rehashed the night's business. Eli found it easy to steer January into their midst without anyone taking particular notice. Too early in the day, he figured. Or too late.

"We'll talk when we get to the livery," she said, almost too low for him to hear. "Best not to speak while we're in this crowd."

Taking a short detour, Eli retrieved Henry from where he'd hitched the patient bay to the back of T.T. Thurston's Ford delivery wagon where it had been set on blocks for the winter. T.T. had discovered the truck prone to getting stuck on roads meant for horse and buggy in bad weather. Henry, glad to see him, shook like a dog when Eli removed the tarp keeping the cold from him.

"Handy." January gave the horse a pat. "He'll give you an excuse to go to the livery." She looked around. "I'll meet you there."

Before he had a chance to question her decision, she flitted away. The last he saw of her, she stood in line with the girls from the brothel, who'd gathered in front of the bakery.

Eli's hand barely refrained from drawing his gun as he recognized one of the men in line with the girls. Recognized from a wanted poster, if his knowledge was called to question, and also as one of the men he'd seen arrive at the train station.

What kept him still was the way January turned up the collar of her oversized coat, and pulled her cap down. So. She was smart. She'd taken a guess at the stranger's identity. And by great good luck, it appeared the man was still half-drunk from his overnight carousing, too stupid with hooch and in need of sleep to notice anything going on around him, let alone a woman with a scarred face.

Eli kept his gun hand free and rode on past the group just now making their way into the shop. January barely flicked him a glance. The outlaw none at all.

* * *

JANUARY, having taken a roundabout route, reached the livery several minutes after Eli. She saw at once he'd been worried about her late arrival. As had Squirt and Dr. LeBret.

She hefted the box of donuts she'd bought at the bake shop. "I had to wait my turn at the bakery. These are still warm, though."

Even Sam, tempted by the smell of fresh donuts, roused enough to claim his share before going back to his chosen stall to sleep another hour.

Doc LeBret sat on the chair next to Southbrook, holding a mercury thermometer upright in the marshal's mouth. He took it out, noted the reading, and shook it down. "100 degrees. Not bad for a man knocked on the head and left laying out in this weather."

Southbrook, they were all cheered to hear, mumbled something, to which Doc said, "Yeah, I know. I got something for that." He fumbled in the black satchel at his side. "I need some water," he told Squirt. "Drinking water fit for men, not horses."

Squirt hustled to bring a dipper of water.

A smile twitched January's mouth. "Was that you I

heard coughing when you went past the Barefoot a while ago, Squirt?"

"Prolly." He grinned at her. "I was layin' it on pretty thick. Musta worked, cuz I ain't seen any strangers with their eyes on this place. I noticed something else, though. Something not so good."

"What's that?" Doc got the question in before January.

"I never knew Bud Knowles to keep the Barefoot open beyond midnight. Or maybe only on Saturday nights. But this ain't Saturday and the lights have been on all night. Men looked to have taken over the place. How'd you know 'bout the coughing, anyways, Miz Billings?"

January blinked. "Haven't you told them?" she asked Eli.

Doc was holding a cup up to Southbrook's mouth. "It's just headache powders," he urged the marshal. "It won't knock you out. Same thing I dosed T.T. with." Then, setting the cup down, he raised a grizzled eyebrow at January. "Haven't told us what?"

Eli shook his head. "I waited for you. You had us worried. What the dickens possessed you to get in that bakery line anyhow? One of the men in line there is on the wanted list. He's supposed to be in prison right now." He said it decisively, as if he might've had a hand in putting him there himself.

She barely raised a snort. "I saw him. I'll surprised if he isn't an opium eater, the strange way his eyes looked. It's no wonder he wasn't paying attention to anything around him."

"Opium eater?" That piece of information made

Southbrook sit up—so to speak—and take notice. "Where'd he get opium in this daisy patch?"

Eli's mouth tightened. "Could be what this gang is doing here. Setting up a supply run for the opium trade."

January's donut suddenly lost all taste. She and her dad had lived near an opium den one time for a few months. It was an experience she didn't want to repeat. There'd been men—and women—lying out on the bare ground. Some had been sick. Some had been filled with euphoria. All had acted as though they weren't quite...there.

And yet, she'd rather fight opium traders than a gang of men out for revenge. Especially a gang egged on by a woman like Ruby Pasco, who had her own axe to grind.

Her brow creased in thought. "I don't think so. About trading in opium, I mean. The Orientals have a lock on that, and they stay pretty much in the big towns. Not enough money in it otherwise. I think these people are here for something else."

"What?" Southbrook and Doc spoke at the same time.

"Or *someone* else," Eli said.

"Who?" Squirt asked the question this time.

But neither Eli nor January had a chance before they heard the livery door open and a voice called out, "Yoo-hoo? Is anyone here? I need to rent a horse."

A woman's voice. One easily identifiable to January and Eli.

Eli blanched. January saw him. She probably did the same.

"Me," Eli answered Squirt's question in a low voice.

"Or me," January whispered as tripping footsteps headed toward them.

Squirt huffed and choked out a long and very loud cough, motioning the rest of them further into the room and blowing out the lamp.

"I'll do this," he said. "Stay quiet."

Whipping out a red handkerchief the size of a table-cloth, he started blowing his nose into it as he walked out and closed the door partway behind him.

"Do for ya?" they heard him say.

"There you are." Ruby Pasco sounded impatient. "You've kept me waiting, sir. That's not good if you want my business."

"Pardon me, ma'am," Squirt said, and repeated, "What can I do for ya?"

"I need a horse and directions to a ranch outside of town."

Setting one eye to a crack in the door, January saw Ruby back away from Squirt and his rasping cough.

"Which of these nags is your best horse?" Ruby demanded.

Squirt, laying his supposed illness on thick, coughed again as he went toward her.

Ruby put up a hand as though to stop him, no doubt put off by the harsh sound.

"I can get a good'un for ya," he was saying, his voice hoarse.

January figured his hoarseness real by now. All that forced coughing must be wreaking havoc on his vocal cords. Her lips curled upward. Who would ever have guessed Squirt at the livery stable to be such an accomplished actor? Not her.

"I'll bring Roxy on out," Squirt went on. "She's got

spirit but she ain't wild, if ya know what I mean. A steady goer."

A horse was led out. A minute or so passed, then Ruby said, "She'll do, I suppose. Saddle her up—no, not that one. I don't ride side-saddle like some old lady."

Evidently Squirt had started for the mocked piece of tack.

"Yes, ma'am. You're the boss."

She chuckled. "And don't you forget it."

The horse emitted a grunt when Squirt tightened the cinch—unless that was Squirt doing the grunting. The metal parts of the bridle clinked as he slipped it over the mare's head.

"Give you a hand up?" Squirt, ever helpful, made the offer.

"No thanks. I don't want to get too close in case what you have is catching."

Reminded, Squirt made another try at blowing his nose, honking and whistling. "No, ma'am. Nobody wants this."

It was when Ruby asked for directions to the old Winkler ranch—now Eli's ranch—that he stuttered a little at playing his part.

"The Winkler ranch?" he repeated. "What ya gonna do out there?"

Ruby turned cold. "None of your business."

Peeking past the ajar door, January saw him glancing a bit desperately their way. She jerked her thumb at Eli. Scowling, he moved silently forward and nodded to Squirt.

"Ah, yes, ma'am. I reckon you're right about that." So saying, he gave instructions on how to find the ranch.

"One last thing." Ruby reined the horse around and

waited for Squirt to open the barn door for her. "If you're smart, you'll keep this transaction to yourself. In case anyone asks, that is. I mean anyone! Understood?"

"Yes, ma'am." Never was a man meeker than the simple livery hand named Squirt—for now, at any rate.

Different for sure from the one who spun to face Eli after watching his customer take off on the long way out of town.

"Good man." Eli already had his saddle on Henry and was leading him to the rear entrance. "I can't trust her not to burn the place to ashes. That or steal anything not nailed down. I'd best find out what she has to say, then I'll be back."

Though he appeared plenty confident, January was not so much. "Be careful," she said. "She may just mean to shoot you dead."

Eli turned to grin at her. "There is that."

Swinging aboard the horse, he urged the animal into a lope. He'd have to ride hard to get to the ranch before Ruby.

# CHAPTER 7

Eli took a lesser-known route out of town, urging Henry across rough country while taking shortcuts he'd become familiar with in the last few months. These were old cattle trails for the most part, and he was glad he'd selected the sure-footed Henry as his mount today. Windswept, his prime racehorse, wouldn't have fared so well.

A question plagued him. *What does Ruby want from me?* Revenge, yes, though he wondered what form it would take. But there must be more for her to have teamed up with Holzer and brought a whole set of outlaws into The Falls. This might be his only chance to ferret out their plan before they struck.

The situation made him almost glad to see her again, if only to refresh his memory of her tricks and taunts.

When she married his father, she'd left anything to do with the house and its upkeep to Mrs. O'Leary, housekeeper for the Pascos from the time Eli's mother died years before. The mundane aspects of married life were of no interest to Ruby. As for something to keep her occupied and amused, she traveled: New York City, New Orleans, San Francisco, and Seattle had been just some of the cities on her itinerary. She bought clothes and jewels and lost the jewels gambling. She flirted. Flirted with him in an attempt to seduce him right under his father's nose. When that didn't work, crime tempted her. Even the sometimes rough living connected with the outlaw life didn't faze her. She thrived on the thrill of stealing what didn't belong to her. In that, she apparently had never changed.

His fault maybe, as he'd gotten out of her way by going into the bounty hunter business. Mostly, he admitted, as a method of removing himself from her and his father. But he was good at catching criminals, with a talent for guessing what they'd do, where they'd go, and what he had to do to bring them in.

The money, particularly when he captured higher profile criminals, was good. Paid for his ranch with some left over, and allowed him to get out of the business before someone shot him in the back.

Ruby, impressed and thrilled by his reputation—plus the danger involved in his work—came after him. He'd eluded her until last spring. Until he'd bought this ranch, in fact. Now here she was again, showing up in his life when he'd believed her finally out of it for good.

With these thoughts racing through his mind, he reached the ranch well ahead of her. Time enough to run a brush over Henry and get a fire started in the stove. A little warmth in the rooms would give the impression he'd been home all along.

All too soon, a knock on his front door announced she'd found him. She'd made good time, but then, she had always been an excellent rider—though often careless of her mount.

He took a deep breath before opening the door. Unsure of what he'd find, his hand hovered close to his gun.

"Darling Eli," she cooed, a smile as false as her heart wreathing her face, "were you expecting me?"

"I was expecting someone. Not necessarily you. The Broomhandle Mauser stolen from the mercantile in town indicated somebody might be looking for me."

She brushed past him, breasts almost touching his chest where he wore his Mauser as she strode into the house. As if thinking she'd be welcome? After the way he sent her off in the wrong direction last time they met?

Eli shook his head at her brazenness.

He remained by the door. "What are you doing here?" He cocked an eyebrow. "No. Wrong question. What do you want here? What do you want from me?"

Her laughter trilled. She turned back toward him and walked right up close, reaching out to grab his shirt collar with both hands. "Why, darling Eli, can't you guess?" Her full lips pouted. "I want everything from you. I'm still mad at you for abandoning me on a mountain trail, you know. I was practically penniless at the time. You owe me."

"Owe you? You're lucky I didn't turn you in for the reward. I heard you got in a spot of trouble afterward."

She ignored everything he'd said. "Or maybe you'd prefer I go back to your father." She was teasing him, rubbing in how she'd managed to cause bad blood between father and son.

Eli stiffened. "He divorced you. You'd get nothing from him."

"You think not?" Her laugh came again. "A bet, dear stepson. This place against your father's. He fell all over himself the first time. Couldn't wait to have his way with me and then couldn't keep his hands off. This time would be no different. Turn me down and you'll see."

His innards shook with rage, even as he admitted to himself there was truth to what she said. His father had been like that in the past. No longer. Not even if he still desired her. A wheelchair had put a stop to all that monkey business. Perhaps she didn't know. Gripping her hands, he cast them aside and stepped away.

"And if I win the bet, will you go and leave us alone?"

"Oh, you won't win, Eli."

"No?"

"No," she said.

The smile he forced onto his face was as cold as the look she flashed at him. She'd always used kohl and a trollop's heavy mascara around her eyes, but nothing had ever obscured the hardness in them. No matter what she said now, he'd never believe her. What he wanted was to discover why she and the gang of criminals she associated with were gathered in this town. What was their purpose?

He heard her blathering something else, taunting as if from a distance.

Although she wore regular female riding gear today, split calf-length skirt, a long coat, a snowy white muffler and matching hat, he couldn't help being curious as to the garb she had worn that day at the mercantile when the Mauser had been stolen. Garb that roused T.T.'s curiosity. All right. He'd start there.

"That was you in Thurston's store, wasn't it? The one he described as little and hiding behind those two galoots?" Eli figured she'd take umbrage at the word hiding, and he wasn't wrong.

"Hiding? Me? I wasn't *hiding*."

"No?" He forced another grin. "What would you call it then?"

"Staying in the background," she said. "I've got a different role to play and need to come into it clean."

"Come in clean?" His tone mocked. His intention. Ruby had always been prone to losing her temper when she believed men didn't take her seriously enough. As if determined to prove her superior intelligence as well as her sexual desirability. "You don't know what that means."

She flounced, as if she thought he'd misunderstood her. "Desi and Krak are nothing to me, as I'm sure you know."

Well, yes. He did.

"Both of them stupid and ugly," she went on, "and without a dollar in their pockets. Arden is not pleased with them, I can tell you, and neither am I. They were supposed to simply keep me safe on the way here, not draw attention to me. I believe I'd have been better off without them along." She became pensive. "Although Krak did shoot a man who may have recognized me outside of Billings, so I suppose he served his purpose." She sighed and rolled her shoulders back, her breasts lifting. "But Desi thought he had to have that gun. 'Just like Pasco's,' he said. As if it's all up to the gun and not the man."

She may have meant the last part as a backhanded compliment. Hard telling when it came to Ruby. But her naming of Holzer had caught his attention.

"Arden? Arden Holzer?" he said, soft, as if it didn't matter. As if he didn't already know the outlaw was in town. "I thought he had another few years to go in Walla Walla."

Her lips pursed. "Oh, forget I said that. I misspoke."

She hadn't, as he well knew. Ruby never said anything she didn't want him to know. Holzer's presence was not a secret she wanted to keep.

Eli stifled any kind of reply to this. He wasn't particularly interested in either Arden Holzer—at the moment, at least—or even Desi Holloway's desire for a gun like the Broomhandle. The point was to discover just why Ruby needed to come in clean. He decided on a direct approach. The sooner he got answers, the sooner she'd leave.

"What are you really doing here, Ruby? All this talk?" He shrugged. "It doesn't mean anything."

She strode around the front room, examining his few possessions with a sharp, and possibly disdainful eye. A couple used chairs he'd bought from Thurston who'd taken them in trade when the owner ran out of money for food. Ditto a small table. A bookcase he'd put together himself, though knowing January Billings was twice the carpenter and cabinetmaker he'd ever be no matter how long he practiced.

Not that the profession was anything he strived to master.

It didn't matter anyway, since these second-hand things were only stopgap. Eli congratulated himself on having nothing much of value in his home. The less Ruby knew about his finances, the better.

In fact, she frowned, passing on through the room and entering the kitchen where she shed her coat and gloves. "It appears you've fallen on hard times, Eli. What's the matter? That horse you cared so much about didn't pan out? God knows he caused enough trouble."

*For her or for me?* Inwardly, Eli flinched over the question. Outwardly, he shrugged.

She sat on one of the chairs, scooting about as if to find a comfortable position. "I could use a cup of coffee to help warm me up. Surely, you won't deprive me of so small a favor?"

Figuring she didn't leave him much choice if he wanted her to talk, Eli went through the motions of grinding coffee beans and putting them, with water, in his percolator. He served her coffee in one of his two good cup and saucer combinations and took a thick crockery mug for himself, then sat opposite her at the oak kitchen table.

He knew his brew was good and took great pride in its quality.

"Ready to talk?" he asked after she'd taken her first sip.

"I've got nothing to say about why I'm—we're—here. There are several associates in our group."

*Associates?* Gang of outlaws, she meant.

"Your group? How many?"

She smiled coyly. "Oh, you'll find out. Maybe you'd like to join us, darling. Given how broke you appear, I'm sure even a small cut would help you out."

A tease. Eli surprised himself with the resentment he felt. He shook his head.

"No?" Her laughter tinkled. "But today, I came to see you because I don't want you to come to harm. And to warn you to stay here on the ranch for the next few days. Believe me, it will be to your advantage." Her face, its smooth alabaster complexion belying the way she lived, showed only sincerity. "And I wanted to ask if you ever see January Billings. Or if you know what happened to that young girl who took your horse. I can't remember her name. Something that started with a Z, as I recall."

"Yes. Zora Winkler. We rescued her. Her and three other girls. I heard she went to live with some cousins back east." He thought it prudent to say as little as possible about January. Ruby had always been a jealous creature, with a strong dislike of other women.

He wasn't pleased when Ruby's gaze sharpened, her attention caught on the "we" he'd mentioned.

"*We* meaning you and who else? Although really, Eli, you have a strong propensity to act as a knight determined to save the maiden, don't you?"

He stared at her, ignored her first question and answered the second with a question of his own. "Do I?"

Her laughter tinkled. "Even me, at one time."

Eli nodded. "Until I learned you didn't need saving. The other way around. People need saved from you. People like Zora."

Her eyes narrowed. Clearly, she didn't care for his opinion.

"What are you really doing here, Ruby?" The inquiry came coolly, without inflection as he finished his coffee. He hoped she'd soon do the same. "Unless you planned on hitting me up for money. You're out of luck if you did."

"No need. I told you, dear stepson." She grinned at the appellation. "I came to warn you to stay out of town. Keep your nose clean and ignore anything that happens there in the next few days."

Unable to sit still, he stood up and went to the stove, lifting the plate and stirring the embers until the warmth loosened tense muscles. "Does this warning come from the goodness of your heart? Because I've never known you to show any kind of consideration before."

She flounced up from the chair and said, her voice hard, "Just stay out of my way. You can come out of this alive or face the opposite. I...well, let's just say, all will go more smoothly without you horning in on the job."

"What *job* is that? What are you and those men you're with planning?" He didn't let on he knew about more than Holloway and Krakowski. Or Holzer. He still wondered why she'd mentioned his name.

At this question, she winked, though not as prettily as she probably thought. "Oh, you'll find out, darling. It'll be a surprise."

With that, she put on her coat and went out to her mount, riding away at a fast canter without saying goodbye or giving as much as a farewell wave. She didn't look back.

Eli hoped she wouldn't run the horse too hard. Though Squirt's animals were sound, they weren't meant for hard trails and Ruby had never showed much concern for those she used. Sometimes, used up.

Puzzling over the woman's strange visit and supposed concern for his welfare, he rinsed the cups and scattered the fire in the stove to be certain it would go out without catching the house ablaze.

Stay here and keep his nose clean? When he lived here? When his friends were here? When January Billings had been selected to face a gang of outlaws on her own? He'd been drawn in because a gun like his preferred model had been stolen. He considered the incident almost an invitation.

Eli chuckled aloud over the idea.

Ruby Pasco was a fool if she thought he'd bide by her advice. But then, he didn't think she did. He thought it more likely she knew what he'd do, and planned to be there to see him caught in the fight. The one he knew lurked right around the corner.

Eli left Henry at home for this trip and saddled a gelding he didn't think anybody hereabouts had seen. He'd gotten the horse in a claiming race up in Canada and, while not the fastest on the track, he had a better than average turn of speed. Eli wanted to get to town fast, before the anticipated war began in earnest.

He started along the route Ruby had taken instead of using the short cut with its rougher trail, and had gotten no more than a mile from his ranch headquarters when a shot startled the horse. Pinning back his ears, the gelding hopped about in retaliation of the close buzz.

Eli hadn't even had time to let out a surprised yell, let alone get his gun out, when another shot sounded. This time a bullet scratched across the top of his saddle horn. Unaccustomed to gunfire and sensing danger, the horse pitched a fit, almost tossing Eli out of the saddle. Instead, Eli dug in his spurs, setting the horse into a run.

Not that he figured to outrun a bullet, but at the spurt of speed, he hoped to put the shooter's aim off.

Whoever was shooting, and he had his suspicions,

got left behind as he steered the gelding around a huge basalt boulder where the road curved. Then, instead of following the road, he slowed and urged the horse into the trees bordering it, where heavy foliage provided cover. Later, when they neared the road again, he stopped. Waited. Listened. Reached for his Mauser when he heard sounds of movement in the underbrush.

After a while, a doe ambled out of the trees a hundred yards beyond him. Relieved, he urged the horse on. Even so, Eli didn't let down his guard. He kept his eyes open, watching front, back and sideways.

He saw no one. Whoever the shooter had been, there was no sign of him now. Probably, he figured sourly, gone to ransack his house while he was gone.

# CHAPTER 8

JANUARY SNUGGED THE CAP SHE WORE OVER HER HAIR, pulled the ear flaps over her cheeks, and tied the strings under her chin. It was a Norwegian kind of cap, one her neighbor Pinky Langley had knit for her, and it hid most of her face. Most importantly, it was warm and covered the telltale scar. Pushing a few errant strands of hair beneath the cap's edge, she stowed her boot gun in her coat pocket. The other pocket held a folding knife. She came prepared nowadays, although her weapons weren't always so ready to hand.

"Where do you think you're going?" Doc LeBret growled, eyeing her preparations.

Marshal Southbrook, who'd been lying with his eyes closed, opened them to look at her.

"Someone has to go out and see what's happening around town. With that woman on her way to Pasco's ranch, this is my best chance. She's the only one who would recognize me."

Doc squinted thoughtfully. "I dunno, January. You

are kind of unmistakable, if you don't mind me saying. Kind of notorious, too. I figure there'll be some who've heard of you and gotten a description."

January tried hard not to show her displeasure at this assessment. The trouble being he was probably right.

Unmoved, Doc winked at her.

"Is that the woman who was in on stealing Pasco's horse?" Southbrook asked.

"Yes. Pasco's father's ex-wife and Eli's bitter enemy." She figured these men deserved to know as much as she could tell them about Ruby, even though she didn't like revealing Eli's private business. Let the men press any other questions they might have directly onto him—if they dared.

Rising from where he'd been sitting beside the marshal, Doc looked more than a little disgusted. "She's got some nerve, showing up here again."

"Oh, she doesn't lack for nerve. I can guarantee that." January huffed out something between a laugh and a snort.

The information was enough to have the marshal pushing up on an elbow before collapsing onto his back. "Wasn't she in on the kidnapping, too?"

"She says not. Evidence points otherwise. But definitely the horse stealing, and party to my abduction, as well, although at the time she acted the role of a victim." Try though she may, January failed to hide her lingering bitterness. "She's a pretty good actress, unfortunately."

The men, Doc and Squirt, shifted uncomfortably. Although she didn't talk about it, news had wended its way around town about how she'd taken down the gang of men who stole and sold girls, often shipping them off by boat to foreign lands where no one could track them.

Deemed unsuitable for the gang leader's purposes due to her scar and age, January had been abandoned to a madman. But instead of him killing her, she turned the tables and disposed of him. All the facts were not commonly known, which suited her just fine. She didn't want to think of the fight, let alone talk about it.

The marshal flopped down on the cot with a sigh. His eyes closed again. "If you're going out, you should have somebody with you, Deputy Billings. Somebody you can trust to watch your back."

January huffed out another of those snorty laughs. "Got anybody to suggest, marshal? Because I wouldn't be averse to the idea. I'm not eager to get shot again. Once was adequate, thank you."

Southbrook's mouth curled under his mustache. "Yeah. I heard about that. How about Langley. He's helped before, hasn't he? Or that young feller you got working for you? Or Bo Cobb."

Her head shook in a negative fashion at his every suggestion. "Bent Langley's got a family. I can't put them at risk. Bo Cobb is slowing with age, and Johnny Johnson has almost died under my watch once already. I don't want him walking into danger for my sake, ever again."

Squirt muttered under his breath.

"What's that?" Southbrook said.

"I said, we oughta kick Dabney's...behind. This is his job. We're paying him sheriff's wages, ain't we?"

January made a throwaway gesture. "Never mind. He'd be more trouble than he's worth. Besides, I don't plan on taking any drastic action. Not until I know what I'm up against, and then I'll ask for help. This is just a simple a scouting mission, that's all. I need to find out what these men—and Ruby—are doing here."

"What do you suppose is going on, Southbrook?" Doc looked up from packing his medical bag as he prepared to leave, tucking a vial of liquid within a special strap. "You got any idea? Must be something big."

"No. I don't know. Just be careful, Mrs. Billings." Southbrook crooked his arm, covering his eyes as if the light hurt them. "Your intentions may not jibe with their intentions."

In January's estimation, it seemed certain they would not.

Marshal Southbrook spoke the truth. Even she didn't know exactly what her intentions were as she slipped out the livery's side door. Easing along the edge of the building, she waited to fall in behind a cluster of folks walking toward the town center. A street which, she observed, seemed as busy as most Saturdays. Odd, for an early Thursday morning. Maybe, she decided, because the splatter of snow had stopped. The sun, when it peeked through the clouds, provided a growing warmth, while a breeze worked at drying the mud.

Hours had passed since she'd arrived in town and gotten trapped under the loading dock with Eli. The stores were opening for business. Next to Squirt's livery, the traffic around Peevy's feed store appeared normal, with two wagons pulled up outside waiting to load bags of grain. A stack of salt blocks sat outside under the eaves. They were half-covered by a tarp, ready for ranchers stocking up for the winter. A few souls lounged around the store, all appearing to have business there. Across the street, the blacksmith was shoeing a horse for his first customer of the day, his forge glowing as he worked to fit shoe to hoof. She strolled on, joining an unusual number of folks riding up and down the street. Women walking. Dogs trailing their owners.

At the drug store, the outlook changed. Patrons, mostly women, seemed to intrigue a man who looked a little out of place. He leaned against the building, one foot braced against the wall as he cast a sharp eye on every younger woman who went past him. He paid the older women no mind at all. It struck her that he was looking for someone in particular. Her next thought was that it just might be her. The thought intensified as she caught sight of another man who held down a similar position on the other side of the street.

The milliner? January chuckled to herself. If they thought to find her at a store like the one belonging to prissy Mrs. Gowers, they didn't know her tastes very well. They were definitely barking up the wrong tree, especially considering this weather. She'd stick with her homemade Norwegian cap with the earflaps hiding her scar, thank you very much.

Despite her amusement regarding hats, she worried about the number of men available to take on this sort of duty. How many men had been imported to The Falls, anyway? What was their purpose here? Three or four might, emphasizing *might*, be manageable for her to combat, as long as she needn't take them all on at once. But more?

She shuffled past yet another stranger, apparently unworthy of his notice.

T.T. Thurston's mercantile bore the biggest crowd January had ever seen there. More even than at Christmas last year, when folks had been putting in gift orders on a day she'd inadvertently selected to bring in butter and eggs.

January was relieved when she got inside the store and looked around. A relief that didn't last long. Over at the pot-bellied stove, the usual group of older fellows warmed their hands and gossiped. In the tools department, someone was about the business of selecting a new rope, while another hefted an axe, trying it for weight. Several people browsed the double aisle that separated the grocery section from the hardware and dry goods, while a fellow sorted through the small variety of coats T.T. had in stock. January didn't blame him, as he wore only a light canvas jacket.

Young Timothy Thurston walked toward him, and judging by the boy's expression, he was none too sure of himself.

A couple men leaned over the gun display case, eyeing the wares with avid eyes even though it lacked the stolen Mauser Broomhandle as an enticement. She didn't recognize either of them. They were the ones who raised her hackles.

*Too many people.* The thought flashed through her mind. *Too many strangers. And lots of curious local browsers but nobody who seemed to be buying much.*

"Can I help you find something?" January heard Timothy say to the fellow fingering the heavy jackets.

T.T., once again seated on the stool tending the cash register, watched the activity warily while his wife rushed about the store selecting goods to fill regular patrons' orders, then wrapping and tying their selections into bundles.

News not only of the robbery, but of strangers invading the town had gotten around. A few ladies January recognized proffered shopping lists to be filled, but she believed they may have been here more to satisfy their curiosity than to shop. Perhaps their husbands had sent them? January twitched with amusement—and maybe a bit of gratitude for their prudent thinking.

The ladies, although they glanced her way, did so without recognition. She'd tucked her mahogany colored hair under the bright cap and with no visible scars in view, they had no reference. Hunching her shoulders and shuffling her feet, because nothing is more identifiable than the way one moves, she approached the counter where T.T. sat. The small changes in her appearance proved an excellent disguise.

He stared at her blankly, his eyes still dull and confused from yesterday's blow to the head.

January made a mental note to inform Doctor LeBret he needed to check on this patient, in between standing guard over Southbrook.

"T.T., it's January Billings." She spoke softly to his unfocused gaze.

"Eh?" he said, too loud for her comfort. "Speak up."

Pasting on a smile, she reached for his note pad and wrote down her name and a single sentence. *Don't say anything.* This time, awareness crept over him and he stared hard at her, finally nodding, his face flushing as if embarrassed by his lack of recognition.

*We need to talk.* She mouthed the words slowly and

distinctly, at which he nodded again. Evidently, he took her warning seriously. "Edna," he called out to his wife, "I'm gonna show Mrs. Schutt the order we're holding for her. It's in the back room."

Her admiration for T.T. grew. Calling her by her maiden name would confuse people. Members of Ruby's gang would never have heard it. A glance around showed the name had passed over Edna, as well.

Rising from his stool, and wobbling a bit as he did so, T.T. led her to the back of the store. Holding a finger to his lips, he checked the loading dock before saying a word and shook his head, wincing at the motion. "There's a feller I've never seen before out there pacing up and down the alley. Looks to me like he's on watch." T.T. held his voice to a low rumble. "What's going on, Mrs. Billings? Something is, aside from me getting robbed and knobbed. All these strangers in town just don't seem right. And they're acting suspicious, poking around in places they got no business."

"I hoped you could tell me what's going on."

"Well, I can't. But I question if this is about stealing a Mauser Broomhandle from this store."

"I agree." Her mouth pursed. "But the theft may have given us warning of something more serious in the works. Have you heard any talk?"

"Some. Mostly it doesn't make sense."

"Anything to say why so many people are gathering in your store?"

He glanced outside as a man walked past. Holding a finger to his lips, he said, "I think they're looking for you."

"Me?" She blinked. So her judgement about those

men outside had been correct. "Why me? Do you know?"

T.T. shrugged. "Not for sure. I doubt their good intentions. But there's something else, too."

She thought a moment. "Doubt regarding their good intentions goes without saying as long as Ruby Pasco is involved. I wish I knew if it's because I'm the deputy, or because I'm who I am." Her mind shifted a cog, to another thing he'd said. "This 'something else' you mentioned, what is it they're saying that doesn't make sense, Mr. Thurston?"

"Talk about the train schedule, about the army paymaster. About horses." He stopped, frown lines deepening with his thoughts. "Thing is, I got to wonder if that's one of those fish things folks talk about."

*Fish? Had the blow to his head scrambled T.T.'s brains? He most certainly doesn't seem himself.* Then the penny dropped.

"Do you mean a red herring?"

"Yeah, yeah. That's it. Sorry, but I don't see what army paymasters, horses, or trains have got to do with us. Still, could be Squirt had better keep a close look out on his animals. But that isn't all."

January didn't see the relevancy either and shook her head. "What else?"

"The telegraph operator was in earlier, buying some bright-leaf tobacco. Said he was having trouble getting messages through as there's some kind of trouble on the line." He stopped and pondered a few seconds. "But the main thing concerns Leonard Pearson. He's been walking back and forth 'round and 'round the bank building like he lost something. If I ever saw a worried man, he's it."

January's eyebrows raised. Leonard Pearson was the bank manager. "Did you talk to him?"

"No, but I've never seen the day when he came to work more than an hour early, let alone inspecting the place like he's doing. He's dang near as lazy as Albert Sims used to be. Besides—"

January had no answer to that. She'd never had cause to deal with the man, but from what T.T. was saying, Pearson was not in the habit of arriving early. "Besides what? Do you think something is wrong at the bank?"

"I do. Besides," T.T. went on, "while he may not be a real friendly fellow, I've never known him to ignore Edna when she tells him good morning. And I think he's an honest gent. As much as any banker ever is, at least. He's worried about something. I guarantee it. What's more, I just seen the old fellow, Ollie, that does odd chores around the bank. He's here today, too. That's never happened before, and I ought to know, seeing as how the bank is right across the street. It's in plain sight out my front window."

Small things, none of which added up to anything sounding good.

"Do you think Mr. Pearson would tell me what's worrying him? Me as deputy sheriff, I mean." She'd made a few deposits and written a few checks since the bank had changed hands, but had never met the banker in person.

"Dunno about him," T.T. said. "But could be that Ollie would. He visits with Squirt from time to time, so with Squirt helping you right now, I figure Ollie'd do the same. He might not know everything going on, but I suspect he's heard a thing or two."

January nodded. "Any information, no matter how tenuous, would help."

"I'll send Tim to see if Squirt can have a word with him, first thing." T.T. poked his head out of the store-room, waved to get his son's attention and motioned him over.

She studied the storekeeper for a moment. "Whatever is going on must be big, T.T. You take care and keep your head down."

Grinning wryly, Thurston gently rubbing the offended appendage. "Kind of late for that, missy, but I'll do my best. Wish I could give the same advice to you. I'll try to get word to you if I hear anything new."

Her smile flashed. "Thanks. I'll do the same."

Returning to the front of the mercantile, she made a small purchase on the premise something to carry made an excuse for walking from store to store in her guise as a shopper. Resuming her slouched stance, she saw young Timothy Thurston dash across the street to the bank and go around to the alley. A few minutes later, he returned, a gray-headed old codger following.

T.T. looked to have come through with the plan to talk with Ollie. Satisfied, she moved on. Her gaze moving from side-to-side, she spotted far too many loiterers for this time of day. Something that felt like a cold blanket had settled over the town, where even the locals looked at each other askance. Instead of appearing busy, they struck her as furtive.

A tingle of fear raised the hair on her arms.

January fell in behind two of the prostitutes from Fat Mary's riverside brothel she'd seen earlier at the bakery. Alone now, the women had walked alongside a man earlier. One who'd not only been wearing a gun belt, but carrying a carbine. Not a local. A local wouldn't have been toting his carbine around in town.

The two prostitutes were talking, their voices loud enough for January to catch much of their conversation. She couldn't help blushing a bit. Even though she'd been a widow for over a year, she'd never heard of some of the things they described. That they laughed over.

"Don't think I've ever been with as randy a fellow," one said.

The other giggled, a tired sounding giggle. "The two of us, and I thought he'd never go to sleep."

"Remember? He said he hadn't had a woman in two years. Imagine!" Heads together, January didn't catch what the first replied. Not until she added, "But he paid well. Guess he'd been saving up his money."

The tired giggle came again. "Poor Mr. Nelson Peel. *'And don't forget the mister.'* Remember him saying that? Like he thinks he's *somebody*."

January missed a step. *Peel?*

The first stopped in mid-laugh, before saying, "I don't know though, Sally. There was something about him. Something that kind of scared me."

January saw the other woman nod. "Yeah," she said. "I caught fright, too."

If the name mentioned made the connection she believed it did, they had good reason.

*Nelson Peel?* Sadly enough, in certain circles, he *was* somebody. Even January knew his name. To a great deal of ado, Ford Tervo, the deputy U.S. marshal from this territory, had chased him down a while back and put him in prison. How had Peel gotten out? More importantly, what was he doing here?

But January thought she knew. Revenge. She had,

after all, captured his brother and been party to putting him in prison where he was serving a twenty-year sentence.

Less, in her opinion, than he deserved.

But plenty to make his brother want retribution.

# CHAPTER 9

JANUARY COMPLETED HER CIRCUIT OF THE TOWN, TAKING the side streets and back alleys to the livery when done. She had a lot to report to Southbrook. Maybe by now Squirt and Ollie had conferred and she'd know better what she had to deal with. She only wished her own news was better. And that it didn't contain the news about Nelson Peel. She itched with the need to talk to Eli.

Johnny and Pen were waiting for her at the livery—a surprise. Johnny looked so worried, his young face drawn into tight lines, that her first thought was for her ranch. The new house. Had those intruders managed to burn it down? Or worse, had they attacked the ranch and harmed the animals? As for Pen, her dog greeted her with a wagging tail and a welcoming lick on the hand. Then another on the face.

"What? Am I dirty?" she murmured, hugging the dog. Come to think of it, maybe so. She hadn't had a chance to wash since huddling under the loading dock with Eli. The shelter hadn't been without its detractions.

As a matter of fact, it had stunk of garbage, mold, and old dirt. And that had been several hours ago. It seemed so far in the past it no longer counted.

"What's happened?" she asked Johnny, the question taut with fear that drove everything else out of her head.

"It's all right," he hastened to say. "We're all right."

Her glance fled to Southbrook, who appeared to have recovered somewhat in the hour she'd been gone. She found him sitting on the edge of the cot, pale as a snowman, and looking as if a puff of wind could blow him over. He didn't appear too concerned. Squirt stood by a galvanized bucket dipping out water for another pot of strong coffee, while a skinny little man with a hump on his back sat on an upended chunk of stove wood and munched on a bread and cheese sandwich.

Ollie, she surmised.

The old fellow rose from his makeshift chair as she walked in and, like a real gentleman, shook her hand.

She glanced at Johnny where he stood warming chilblained hands at the glowing pot-bellied stove. "What is it, then? What are you doing here? You're supposed to be looking after the ranch while I'm gone."

Johnny's mouth twisted. "Well, yeah, but something came up."

"What?" She made an effort to tamp down her impatience.

He gave her a look as though to question her tone. "I'd let Pen out of the house and started the morning chores when I saw smoke. It was coming from somewhere around the bridge, near your new house. Thought I'd better take a look. Pen didn't want to go inside, so I let her come with me when I rode over to check. Hope that was all right."

January's brows pulled together, anxiety rising. She nodded, although she wasn't sure about his decision considering the house had already been broken into. "And? The smoke?"

He scrubbed his hands together one last time and moved away from the stove. "It was coming from the bridge house's chimney. Somebody had to have broke the new lock to get in. Whoever it is built a fire in the fireplace and has taken up residence." He hesitated. "I didn't know if I should put the run on whoever it is, or if I should tell you first."

She eyed him grimly. "You'd better be telling me first."

He nodded. "I am."

"You did right, Johnny." A tiny bit of her anxiety faded.

"Could be worse," Squirt said. "Be glad the smoke is coming from the chimney."

Anger rushed through her. "Considerate of the housebreaker, I guess. Nice of him not to have set the place on fire. Yet."

Johnny shook his head. "No, ma'am. And it's *them* staying there. There's two horses tied on the south side of the old chicken coop out of the wind. Out of sight from the road, too." He took a breath. "You want me to go back and get them out of there or do you want to make an arrest?"

Southbrook lifted his head and looked at her. January figured she knew what he was thinking. Most likely the same as what ran through her mind. She'd bet they both were thinking a confrontation would put Johnny in a whole lot of danger. Not something she'd consider for even a moment. And she didn't have the time, just now, to do anything about the situation.

"Neither. We'll leave them for the present. If they're decoys for this group in town, well, at least they aren't in the way while they're out there. And if they're simply someone who's cold and needs shelter..." She trailed off.

"I could do it," Johnny said, bragging a little, at which she conjured up a smile and said, "I know."

Southbrook nodded and sat back as Squirt tossed another chunk of wood into the stove's firebox.

"You warm enough?" Squirt asked the marshal. "Doc said you ought not to get chilled."

"I'm good, thanks." Southbrook glanced around. "Who wants to talk first?"

"Shall we wait for Eli?" January asked. She pulled a pocket watch from inside her coat. "I expected him back by now."

As if her words had been a signal, they heard a horse outside the barn and a man grunt as he dismounted. Squirt went to look.

"It's him," he said and shook his head. "Pasco. He's rode that horse hard."

* * *

ELI SPOTTED the mare Ruby had ridden to the ranch in Squirt's corral as he drew up outside the livery. The hostler'd had time to brush the mare down, so Eli figured he was safe to openly enter the barn. He doubted Ruby would be waiting anywhere near the stable on the off chance he'd show up in town. Why should she? Simply to see if he was still alive?

Squirt came outside to meet him. "What took you so

long?" he demanded. "That woman got back a quarter hour or more ago."

Eli pointed to the damage on his saddle where the bullet had grazed it. "I was waylaid. Got lucky when my saddle bore the brunt of the attack. Made me think it best to take the long way into town, though." He patted his horse's neck. "This poor fella banged his ankle on a boulder and got a gash. I'm hoping you've got something for it."

The wrangler bent to lift the horse's foot. "Waylaid? You mean somebody shot at you? Who?"

"Don't know. I didn't see who." Eli shrugged the question aside. Truth be known, he had no idea which of Ruby's gang had lain in wait for him and it probably didn't matter a whole lot. He knew it hadn't been her personally. Whoever had tried to bushwhack him had used a rifle, and Ruby hadn't had one in her possession. Holzer was noted for using a rifle, but he disliked riding outside of towns.

Squirt peered at the horse's small wound. "I got some salve that'll do it right. Bring him on in. I'll put him in the back stall across from Mrs. Billings' Hoot. Hell of a note," he added, "when I've got to hide horses from outlaws. Good thing this 'un ain't that racehorse of yours."

Eli didn't disagree. "So Mrs. Billings is still here?"

"Yeah. She's been out scouting the town and talking to folks and just got back. Took her about as long as it took you. Southbrook is still here, too. It's a regular dratted party. Doc had to go tend to his patients. Didn't want anybody to come looking for him and find Southbrook holed up."

"Good plan." Eli finished stripping his tack from the

horse and set his saddle on the rack the livery provided. Squirt, talking gently to the animal, led the gelding away to be tended.

While eager to check in with the marshal and January, the results of Eli's own meeting with Ruby had proved disappointing and wouldn't show much headway. He wished Ruby had been more forthcoming—or that he'd asked better questions. Made him mad all over again to think of the way she talked right through him. Maybe the folks here had gotten a handle on what was going on.

Pen rose from sitting beside January when Eli entered the overcrowded room where everyone was gathered. Tail wagging, she bounded over to greet him. They were friends. He'd carried the old dog on his horse when she'd gotten weary as they trailed January in the chase to save Zora Winkler. He thumped her side, scratched her ears, and murmured a bit of nonsense to the dog.

"You're that bounty hunter," Ollie said upon introduction.

"Used to be. Now I'm a rancher," Eli replied.

The old man stared doubtfully at him. "Huh."

Pleasantries soon dispensed with, they got down to business. Southbrook took the lead. Eli noticed that although January raised the earflaps on her ridiculous cap, she was back to keeping her head turned, hiding her scarred cheek from display.

The marshal rubbed his temples as though to scrub away a headache, and nodded to Eli. "What have you learned, Pasco? Did the woman tell you anything?"

"Nothing much. Going to meet her wasn't worth my time. I still don't understand why she bothered to ride all the way out to the ranch." Probably to set him up for the ambush, he finally concluded. She'd always been smart and had probably figured he'd follow her back to town. Easy to have one of her outlaw friends kill him so she could claim innocence.

"Ruby Pasco..." He noticed the way the marshal's eyes sharpened at the name. "She and I have a history. It's personal and it's not good. I don't know as it has anything to do with the situation here in town. I did learn there are more men, several of them recently released from prison, arriving here than seems logical. I'd say they've got plans for a big haul. I just don't know what it is."

Eli wasn't telling the whole truth. If it weren't for him, and Ruby's vendetta against him, these people might have chosen another town to harass. And he suspected a good many of the men were those he'd captured and helped put in prison. His popularity was doubtful.

January knew the story behind Ruby and himself—or some of it—but she kept silent. He was grateful.

"Ruby told me Arden Holzer is the organizer of whatever is planned," he added. "He's smooth, logical, and ruthless. A killer who's supposed to be incarcerated."

Eyes narrowed, Southbrook said, "How do you know all this?"

"Because I'm the one who brought him in and had him arrested a couple years ago." Eli didn't flinch from the acknowledgment. "We already know some of the other men involved."

Southbrook's mouth grew taut. "Confirmed." He turned to January. "Deputy Billings? What did you discover while you were looking around town? Did Thurston provide any insight?"

Soft-voiced, January said, "I don't know what this means but Mr. Thurston mentioned seeing Mr. Pearson, the banker, acting strangely the last few days. Pacing around, being short with customers, seeming preoccupied but at the same time, extra vigilant. T.T. suggested talking with Mr. Ollie, since he works at the bank. That's why he's here."

Southbrook nodded. "You must've drawn some conclusions on your own. Anything else?"

January's smile flashed. "Oh, yes. Here and there. Among other things, I understand the telegraph is not working properly. In an odd sort of malfunction, it seems to be cutting in and out. I don't know about you, but to me this sounds as if someone is listening to the messages and controlling access. As Mr. Pasco said, this is a gathering of convicts. Arden Holzer isn't the only one. There are several others of particular reputation, a certain Nelson Peel, for one." She glanced at Eli out of the corner of her eyes as she said the name.

A name that resounded in Eli's ears like a cracked cathedral bell. Only not nearly as musical.

January was still explaining. "Put them together with Pearson's behavior and the telegraph, and my guess is there's a bank heist in the works."

Eli startled erect from where he leaned against the wall. "A bank heist? Is there enough money deposited here to warrant involving this many men in a robbery?" His brows drew together as he pondered. "It makes sense, I guess. Holzer has tried bank robbery before—and succeeded, for a while. Until I caught up with him and brought him in." He refrained from adding the bounty had added nicely to his bank account and helped to buy his property. "But if that's the case, where's the money coming from? With this many men involved, it's got to be something special."

"Yes. I agree." January's gaze seemed to warn him to say no more. She turned to the marshal. "Marshal Southbrook, have you heard anything about a payroll deposit or a land sale underway? Something that puts a large amount of cash on deposit in the bank?"

Eli watched the marshal shake his head. He couldn't see any signs Southbrook was holding anything back. Whatever was going on, he wasn't privy to it.

"Something secretive, then," Eli said, "kept under tight wraps. Sounds like a transaction the government may be behind. Or a big corporation." The idea set him to thinking, and from the look on Southbrook's face, a similar thought had begun percolating in his mind.

"If so, how did these fellows find out about it?" Southbrook was still frowning. "And why haven't I—or Dabney, for that matter—been warned to be on the look-out?"

"Ruby," Eli bit out. "She manages to have connections in every corner. Men confide in her. Men who should know better." *Like my father.* And a moment later, *Like me.* At least he'd learned quickly what a trickster she was. Not all men did. Ever.

January, not one to be left behind, had noticed the marshal's expression. "What are you thinking, Marshal? I can see you've had an idea."

Southbrook held up one finger.

"Ollie," he said, "it's time to speak up. What have you learned?"

The older man shot a glance at Squirt, who nodded.

Reassurance between friends who trusted each other, a trait Eli admired.

Ollie brushed bread crumbs from his chin whiskers. "It ain't what I heard so much. It's what I seen, so mostly, this is just what jumps into my mind. It ain't something Pearson told me. It's a guess."

Heads nodded encouragement.

"I reckon you all remember Albert Sims and Marvin Hammel," Ollie said, then flushed crimson as he appeared to remember he was talking to January Billings, who had rid the territory of these same bad people.

Eli had heard a bit about it more than once, though not from January herself. Sims, the banker, and Hammel, an influential landowner, had been bilking men out of their property by shutting off their river access to water their cattle and crops. His idea had been to buy their land for a song and start an electric power plant to service the northern mines. The two had intended on flooding the rich land along the river to store the water. Somehow, January and her late husband had foiled the plot.

She'd been unmarried then, her last name Schutt, hence the S-shaped scar on her cheek, courtesy of her mad grandfather.

"What about them, Ollie?" Eli asked quietly. "What's the connection with Pearson?"

"Don't know as there is a connection. But I figure he might be getting hoodwinked. Tell you what I think. First off, folks don't much notice an old man like me." Ollie sounded just a little bitter at the idea. "I'm around a lot, keep my mouth shut, just do my work. But I keep my eyes and ears open." The tips of those ears remained red as he talked. "Back when Sims had the bank and was in cahoots with Hammel, they was talking with men from British Columbia about flooding the area for their dam. Everybody knows that now. The plot fell through, and thank God it did. This here is too good of ranch country to destroy. But then I seen one of those same Canadian fellers what hung around Sims in a meeting with Pearson. Him and some other feller, an American."

"When was this?" January leaned forward as if to encourage the old man.

"A couple weeks ago." Ollie lowered his eyes as they all stared at him. "Happened just at closing time and them two fellers got off the train and come directly to the bank."

"How do you know they came directly?" Southbrook asked.

"Because Pearson sent me to meet 'em at the station. I carried a satchel for one of 'em. It were fair-to-middling heavy, too. Then Pearson sent the teller home five minutes early and locked the bank's door. I 'spect you know closin' early ain't like him, so when he told me to skedaddle on out and chop some wood, I knowed somethin' was up. I didn't trust 'em, so I went out—" His face colored up again as he admitted, "—but I stuck my ear against the door and listened."

"What did they have to say, Ollie?" Southbrook's eyes were narrowed, sharp on the older man.

"I couldn't hear everything." Ollie shifted his back as if the hump hurt. "But one feller says, 'This'll be your portion provided the transaction remains secret,' and Pearson whistles and says, 'This is a lotta money.' So the feller says, 'Worth your while, I'd say.'"

"Did you see money change hands?" January asked.

"No, ma'am. But Pearson says, soundin' kinda worried, 'You sure this is all in order and legal? It doesn't seem...' but the other feller cuts Pearson off and says, 'Mind your Ps and Qs, Pearson, and you'll come out fine. Don't, and the results won't be to your liking. Men will be arriving soon. We'll meet again when they get here.'"

Even Squirt blinked at this. "Sounds like a threat to me. You mean to say Pearson actually stood for a man talking to him like that?"

"Well," Ollie said, "I reckon he did. Don't know. I told you. I couldn't hear everything. But I didn't figure I'd better stand there no more so I skedaddled on off to where I shoulda been. But what I do know is that Pearson ain't been the same since."

"That's it?" Southbrook said.

Ollie nodded. "Except when them men left, they wasn't carryin' the satchel. When they left, I heard one say they'd be back."

Eli's thoughts were racing. "And has a second meeting taken place?" He caught the way January's gaze fixed on him.

The old man looked almost relieved to be asked. "It has. A few days later, at night. A meetin' on the sly."

"On the sly?" Southbrook said as if questioning what the word meant.

"Sneaking." It may have been Johnny who spoke. Eli wasn't sure.

"What else would you call it when they met in the office along about ten o'clock in the evenin'." Ollie paused to sniff his considerable nose. "I should've been gone home, I suppose, but truth to tell, I weren't feeling too perky for most the day and it took longer to get through my chores than usual. I was just about to leave when they showed up and sort of trapped me inside. Couldn't help seeing who they was and overhearing their confabulation."

"Yeah?" Southbrook made an encouraging sound and Eli, who'd resumed leaning against the wall due to a lack of chairs, stood up straight.

"Yeah." Ollie nodded vigorously. "Now, I ain't sure but what Pearson is gettin' duped by these out-of-town-ers. Some of them is pretty hard-looking fellers. Threat-enin'. That's the word, even to a feller like Pearson, who's...well, never mind about him. Anyways, takes somebody smarter than me to figure out what's going on. I've been worrying over it." He turned to South-brook. "That's why I'm here. T.T. said I should tell you. You or the lady." He nodded toward January, who smiled at him. "Said you'd know what to do."

"What did they have to say, Mr. Ollie? What's got you in a turmoil?" January's voice was calm and a little of the high color in Ollie's face faded. "Is there anything else?"

Ollie nodded his grizzled head.

"What is it?" Her question sounded merely curious.

"One of those Canadians from before? He's in town right now, and if you ask me, he's up to no good."

The blood rushed to Eli's head as he waited for Ollie's next words, sure to be important. He wasn't disappointed.

"It's the one I heard called Nelson Peel."

Eli's fists clenched. Peel was the brother of a very bad man whose illegal operation he and January had taken down when they first met. Nelson Peel hadn't been involved in that case, but he might be planning to take a hand here because of it.

"He's the fancy dresser who's been walking around town smiling and friendly," Ollie said. "Only he ain't friendly at all. He's the one who clunked Southbrook here on the head and left him alayin' on the ground in the snow. I seen him do it and told Squirt."

"You did?" January said, sounding astonished. "Squirt, I thought you found the marshal."

Squirt wriggled a little. "Well, see, Ollie being a little shy, he told me, and we figured it wouldn't matter which of us actually found him, as long as we got him some help. It don't, does it?" He looked to Southbrook for an answer.

"Nah." Southbrook started to shake his head but changed his mind. "Guess I don't know. Looks like I've got a bone to pick with this Nelson Peel."

Eli huffed what was almost a chuckle. "You might have to get in line."

# CHAPTER 10

A PIERCING WHISTLE FROM OUTSIDE BLASTED LOUDLY enough the old burro Squirt kept around to help calm the horses was startled into braying. From one of the empty stalls, Sam said, "Wha..." and Pen barked. The rest of them, except for Eli, froze in place. He reached under his coat for his Mauser.

"Hey there, you in the livery. Open up." A thump against the side of the barn provided punctuation. "You in business or just there to clean up manure? I need a horse."

The demand forcefully interrupted their meeting, leaving a whole lot of business unspoken.

Squirt scowled fit to frighten the bogeyman. "Must be a drunk. Hold on and I'll run him off. I don't rent my horses to drunks."

But it turned out the customer was not intoxicated —just demanding and belligerent. Squirt, somewhat reluctantly, supplied him with a red roan mare and watched him ride off along the road headed east. If he stayed on it, the road would take him to the bridge at Kindred Creek and January's half-built house.

The direction drew Eli's attention a second after January's, bringing a new consideration to the situation. The two of them stood alongside Squirt watching the man ride out of sight. Squirt scratched his head as if worrying about his horse. Not that January blamed him. She couldn't help but worry about her house and it was just rocks and boards. *And hours and hours of labor.* But not, at least, a living creature.

January's thoughts drifted to the people Johnny said were camped in her house. Who were they? More outlaws? If so, why were they hiding there? Something to worry about later, she figured as the discussion resumed.

They'd just settled again when the sound of a single gunshot, more disturbing even than their previous interruption, made them all jump. It put a stop to her speculation. The report was a little muffled, as if coming from behind closed doors.

"Dang." Squirt, gawking around, was the first to recognize the location. Perhaps from having heard its like before since in the old days, even a law-abiding town like The Falls sometimes got rambunctious. "If I ain't mistaken, that come from the Barefoot."

"You're not mistaken." January flipped the lapel of her coat outward so the deputy's badge pinned there was revealed. "I'll go see what's going on."

She couldn't hide her dread.

"Not alone, you won't," Eli said.

He spoke to her back as she'd already let herself out of the livery and set off at a quick jog trot toward the saloon. Squirt called something to her that she didn't hear. Eli followed only a few steps behind. With his longer stride he soon caught up.

She barely had time to get her .38 from holster to hand before she reached the Barefoot. Eli had his Broomhandle out, although, like her, he held it at his side. Stopping short of the saloon's door, January raised up on tiptoe in an attempt to peer through a small window placed high in the wall to let in a bit of light.

"See anyone?" Eli loomed above her, trying to see over her head.

"No. Nothing but shadows. The window is too dirty. I'll have to take a chance on the door." Her heart was thumping to beat two of a kind. "Stay out of it, Eli. This is my job. Let's hold you in reserve." Caught up in alarm, she forgot their previous stiffness.

Inside, there was a crash, the sound of glass breaking, then a second shot followed by a hollow-sounding thud. January chose that moment to slip through the door, entering as she heard Bud Knowles bellow something about a crazy fatherless son.

"Hold it. Stop right there." Knowles stood behind the bar as if deciding whether to fire the shotgun in his hands, or to duck—not that the bar's wooden front made for a bullet-proof barricade. "You men get outta my place. You want to fight, kill each other, do it outside."

His demands went unheard, or maybe just ignored. Knowles's normally pleasant face was contorted in an angry grimace. He raised the sawed-off shotgun and had it leveled on two men fighting for possession of... something. January couldn't tell just what. One of the men had a gun and was trying to level it on the other. They both ignored Knowles's shotgun.

A glance showed her a body already lay on the floor, blood seeping from a hole high in his chest. Whoever it was, he wasn't moving. *Possibly dead.* January made an estimation without pausing. *Probably dead.* She stepped between the two men and slammed the barrel of her .38 onto the hand holding the gun. The gun dropped to the floor.

With a triumphant cry, the second gent made to pounce on it. But he moved a second too slowly, as the toe of Eli's boot caught the trigger guard and sent the pistol spinning. All the way across the floor where it skidded out of sight.

"You are under arrest, mister." January spoke into the disarmed man's angry face. He hauled back his arm and readied himself to slug her. Instead of dodging, she lunged forward, slapping his face hard with the barrel of her .38, then skipped backward out of reach as stunned, he slumped.

Blood coursed from the split over his cheekbone, though January found herself unmoved and unsympathetic. "Settle down, buster. You're going to jail." Snatching a pair of metal cuffs from her coat pocket, she yanked his arms behind him and clamped them on. If he'd thought he was competing with a delicate woman, he was mistaken. She may have been slim and fine-boned, but she had whipcord muscles from the work she did every day.

Blinking a little, she saw Eli had the second man's arm twisted to his back and was pushing him out of the way. Both men were still yelling, Eli's captive trying to tell his side of the story. January's simply cursed, vividly, she noticed with half a mind, blaming her for spoiling a good fight.

Bud Knowles had his shotgun pointed at the floor now. Taking a good look at him, she thought he looked a little pale. His gaze fixed on her with relief.

"Dang." He exhaled a sharp breath. "I sure am glad to see you, Mrs. Billings, and not that lily-livered Dabney. Thought I was gonna have to shoot somebody."

January felt a little pale herself. "Who shot that one?" She nodded toward the body on the floor.

"Him." Bud indicated her prisoner. "He picked a fight over nothing and drew his gun."

"Nothing?" January repeated.

Her prisoner began a denial. "Shut up," she said.

"Unless you consider the shape of the kid's doggone hat something, I suppose." Knowles pointed at a crumpled brown hat on the floor. "The kid didn't even have a gun. Cold-blooded murder, I call it." Bud shook his head as if he still couldn't believe a man getting killed in his normally calm saloon. Let alone for such a trivial reason.

Even January knew local men gathered around his tables of an evening—sometimes an afternoon—as groups of friends. They had a drink, played penny-ante poker, and caught each other up on local doings. There hadn't been a lethal shooting since Knowles had bought the place. A couple accidentally misplaced bullets, is all.

Panting a little—and come to think of it, she had been running—January took a moment to decide what her next step should be. Then she had it. "Can you check if this man is dead?" A jerk of her head indicated the man on the floor. Had that been a tiny rise of his chest or was she seeing things? "And send someone for Doctor LeBret. If he's dead, we need Doc to make the

pronouncement. If he's not, it looks like he could use some help."

His relief apparent at having something to do, Bud knelt beside the man. "No rush. He's dead all right," he reported.

Question answered. She'd been seeing things. "Do you know who he is?"

"Works at the Inman ranch, I think. Him, too. Them Inman ladies are gonna be upset." Bud nodded his head toward the young hand who'd been wrestling with the gunman. He'd collapsed onto a chair when Eli released him. January saw a tear slide down his cheek.

He let out a moan. "You got that right," he said. "She'll can me for sure. Jack and me wasn't supposed to be here. We was supposed to pick up supplies, then get right back home. We just thought we'd like a drink to keep us warm on the way."

A set of twins who owned a large ranch southeast of town, the Inman ladies were important people in the community. And with one of them married to the retired sheriff, it made them even more influential. Nobody wanted to get on their bad side, especially their ranch hands.

At last January turned her attention to Eli. He hadn't said a word as he watched over the kid who'd fallen silent now. In shock, she suspected, over his friend's death.

She gestured Eli closer. "We won't be able to keep this quiet for long. Whatever is in the works is apt to start as soon as news of this shooting gets out."

Eli nodded. "I can hear people talking outside already." He grinned suddenly. "I locked the door when I came in. Figured something like this might happen."

A benefit of his wide experience, January thought. "The back exit empties onto the loading dock." She jerked her thumb at the man she'd pistol-whipped. "We'll take this one out that way and get him over to the jail. Move quickly enough and maybe we can keep the news to ourselves a while longer."

"I'll take him," Eli said. "You can see this youngster goes out the front and doesn't talk to anybody. The quicker he's out of town, the better. If you have to say something, tell those folks there was an accidental shooting." He glanced at Bud. "All right with you?"

Knowles wiped sweat from his face. "You bet. Won't be the first." His face drew in, sober and scared at the same time. "I'm shutting down and not letting anybody in. I've had enough of these blowhards who've showed up in town."

To January's knowledge, Knowles had never closed the saloon before. The glimpse she'd had of him earlier, when Arden Holzer had been here and before Eli whisked her away, must've put a scare into him.

Next, she turned her attention to the ranch hand. "You. Promise to mount your horse and ride out without talking to anybody and you can go. Leave town immediately. Let the Inman women know about the shooting. Tell them the town is locked down and that there's trouble brewing. Tell them to keep their riders away from town."

The hand nodded his head so vigorously she wondered it didn't fall right off his shoulders. "Yes, ma'am. But what about Jack? And what about him?" He stared at the outlaw as if wishing for a lightning bolt to power on through him.

"I'll see to your partner. As for him—" She cocked a

thumb at the killer. "Don't you worry about him. He's my job. A judge and jury will see he gets what's coming to him."

The outlaw stood sullenly wiping blood from his face onto his shoulder—January hadn't been gentle either time she struck him—his eyes glaring hate.

She eyed him right back before saying, "Stuff a rag in this one's mouth, Eli. And watch yourself. He's plotting something."

Bud Knowles, Johnny-on-the-spot, tossed Eli the soiled rag he'd been using to wipe spills off the top of the bar. "Use this."

Chuffing a short laugh, and encountering some difficulty due to the prisoner's objections, Eli complied. Turned out he had a real knack at handling prisoners who protested.

Southbrook had passed the jail's key to January earlier, when it became clear he was not yet in any condition to take up his work. In turn, she slipped the key into Eli's hand. "See if you can get him to talk. Maybe he even knows what those outlaws are cooking up."

"I imagine he's only here to lend another gun. He doesn't strike me as smart enough to be in on the planning."

"I expect you're right. Meet us back at the livery when you have him locked up." She spoke quietly, so the prisoner couldn't hear.

Eli nodded. "And you be careful when you walk out of here. Be ready to duck."

"I will. You too." She almost wished he hadn't said that, as if saying it out loud would increase the danger.

Knowles led the way to the rear of the building, Eli

and the outlaw following. The prisoner kept up a steady mutter through his gag, right up until Eli sank his fist into the man's skinny gut. With him doubled over and gasping for air, they trooped through a storeroom redolent of beer from a keg whose tap dripped to the board platform it sat on. The sharp yeasty smell permeated the wood and filled the air.

Other spirits blended with the brew, until January believed she might become dizzy on the fumes alone. "I'll step out first and see if the way is clear."

She studied the alley, finally pronouncing it safe. "Leave him gagged and cuffed. Don't take any chances with him." Not that Eli needed the warning. He had a whole lot more experience than she did in this kind of situation.

"Yes, ma'am." Eli grinned at her anyway. "Does this make me a deputy deputy?"

The playfulness of his words surprised a laugh out of her. "I think it does."

\* \* \*

Eli, pleased he'd done something to relieve the tension he saw in January's face, poked the outlaw in his ribs. "Move."

Flinching from Eli's prodding, the outlaw broke into a shambling run, awkward considering his hands were confined behind his back and he was still short of breath from the blow to his gut. Eli had no sympathy to spare. The sheriff's office was on the same side of the street as the saloon, so only one spot along the way gave him fits. They'd be in plain sight while crossing a lot empty except for a stack of lumber awaiting a new construction project.

He stopped the outlaw while they remained concealed behind the harness shop. "Wait." He scanned the area between the buildings and had just decided the way was clear when he saw movement on the other side of the lumber. A man stood behind it, mostly hidden until a shift in position put him in sight. A stream of smoke rose as the fellow lit a cheroot.

Eli's fingers clenched around his prisoner's arm, holding him motionless. An imprecation under his breath did nothing to get the watcher moving. He wasn't sure how long it took before the figure slipped from hiding and walked toward the saloon and a group of men gathered there. Eli took the chance to push his prisoner forward. As he did, he spotted January.

She had just opened the saloon's door and stepped outside with the young ranch hand. Gripping his arm, she marched him toward his horse.

Someone rushed forward to meet with her, waving his hands as if attempting to raise a wind. Voices rose, carrying across the way. She'd timed the exit just right. Something to divert the curious—and any of Holzer's men who might be watching. That included the man behind the lumber who might have been one of the outlaws. Or simply a local stopping out of the wind to light his cigar. Whichever, he'd moved on, beyond concern.

A prod with the barrel of Eli's pistol forced his prisoner to pass through the open area at a trot. They continued jogging until they reached the jail. Eli, fingers a little clumsy with haste, unlocked the door and shoved the outlaw inside.

The first thing he noticed was the chill. Southbrook had been out of the office for a good many hours by now, laid up over at the livery. The fire in the stove had gone out. Eli manhandled the prisoner, who dug in his heels and was making noise through the towel in his mouth, into one of the two cells the jail boasted and locked it.

January, he remembered, had told him to question the outlaw. Not expecting to learn anything of the gang's plans, he made a try.

"You cold?" he asked.

A glare and a nod answered him. Laying a fire, he stuffed a couple chunks of wood into the stove's fire box. Even so, he doubted the consideration would soften the fellow up.

"Stand in front of me and I'll take the gag out of your mouth." He could see the offer surprised the outlaw, who hurried to obey as though thinking Eli might change his mind.

Grasping a corner of the rag, Eli yanked. "What's your name?" He dropped the soggy rag on the floor.

"I ain't tellin'." The outlaw turned. "Take off these cuffs. My hand hurts where that bitch hit me with her gun. My face, too. My mouth don't work so good when I'm hurt."

"Bitch?" Eli repeated the word softly. "Could be it's best you *don't* talk. For sure best not to say that word again. Do, and it could be you tried to escape and I had to shoot you."

The man's mouth opened and closed. Blood from the cut on his cheekbone dribbled toward his chin. "What?"

Eli stood next to the cell bars and shook his head.

"You heard me. Now, your name? I've got to book you into the jail with some kind of identification."

"Yeah? Well, I ain't talkin'. I'm a sick man."

"Sick in the head, is all. So is any man who lets himself be taken in by people like Holzer and Peel." Just saying the name "Peel" made him feel queasy, and he could only imagine how January had felt when she heard it.

As he'd expected, the man took offense at the 'sick in the head' comment. Or maybe it was the easy way he named Holzer and Peel.

"You won't be talking with a loose tongue when they get done with this town." The outlaw tried to sneer, but the muscle twitch stretched the gash on his cheek and he huffed out a stifled moan instead.

Forcing a chuckle, Eli said, "You think so? I say they're more apt to get shot out of their saddles if they venture too close to the bank. We've got people all around it," he added for good measure. "The people in charge, they're not fools."

A telltale blink showed him the bank was most certainly the target. No surprise there.

"So," Eli continued, "what's your first name, Oldham? I know you've got a brother and I'm not sure which of you is which. I hear you're both cut from the same cloth."

The prisoner's jaw dropped. "You know who I am? Then why'd you ask?"

Eli almost laughed out loud at the outlaw's shock. As a bounty hunter, he'd seen sketches, photographs, and written descriptions of most every outlaw in a four-state area who had a price on his head. It had been a while for this one—and his brother—but Eli had an excellent memory.

If Oldham's surprise when he mentioned the bank had been obvious, it was nothing compared to his being identified.

Eli cocked an eyebrow.

"Willie," Oldham admitted after a while. "I'm Willie. Otis is my brother. But he ain't here. He's over in BC."

"Doing what?"

"Doin' what? I dunno." Oldham looked away.

He knew, all right. Eli figured the other Oldham was part of the Canadian connection. Maybe even the reason the gang was holding off on robbing the bank. Seemed he'd heard Otis was the smarter of the two, although that probably wasn't saying a whole lot. But Willie was noted for knowing how to blow a safe.

"When do they plan to carry out the heist?" Eli demanded.

"Heist? You mean a robbery? Who says anybody is planning a robbery?" Willie stubbornly denied the foregone conclusion.

Eli huffed out a short laugh. "I say so. Evidence says so. You might as well tell me about the plan."

But unfortunately for Willie Oldham, he didn't know anything of importance, and Eli, feeling the need to get back to January and the others, soon gave up. This man was a pawn on a large chessboard. Expendable.

He checked the cell was secure, made sure the fire was safe inside the stove's firebox, and prepared to leave.

"Hey. You can't leave yet." Oldham pressed his face against the bars. "You said you'd take these cuffs off me."

"I said I'd consider it." Eli opened the outer door

and stuck his head out, scanning his surroundings for potential troublemakers.

"Well?" Oldham's temper seemed to be rising along with his voice. "Consarn it! Take 'em off."

Eli turned. "Yeah. About that. I did consider it. Decided it wouldn't be advisable." He shut the door on Oldham's complaint as he left, carefully relocking the door behind him. A heavy door, he noted. One made of thick planks that efficiently muffled the outlaw's increasing invective.

# CHAPTER 11

THE INMAN'S SURVIVING RANCH HAND SOON DISCOVERED January had a sympathetic ear. He alternately sobbed and talked as they waited while Eli and the outlaw made their way to the jail. He rattled on, frequently repeating himself, glancing at Bud Knowles now and then for verification as if he couldn't believe this had happened. Knowles simply nodded and let him speak uninterrupted.

January listened, also remaining quiet for the most part. That the kid needed to purge his rage was obvious. Finally, he fell silent and she asked, "What's your name, mister? What's his name?"

No mistaking who she meant.

"Harry. My name is Harry Fuller. He's...that's Jack. Jack Blair." Glancing toward his dead companion, he sniffled, his hands trembling. He was twenty years old, he said. One year older than his friend Jack, laid out on the barroom floor waiting for Doc to arrive and pronounce what they already knew. Jack was most definitely dead.

Harry, she'd concluded, was shocked to the core. He maintained the two hadn't done anything to provoke Jack's killer. They'd been quiet, just having a shot of whiskey before starting back to the Inman ranch in the cold.

"Is that true?" she asked the barkeep.

Knowles nodded agreement.

This wasn't the old days, Harry kept saying, with adventures like they read about in the dime novels the hands read so avidly. Those were just stories purchased to pass away an evening in the bunkhouse.

"Folks don't walk into a saloon and start shooting," Harry insisted, despite uncontroversial proof otherwise. "Not over nothing. Jack's hat? Why would anybody do that? It don't make sense."

*Jack's hat?* It didn't make sense to January either.

"We didn't do anything to cause that feller to shoot Jack. Nothing." Tears leaked from his eyes and he looked away.

January, who knew all too well people did do such things and even worse—after all, she had personal experience—shook her head sorrowfully. "I believe you. You're lucky it wasn't you he shot," she said. "It could've been just as easily. If I hadn't gotten there when I did, you might've been next. Then Mr. Knowles." She doubted what she said made Harry feel any better. It sure didn't her.

Behind her, she heard Knowles make a sound, a sort of growl deep in his throat. Agreement? Or an indication he'd have had something to say about that. She thought the latter.

Minutes ticked past, until she figured Eli'd had time to get the murderer locked in a jail cell. Time for her to remove Harry from the room where his friend lay dead. The whole big room reeked of burnt gunpowder and death.

"Let's go, Harry. Remember not to speak to anyone. Anyone at all. Understand? I'll do any talking that needs done."

His head hung. "Yes, ma'am."

January felt weary and strained beyond limits, walking outside beside the young ranch hand. Strange to feel twice as old as the kid she escorted, although she wasn't such an awful many years ahead of him. Closing the saloon door behind her, she took a breath. People still milled around the front of the saloon, talking, gesturing, spitting. Several shouted questions at her, all wanting to know what was going on.

She marked out a path through them without answering.

Some of the folks January knew as locals. One or two caused her to narrow her eyes and memorize their features. But most prominent was Mort Erickson from the weekly newspaper, his notepad and a chewed pencil at the ready, as he waited to take down a statement. Or even a single word that might slip from her mouth.

His wife stood beside him, her gaze bright and eager. She, January had heard, was the brains of the two, and would be figuring out the next question for her husband to ask.

Silly, January couldn't help thinking. Why didn't Mrs. Erickson just do the job from the beginning and save everyone's time?

The moment she and Harry stepped beyond the door, they were pelted by questions flung about with increasing velocity.

"Where's Dabney?" "Shouldn't he be here?" "Where's the marshal?"

The questions came rapid fire. She couldn't even tell who was asking what.

"Deputy Dabney is indisposed," she said, tongue firmly in cheek. The answer seemed to surprise no one. "Marshal Southbrook was attacked early this morning on his rounds. He is recovering at home, but will be with us soon."

Gasps and widened eyes from the few women marked this news. A low muttering indicated several of the local men had taken notice of the influx of strangers in town. Her evasive report didn't help. January gritted her teeth as more questions came at her.

Ignoring them, she pushed Harry toward the horses.

"We heard shots," Peevy from the feed store said.

"Has someone been killed?" a timorous woman asked, her hands clasped together as if in prayer.

"It looks like someone has been killed," another woman said.

January had to stop. "I'm saddened to say, yes, someone has been killed. But you can all go home now. The excitement is over. The undertaker will be here directly. Show some respect and clear the way." January took note of Erickson writing furiously, his wife leaning over his shoulder, urging him to ask another question.

Erickson pointed his pencil at Harry. "Who done it? Him?"

She had to answer this, for fear they'd attack Harry. "No. A stranger in town."

More questions were hurled at her.

"Who's dead?" "Who did the shooting?" "Where is

the shooter?" "Did you get him?" "You've been known to shoot people. Is he dead, too?"

The questions came from more than one throat and showed they were aware of her reputation. The knot in her stomach shriveled into a hard ball. It felt like buckshot rattling around and tearing holes in her flesh.

She answered the first question. "A fellow who worked at the Inman ranch has been shot. Jack Blair." She looked to Harry and thought to ask a question of her own. "Was he from here?"

"No. From someplace in southern Idaho," he mumbled.

"Family?" she asked, and he shrugged.

Something she'd have to find out, unless this was at least one thing Dabney could—or would—do.

"Marshal Southbrook has asked me to handle the investigation for now. He'll be with us directly. I'm sure he'll want to speak with you then." She spoke firmly, though she was sure of no such thing. "Please, let this man mount up. He needs to report to the dead man's employers." More evasion.

They'd almost reached the horses when Doc LeBret came hurrying toward them. Their eyes met.

"Inside?" Doc asked.

She nodded and got Harry going again.

It surprised her when onlookers stepped aside and allowed them to pass, their attention caught by Doc's arrival. Harry gathered the reins to Jack's horse, standing at the hitch rail with his own bay. Mounting, his head down, Harry rode out leading Jack's mount. At the first side road, he spurred his horse into a lope and, yanking the other horse's reins, headed out of town. January said a little prayer, thanking God for getting him away before anyone had a chance to ask him about the killer. For instance, who he was and where he was now. Best if no one knew they had him locked up in the jail. She'd prefer not to deal with a lynch mob. Or an escape attempt.

Mrs. Erickson watched Harry go, giving January a sharp nod as if to indicate the questions were finished. For now, at any rate.

January would've laid money the Ericksons were already planning a visit to the Inman ranch. After they talked to Bud Knowles, that is. Best to warn Knowles to be careful what he said, too. She'd give him the same guidelines to follow she'd given Harry.

She stepped back to bar the saloon door. "The Barefoot is closed until further notice. I'm sure Mr. Knowles will let you know when he reopens."

It took a while to convince them. Eli had returned when she reentered the saloon, having arrived the same way he'd left, via the rear entrance. She took a moment, leaning against the wall and taking a deep breath. Then another.

*How odd*, she thought. Her hands were trembling.

Doc had already completed his examination of the body.

"Dead," he said. "Not hard to tell the cause what with that hole in his chest. A shot directly to the heart."

"You did good, Mrs. Billings." Knowles said to her. "Headed Erickson off for now, but you know it won't last. He'll be around."

He'd had an ear to the door listening to the goings on outside, while still finding time to help Doc throw a covering over Jack Blair's body. It was an old sheet, January thought. Probably the one he tore into the rags he used to wipe the bar. What remained of it was blood-stained, most certainly beyond further use. "I know. I think you can put him off, as long as Mrs. Erickson isn't with him."

Knowles managed a laugh, not at all like the hearty one he was known for. "She won't come in here. Might upset her standing in town."

January wasn't so sure. This was probably the most exciting story they'd had to report on for months. A change from lost dogs, tipped over outhouses, and the new teacher who'd come from teaching in some exotic place like Hawaii.

She turned to Eli. "Did anybody see you?"

"Not that I know of. Willie Oldham is locked up tight. I left your cuffs on him. He won't be going anywhere."

"Oldham? You got his name? You must have powerful methods of persuasion."

"Yeah." Eli's grin flashed. "I didn't even have to beat him bloody. Surprised him, too. I recognized him from seeing a poster with his picture on it a while back. He's been locked-up lately, so I don't think the paper on him is valid now."

"Say there, Pasco," Knowles said, "you have a fine memory. You'd make a decent bartender."

Eli spurted a laugh. "Goes with my job. My former job."

January wasn't the only one who thought Eli Pasco would never be completely divorced from his former occupation. Which also meant his life would always be in jeopardy from outlaws who held a grudge. She stowed that in her memory to think on further.

Doc picked up his medical bag. "We need find out

what these people are doing here and put a stop to it. And to do that, we have to know what kind of men we're dealing with."

"I think we do know," January said. A glance at the sheet-covered form told the story.

Knowles took a clean piece of cloth from under the counter and began polishing glasses again. "I can tell you one thing," he said. "About the leader. He and some of his men kept me up all last night, waiting for some other fella. The outlaw you hauled off, he was in here then, too. I couldn't hear what they were saying, but I doubt the headman is gonna be pleased over this turn of events."

January, hesitant to admit to witnessing some of this herself, had one question. "We've heard the ringleader's name, Mr. Knowles, but did you catch any others?"

"One or two. A feller called Newton got a mention. He's the one they've been waiting for. A certain Mr. Peel. He's high up. They all call him *mister*, like he's some kind of bigwig. Even Holzer does. That's all." He glanced toward the body. "Wish the undertaker would get here. I don't like having a dead man laid out in my saloon."

January didn't hear much of anything after the mention of Peel's name. *Peel*. The very sound made her innards quake.

A knock at the back entrance indicated Knowles had gotten his wish. Leaving Eli to take charge then, January figured she'd best get herself over to the livery to bring Southbrook and Squirt, thoroughly enmeshed in this problem now, up to date before they all had conniption fits.

Slipping out, doing her best to avoid notice, she

made her way toward the livery. She soon caught up with a woman carrying a baby. A small boy toddled along beside the woman. They strolled along in front of January, their pace making her a little impatient. Out in the street, she noticed two men on horseback making their way toward the blacksmith shop. She recognized them both as local men minding their own business, the realization easing a knot of fear.

The blacksmith's wide entry door stood open, allowing the smoke wreathing over his head from the forge to escape. The clang of his hammer beating on iron drowned out both the men talking and the little boy chattering to his mother.

It didn't, however, cover the sound of the shot that came from somewhere above the street. Or the mother's sharp scream, or the curse from one of the horsemen whose sorrel mare jumped at the sharp report.

But the noise was all they had to worry about as it became clear January was the target. The bullet dug a trench a scant inch from the toe of her boots.

"Take cover!" Her call rang out, sending folks scattering for shelter. She set out to take her own advice, springing forward.

But then the woman ahead of her cried out, reaching for her son's hand even as the baby in her arms began bellowing. The infant slipped and the woman let go of the boy. The woman continued running, clumsy in her rush, toward the drugstore, urging her boy to run as well. And he tried, but within two steps the little duffer tripped over something—January suspected his own feet were to blame—and fell. His cries joined the baby's, the woman's, and even the horseman's as his mare cut loose with a full-fledged bucking spree.

Another shot sounded. A bullet plucked at January's coat. She reached for her .38, desperate for a target. Movement, more sensed than seen, drew her eyes to the roof of the drugstore, up where the owner had a couple rooms to let when the hotel was full. Was that a rifle barrel poking out the window?

Yes. Sunlight glinted off the barrel.

She fired, the pistol's crack sharp in her ears. The rifle barrel disappeared.

Breaking into a run, she headed for the drugstore entrance, her first instinct being to catch the shooter before he got away. But then, with a few horses pulled away from the hitch rail running amok, and one close to trampling anyone on foot, she swooped the boy off the ground as she passed and carried him, squealing and screaming, toward the nearest building. Her surge took her past the mother, by now crying and screaming herself.

January left the horsemen to their own devices, and from the corner of her eye, saw one of them racing down the street out of range. The bucking horse dumped its rider and followed, leaving the man on his hands and knees in the mud.

She couldn't carry him, too. He was on his own.

A third shot went over her head, the rifleman having found a new position from which to shoot. One January couldn't see from where she was. Hopefully, the shooter's view of her was no better.

January rushed herself and the kid into the dim interior of whatever business they'd stumbled into. Setting the child upright as his mother followed them in, she discovered it to be the pool hall. A few men stood about with cue-sticks in one hand, beer mugs in the other. They'd fallen silent and were staring.

This, after all, was not a venue for women to invade. From their astonished expressions, not even women being shot at.

January pulled the earflap on her hat over her scarred cheek. "Good morning," she said. "Don't worry, we'll be gone as soon as the shooting stops."

A gabble arose. A couple men exclaimed over the boy. To her surprise, they surrounded the little family in a protective shield.

January took the opportunity to get out while nobody was looking and follow down the first side street taking her to the rear of the drug store. This time, she held the .38 in her hand.

Taking into account the noise still coming from the street, a combination of several loose horses clomping and whinnying, and people whooping and hollering, January supposed the shooter would make his escape out the rear of the drug store. When she pounded up, a tad short on breath from her run, she didn't expect to find an outside stairway leading to a small second story. The landing had two doors. No need then, for whoever occupied the rooms there to pass through the store on the way out.

At that point, she figured she'd arrived too late. The shooter must have escaped by now.

Still, she was a woman noted for her careful assessment of the facts. A lesson her father had taught her as they skipped from place to place evading the law he'd only imagined was chasing them.

January spent long moments studying the windows in the two doors. Watching for movement. Watching for shadows, for anything out of place. Just as she was about to move forward, one of the doors opened and a man stepped out. She froze, glad to be concealed behind some barrels stacked behind the store.

The man paused at the top of the stairs, his head turning from side to side as he scanned the area. He carried a bolt-action rifle across his chest where a single motion would bring it to his shoulder.

She recognized him as much for the way he carried the rifle as for his looks. Those were as average as they could be. He wore a plain brown canvas coat over denim britches, and high-top lace-up boots. She couldn't reliably make out his features, mostly concealed by a black felt hat pulled low over his ears. He'd carried a shotgun in an identical way earlier as he patrolled the alley behind the Barefoot Saloon, when he'd missed seeing her and Eli under the loading dock. And he kind of hunched as he walked.

Her anger had carried her this far. Now she found herself wondering if she should take him on. Would a .38 revolver, carried in her hand, be a match for his rifle, held close to his chest? Who'd take action first, her or him?

One difference, she told herself. She was aware of him. He, by the look of things, was not aware of her. Surprise was on her side.

A moment later, she had no choice. He'd supposed the way clear and trod down the steps, clearly intending to make a getaway. And he headed right toward where she stood.

Making her decision, she stepped from behind the barrels.

"Hold it there," she said.

Startled, he stopped, staring toward her as if thinking she'd popped out of the ground like a weed. His gaze settled on her scar.

"Set your rifle on the ground and raise your hands," she snapped, her anger flaring anew. "You're under arrest."

Maybe, if her voice had been stronger, more commanding and without that slight, disconcerting quiver marring the steadiness, he would've done what she said. Maybe.

But he didn't. He laughed. "Under arrest? Says who? That some kind of joke, woman?"

"I am Deputy January Billings, and this is no joke. Place your rifle on the ground. Now." Steadier. Firmer.

Beyond his orders to kill her, she could tell he'd heard about her. About how she'd taken on outlaws before—and won. His face, sharp-nosed like a fox, changed. Grew harder.

In a move she knew he must've spent hours practicing, the rifle dropped *down* into his hands and, in a single blurred motion, he pulled the trigger.

# CHAPTER 12

It could've been funny, him thinking she'd stand paralyzed like a deer in a moonbeam and allow him to shoot her. Only it wasn't.

Instinct took over. January zagged when he must've figured she'd zig.

He had, she thought a little snidely, practiced his fancy move with the rifle for speed, not accuracy. The bullet went low, blasting a hole in the barrel beside her. Liquid splashed out, something smelly she couldn't place. She skipped out of the way; toward him, as it happened.

His mouth sagged open, as if he couldn't believe he'd missed the shot and he worked the rifle's bolt to chamber another round. He was fast at it, too. But not fast enough.

Just about anyone could've warned him he should've dropped the rifle when she ordered him to. Worse yet, he was too stupid to do so now. He reefed the rifle into firing position a second, or maybe even two, too late.

January's .38 spat fire.

A red stain blossomed on the front of his jacket. His knees buckled as he fell onto his face, squirming and kicking and trying to crawl until after what seemed a very long time, he lay still, the rifle caught under his body.

No. Not funny at all—for him.

Nor for her. Sickness rose in her throat. She swallowed it down, willing it to settle.

Shouts arose from the front of the building, even as Mr. Brady, the drugstore's proprietor inched out onto the small stoop and peered cautiously around before his gaze settled on the downed man. Then it moved to her.

The whites of his eyes surrounded the iris, giving him a wild, almost crazed look, strange for a man generally noted for his calm, dapper appearance.

Right now, he acted awestruck. "I saw it. I saw it all. Mrs. Billings..."

She cut him off. "Deputy Billings, sir. With Sheriff Dabney in hiding and Marshal Southbrook out of commission, I have the responsibility for upholding the law in The Falls."

He appeared not to hear her. "You're a hero. A heroine. A...a... How did you know where to look for him? He threatened to shoot me and my wife if we tried to warn anyone."

January worked hard to keep her lip from curling. Mr. Brady's actions—or rather, lack of any action at all—proved he was not the sort to appear in legends. "Simple. I spotted him from the street when he shot at me. It stood to reason he'd come out this way. Is everyone all right in the store?"

"Yes, yes. The ladies, of course, were terribly frightened and upset."

*As if he was not?*

In truth, January still felt a tad shaky herself, stomach churning and waves of heat flushing through her. She took a couple deep breaths to recharge. The deaths of two men in the space of a half-hour took its toll.

Help arrived in the form of Sam from the livery. "Squirt sent me over," he announced, puffing like an overheated steam engine. "We heard shootin' and him and Southbrook said I should find out what's goin' on." He spent a moment staring down at the dead man, glancing from the corpse to the pistol January still held. "You shoot him, ma'am?"

Her head tilted; a bare nod.

"I saw it all," the druggist broke in again, full of importance. "She gave him every chance to give up but he wouldn't do it. He shot first and missed. We've got a regular Annie Oakley in our midst."

Annie Oakley shot only at targets, if she remembered correctly. Or maybe food for the table. She wished she did.

January shuddered. Had Eli suffered this kind of reaction when he'd been a bounty hunter? Is it why he'd quit? What about U.S. Deputy Marshal Ford Tervo, who had taught her to always aim for the largest body mass? He'd told her when in a gun fight, aiming for anything less than lethal was a good way to get yourself killed.

She turned to the druggist. "Mr. Brady, if you'd be so kind as to send for Mr. Hannon at the funeral parlor I'd appreciate it. He's already had one customer this morning, so he may be a while getting here. Please keep everyone away meanwhile."

"Of course, Deputy Billings," Brady said. "He'll want to know who to bill."

January's eyelid twitched. "Depends." She didn't say on what.

"Oh," he said. "Oh."

There was more. He wanted to know what was going on in town, having noticed several strangers, hardcases all, or so he deemed them, prowling the streets these last couple days. January shrugged. It wasn't up to her to keep anyone, except Southbrook and maybe T.T. and Squirt, informed of anything. And Eli Pasco.

People began filtering closer to see what the gunfire had meant, exclaiming over the body. Brady tried to shoo them off, not very efficiently. She backed away. Someone attracted the druggist's attention and he, full of self-importance now the danger had passed, turned to spread the news. Sam, she noticed, wariness trickling through her, had already disappeared. Smart of him.

Spinning on her heel, she left, too, taking a round-about way to the livery. Checking around a corner before walking into plain sight, she actually smiled, or at least discovered a bit of levity in the situation. Having the hub for the town's law and order situated in a livery stable full of horses when there was a perfectly stout jailhouse just up the street sort of tickled her funny-bone.

\* \* \*

JANUARY FOUND Marshal Southbrook on his feet and tracing a path up and down the barn's middle aisle. She couldn't decide if he exercised to regain strength or to work off his anxiety. Over at the side, she heard Squirt and Sam talking too softly for her to distinguish words as they cleaned a stall.

"Well?" Southbrook said sharply as January pushed inside. "What happened? Sam says you gunned somebody down."

*Gunned somebody down? Did he speak in accusation?* The shootout, if that's what he wanted to call it, had been in defense of her life.

"He said that?" January's heart lurched. "A man is dead. That much is true, but he shot at me first. Fortunately, he wasn't much of a marksman. He'd been scattering shots into the street very close to a woman and two small children while trying to get me. What else was I to do?" If her question came out cold, the next one sounded even colder. "Would you think more of me if I had allowed bystanders and myself to be killed?"

As if to prove a point, she took out her .38 and replaced the spent loads.

Southbrook stared. "No, Mrs. Billings. Of course not. It's just..."

"Just what?"

"I've never heard of a woman facing up to a gun before. Women—most women—don't want..."

"Don't want what? To protect themselves? Of course they do. Don't want to shoot someone? Probably not. But people have been trying to kill me since I was ten years old, and I'm still here." She pinned him with a cold-eyed stare. "It was a woman who murdered my husband. There's a woman in town right now who is as heartless and willing to shoot as any man. I'm not talking about myself, you understand. You'd best widen your horizons, Marshal Southbrook."

Southbrook rubbed his hand over his head where she knew the goose egg must still pain him.

"Right," he said. "You're right."

Eli stepped into the barn just then, no doubt bringing a measure of relief to the marshal even though January considered he'd brought the tension on himself. The interruption was a relief to her, as well. She was sick of shooting and death and wanted nothing more than to go home, take a hot bath, and cuddle with her good old dog.

Eli took in the frozen stillness between her and Southbrook as if trying to decide if she needed help. "Has Mrs. Billings told you we've locked a prisoner in your jail?" He sent what may have been a hint toward Southbrook. "He'll need tending to when you have time."

January, though she wasn't about to say so out loud, had almost forgotten the outlaw who'd shot young Jack Blair.

"A prisoner? Who? What's he done?" Southbrook asked.

Eli gave the marshal a questioning look. "Hasn't anyone told you yet? He's the gunslinger who murdered the young ranch hand over at the Barefoot. One of the men Holzer brought to town, a criminal by name of Oldham."

"What young ranch hand?" Southbrook groaned. "Lord Almighty! I've about had enough of this."

He, January thought wryly, had only suffered a simple whack on the head. Wait until he had people shooting at him. What he'd best do was grow a stouter backbone and be quick about it. This town couldn't tolerate another lawman of Dabney's ilk.

"What was the hand's name, Deputy Billings? Do you know?" Eli glanced over at her. "His partner is on his way back to the Inman ranch to report to his boss."

"His name is Blair. Jack Blair," January said.

Southbrook cursed softly. "The Inman ranch, eh? Home of the former sheriff. They ain't gonna be pleased."

"No one is pleased." Eli caught her eye and jerked his head the least bit toward Squirt's room, indicating she should retreat there.

She complied, hearing his voice as he recounted the circumstances of the shooting in the saloon. A minute later, he joined her.

"You cold?" he asked. "I saw you shiver." Without waiting for an answer, he shoved a stick of wood in the stove.

"Cold. Hot. I don't even know," she said, barely above a whisper.

"Sit down." He rinsed one of the coffee cups and poured a big dollop of Squirt's strong brew into it, adding an almost equal amount of sugar from a crock. "Drink this."

January tried to push it away. Drink all that sugar? Not on her tintype.

But Eli insisted. "It's good for you when you're feeling down."

Feeling down? Much lower and she figured she'd be inching along on her elbows. The coffee helped, maybe in a counterstroke against the sugar. Her own spine had just straightened a little when a whistle heralded the arrival of the weekly train coming down out of British Columbia. She and Eli looked at each other.

"One of us had better get over to the station and meet the train." Eli, who'd barely sat down, rose up again and shouted out the door to the marshal. "Southbrook, you feel up to seeing who and how many get off at this stop?"

A single groan answered.

"I'll go," January said.

"No." Eli tried to prevent her, but she got up like she weighed as much as the woman she'd heard called Fat Mary, one of the women she'd seen in the bakery's donut line earlier.

"Yes." She held up a hand to stop him. "They're less likely to recognize me than they are you." But she took off her Norwegian earflap hat and rummaged in her saddlebag for a plain, often-washed blue scarf to cover her distinctive mahogany-colored hair and the scar.

* * *

HOOT, January decided, was much too unique for her to be riding him where anyone connected to Ruby Pasco could see. Ruby wouldn't have been shy about setting her up, and the horse was a major way to pinpoint her. A pale silver gray with black mane and tail was a rare coloration in this part of Washington. There was no other of Hoot's ilk anywhere in the territory that she knew of—except his yearling brother.

In which case, January asked Squirt for a loaner, and minutes later she was on her way to the train depot outside of town on a nondescript brown gelding.

Wheels clattering and throwing sparks, the train

arriving from north of the border pulled level with the depot platform as she loped up. Leaving the horse behind the station, she walked around the corner and paused to speak with a couple ladies she vaguely knew by sight. One was the cook over at the café. The other, someone she'd spoken with in the mercantile regarding the purchase of some of January's butter. The woman had questioned January as to her sanitation process regarding the cream separator. January had passed muster. Today, the woman's excitement ran high as she announced in a high-pitched voice she was receiving a new rocking chair by freight.

January couldn't understand why the housewife hadn't asked T.T. to deliver the chair, shipped all the way from Toronto, until the woman said it was a catalogue purchase coming directly to her and not through the store. The woman rushed off to the mail car as soon as the doors slid open.

Then the train car doors opened and the few passengers stepped past the conductor onto the platform. A woman and two children filed out, a man meeting them with kisses. Then an older lady who required the conductor's help. A man wearing a white collar was next. January thought he was a preacher, but since he wasn't the same fellow who'd married her and Shay, she wasn't certain.

The last passenger gave her a chill. Or maybe it wasn't him, but the man who sprang forward to meet him. A doppelgänger of the man she had shot to death in the spring. This must be his twin, Nelson Peel. January braced herself against the station building. Her head spun and she found it advisable to take several deep breaths. She'd known the first Peel had a twin.

Even known he was here in The Falls. But somehow, the sameness came as a shock.

As for the man he was meeting? He looked quite respectable. Wore glasses. Had gray hair. Was tall and thin. Carried himself with the confidence of someone with plenty of money. If he carried a gun, she couldn't tell. Perhaps his suit was *that* well-tailored. Or perhaps he wasn't armed. He carried a large brown-leather satchel, and from the way he walked, it bore more than a change of clothes.

The two shook hands as if they were good friends. Or maybe businessmen, well met with false camaraderie. Peel put a hand on the man's shoulder to guide him toward Squirt's best buggy waiting at the hitch rail. They got in the vehicle and drove off toward town. A man on a horse followed the buggy. A bodyguard, of sorts, but of which man January couldn't tell. Outwardly, at least, neither man had shown any interest in those around them.

January sighed with relief when they'd gone. Peel hadn't even bothered to look around, and at first she thought that had been all to the good. It was only as she mounted the brown horse that it struck her as strange. An act of some sort. This meeting definitely was not as innocent as it appeared at first look.

A man of Nelson Peel's ilk was unlikely to be so careless, especially considering one of his men had just been killed in a shoot-out, and another—although he might not yet know this part—had been put in jail. She bet he guessed she, or someone representing the law, had been around.

She felt some satisfaction in knowing two of the Holzer and Peel men had been taken out of the equation. How many more remained? That was the question. And who were they? How would she recognize them? She'd sure enough hate to shoot an innocent, local family man by mistake.

Which is why Southbrook and Eli between them, convinced her to send Johnny out on the streets to mingle with folks.

"Keep your ears open, and watch like you've got eyes in back of your head." January shook her finger at him. "Don't talk to anybody you don't know. And watch the ones you do. We aren't sure who to trust."

Johnny, all too eager, in her opinion, to get at the task, slapped his gloves on his leg as if removing dust. "Yes, ma'am. You've told me this a dozen times already."

No more than twice, January felt sure. Maybe three times. Or four.

"It bears repeating," she said. "The last time I asked you keep a lookout like this you took a bullet."

"Wasn't your fault. I should've been more alert."

"Of course it was my fault." She would never forget that. "You wouldn't have been a target if I hadn't put you there."

It was true then and just as true now.

"You be on the lookout for trouble. If you see anybody mixing it up, walk away and report to one of us. We'll take care of it. You hear me?"

Johnny gave her a look. One with a slightly twisted mouth and a highly arched eyebrow. "Yes, boss."

Eli, who had more experience than anyone with gathering information, set Johnny's destination as the hotel where Holzer, Peel, and the fellow who'd come in on the train were staying. The noon meal was traditional. The men were sure to be having their dinner in the dining room about now.

"Sit where you can hear what they're saying if possible," he told Johnny. "Keep an eye on them, but for God's sake, don't gawk."

"Gawk?" Both Johnny's eyebrows shot upward this time.

January bit back a smile at his obvious offense.

But then Johnny patted his pockets and took on a worried look. "I didn't bring but a quarter with me. Is that enough to pay for food in the hotel dining room?"

Grubbing in her pocket, January came up with some money and pressed it into Johnny's hand. "Buy yourself a good dinner. The least the county can do is spring for your meal." Even if she never got repaid, he didn't have to know.

He blushed. "Thank you."

Eli went on with his instructions. "Do a walk around afterward. See what's stirring. If anything."

At this point Southbrook, who'd apparently ceded control to the sheriff's department even if it only consisted of a woman, a ranch hand, and a former bounty hunter, nodded agreement. "See what else you can discover. Right now, all we know is that they're up to something. If we find out exactly what and when, we can take them down before anybody gets killed."

Yet somebody already had. Two somebodies. And one of them at January's own hands.

Southbrook sounded confident. January was less so. She figured the marshal's headache must have improved when he said, "I'd best get over to the jail and interrogate this Oldham galoot. Maybe he's ready to talk by now."

Eli shrugged. "He's a tough case. But he was powerful displeased when I parked him in the cell still cuffed. Could be he's mad enough by now to let something slip."

The marshal left then, his legs hardly gimpy at all though January noticed he kept to the shadowy side of the street. He went one way, Johnny the other.

Watching her hired hand, January's mouth twisted. "That kid walks like he thinks this is all a lark. He's even whistling. Didn't he hear a single word I said? This is apt to be dangerous if Holzer and Peel catch on to him."

"He'll learn," Eli said. "If he lives long enough."

Squirt, who'd paid close attention to the goings on, spat into a barrow of horse manure he'd just scooped up, the steam still rising. "Pasco's right, Mrs. Billings. Johnny's young and gots a young feller's nerve. He's a good man. You can trust him."

"I do trust him. It's the men he's going against I don't trust.

# CHAPTER 13

LEAVING PEN TO SNOOZE UNDER SQUIRT'S WATCHFUL EYE, January and Eli took their dinner at Millie's Café located only a block from the sheriff's office. Not so fine as the hotel where Johnny had gone to keep an eye on Holzer and Peel, but altogether warmer and friendlier. January could only imagine the looks they'd get had they appeared at the hotel wearing clothing stained from hiding under loading docks and riding horseback for miles on end. Here, they were unremarkable.

Eli held the door to the little café for her to enter ahead of him. The place was busy, the air redolent with the smells burnt grease, coffee, and people. Small tables surrounded by four chairs crowded the room, each with a fairly clean, blue-checked tablecloth. Most every chair had a patron's rear-end parked in it. A heavy-set woman wearing a turban over her hair worked behind a half-wall separating the kitchen from the dining room. She stirred, she flipped, she ladled, all while sliding filled plates to a slightly thinner woman whose feet moved so rapidly she seemed to fly. This one wove her way between tables, hands and arms filled with plates piled high with prettily arranged food.

"Mmm," Eli murmured. "Looks good."

January was a little surprised when the flying woman managed a moment to smile and cock her head at the last remaining table in the room. They headed that way.

Conversation hummed like a colony of bees, perhaps more loudly than the speakers intended. Then a sudden silence.

"That's her," a man said, voice loud in the new quiet. "She's the one shot that feller over behind the drugstore."

"Just in time, too," the man sitting across from him said. "He damn near mowed down Mrs. Leider and her boys. They was walking on the street right in front of the pool hall."

"Good thing Dabney wasn't the one on duty," someone threw in. His tone mocked. "He'd a been hiding under his desk."

"Hah! He's never on duty. I heard he's holed up in his house."

They were talking about her taking hold of this situation. And of Sheriff Dabney's shortfalls. A flush turned January's face hot.

Eli held her chair, scooting her in after she seated herself, just as though she were a real lady. His grin flashed. "They're giving you credit." He spoke close to her ear. "Take it as your due."

She pulled the scarf tighter around her scar and shook her head.

The waitress skidded to a halt beside them. "You folks had a chance to look over the menu?"

Eli hadn't even a chance to seat himself yet. Nor to pick up the menu, let alone read it.

"Two specials," he answered anyway. "And coffee, please."

"Comin' right up." She sped away, having barely paused.

Eli settled into his chair opposite. "Hope you don't mind me ordering. I caught a glimpse of what most everybody is eating. Looks good."

"It's fine." Actually, she was a little relieved. "I'm not very hungry." Although she might be, she thought, if her mind's eye would only quit seeing that man twitching and dying in front of her. A sight she couldn't force away.

A shadow fell across their table. January raised her head to find Howard Reynolds from the sawmill offering a scarred hand to shake. The hand lacked the thumb and forefinger, but what could she do but take it?

"Mrs. Billings, you are a formidable woman, and that's a fact. I want to personally thank you for saving Mrs. Leider and her boys this morning. Not only from gettin' shot, but maybe trampled by Bertram's horse when he got bucked off."

*Mrs. Leider? Bertram?* "You're welcome. But what…" A tiny frown pulled at her eyebrows.

A grin crooked his mouth under a grizzled beard. "Her husband works for me. He's my sawyer. The mill wouldn't run without him. He sawed the lumber you been putting in that new house of yours."

"Then I'm doubly glad I could help," she began. "But I'm afraid it's—"

Eli cut her off before she could take the blame for the shots being fired in the first place. "Not a pleasant topic to discuss at mealtime," he said, and Reynolds nodded agreement.

"I figure you're going to hear more, like it or not," he said, and sure enough, another man wandered over to have his say.

"Best to speak as little as possible," Eli advised, his voice low. "The fewer people figure out you were the target, the better. We don't want them putting the blame on you." His mouth twitched. "I've been there, January. I know. If they see you as a heroic victim, you'll get all the cooperation you need from them."

Soberly, she nodded. She'd seen it for herself, after Shay's murder and she'd vowed to get his killer.

The short ribs and boiled potatoes the waitress rushed over to them were surely as fine and satisfying in the stomach as whatever fancy stuff the hotel dished up.

Or maybe not. She'd be sure to ask Johnny when he reported his findings. If any.

* * *

As it turned out, Johnny's discoveries were not at all what January expected to hear.

They'd gathered back at the livery after dinner, with Johnny the center of attention.

"That Holzer feller—an evil-looking jasper if I ever saw one, always grinning like one of them sharks you see in ocean pictures—was plenty upset over something. I still ain't sure exactly what, but he didn't finish his steak." Johnny, patting his lean belly as though contemplating his restaurant meal, settled onto Squirt's cot, leaving the stool for January. "The restaurant food was good, too. Not as good as yours, though," he added thoughtfully.

A little surprised—and maybe amused at Johnny likening Holzer to a shark—she was gratified to find him not so impressed by the restaurant fare when comparing their food to hers. Impatient with herself, she pushed the nonsensical thought away. There were far more important matters at hand.

"Upset?" she repeated. "Did you hear why?"

"Yes, ma'am. I think it has to do with your new house."

January nudged her stool closer to Johnny, wanting their conversation to remain inside this room. "My house? Is it his men who are squatting there?" Expecting Johnny to say yes, his answer jolted her.

"Must not be," he said. "Appears as if that's what has him on the warpath."

"Why? What makes you think so?"

Eli, in his familiar position of leaning against the wall, had shot a questioning look at her hired hand. If he'd been a dog, she thought, his ears would've pricked. So. A line of questioning he wanted her to continue?

Johnny shoved back his hat and scratched through his overly-long brown hair. "'Cuz of the way they were talking," he said. "I heard the shark feller saying something about the new house abuilding at the bridge. Then, later on, he says, 'Take the road north into the mining district. We need to gather our people immediately and that's the best place to do it and stay out of sight.'" Here, faltering, Johnny cleared his throat. "Then he says, 'She can't complain if she's dead.' Then—" He stopped and his lips clamped shut.

*She's* dead? Who could they possibly be talking

about but silly January Billings who planned to live at the bridge?

"Go on," she said.

He took a breath and clamped his hat back on. "This one feller, he says, 'I look forward to taking care of that myself. I owe her.' Miss January, I think he meant you."

So Johnny had figured that out on his own. January couldn't help the way her gaze sought Eli's narrow-eyed glare. A glare, she felt certain, not meant for her, but for the situation in general.

He cursed softly under his breath. "Peel."

She nodded. "My place is the only one around here to meet those conditions. That I know of, anyway. Not unexpected either, I suppose, given my history with the Peels."

"What history?" Johnny said.

Though he knew part of the story, January had no plans to enlighten him further.

She threw a dismissive wave. "I...we tangled with the Peel gang before, remember? Eli and I."

"Oh." Johnny nodded. "Yeah."

"Which means I'd better ride out and see just who is camped in my house." Anger drove out the shake in January's voice.

"Not by yourself. Johnson may think there are only two—" Eli's dark eyes flashed. "And I'd back you anytime against only two, but there may be more. I'll ride with you."

Her heart gave a sharp lurch. "I'll be glad of your company."

Throwing caution into the air like seeds blown from a dandelion, they rode out of Squirt's barn door side by side. But, for safety's sake, did not continue down the main street where too many folks congregated. Instead, as earlier, they went around the corral and crossed through the woods to reach the road north.

That left Johnny, who she requested to walk around town, visiting with folks he knew while keeping a sharp eye peeled for the three men he'd seen in the restaurant. Who they met and talked with, January supposed, might give some idea as to their plans. Plans beyond robbing the bank, at least, which, thanks to Ollie, was her best guess.

At first, after hitting the main road, plenty of traces of earlier traffic showed in the dirt, still wet from the now melted snow. However, the farther they went, the more unsullied the way. Until finally, when they looked back the only outward tracks showing were their own. Johnny's headed in the opposite direction from his early morning trek into town. Birds' distinctive v-shaped prints and scuffs from rabbits were easy to spot, along with the heavier indentations from the hooves of a deer or two. A hawk soared into a blue, blue sky, its harsh cry breaking the stillness fallen between them.

January turned her head to find Eli's dark eyes studying her. He looked directly onto her bad side and inwardly, she flinched. Outwardly, she gave no sign, except for the casually applied forefinger lowering the flap of her Norwegian cap to cover her cheek.

Eli looked away.

"Are you going to run for sheriff?" he asked after a while. "I hear people talk about the possibility. Including your hired hand."

"I've thought about it," she admitted after a moment. "But I'm sure there are people more qualified."

"Men?"

She heard the smile in his voice, and answered with a shrug. "I suppose."

"Who?"

January scrambled for an answer but came up blank. *Yes. Who?* Then she recalled an earlier conversation although frankly, she wasn't as sure about it now. "There's Marshal Southbrook."

"Eh." It was an indecipherable sound uttered beneath his breath. "Who else? There must be more than one candidate."

Another name occurred. "Squirt, then. He's plenty tough and smart."

Eli laughed at this suggestion. "I don't think so. Nobody even knows his last name, let alone his real first. I've got to say I doubt if anybody ever set out to name their son Squirt. He's just Squirt at the livery stable." He paused. "Any others?"

She knew he was waiting for her to name herself. "Oh, sure," she said. She leaned forward in the saddle and patted Hoot's neck. "You."

Hoot tossed his head.

January, under the pretext of soothing her horse, didn't miss the startled look Eli wore.

"Me?" he said. "No."

Exactly what she'd expected him to say. Her grin mocked him.

Sensing his home nearby, Hoot's pace picked up the closer they came to the bridge and her unfinished house. January reined him to a halt just before the structure, built on a knoll overlooking her bridge across the noisily rushing stream, came into view.

Eli stopped beside her. "How do you want to do this? Both of us ride in? Or me wait here until you circle around to come in behind the house and I'll head in first?"

She frowned.

"Or you wait here and I'll circle around." He provided another option.

If her narrowed-eyed look meant anything, it should've frozen him. Not that it seemed to. "I own this place," she said coolly. "I kind of figured to ride up and tell whoever is here to get out. Plain words and a simple instruction to follow."

He drew in an audible breath. "Did you? Without knowing how many are holed up in there or who they are?"

"Yes, as a matter of fact." January clicked her tongue to Hoot, who started forward, but the horse paused a few seconds later when she told him "Whoa."

"Ride on around to the back, Eli. There's good cover if you go around this hill. It shouldn't take more than five-ten minutes. I'll wait here. Wave your hat when you're in position. I'll see you."

His mouth tightening, Eli did as she said, although the set of his shoulders told her plain as day he disapproved of her actions.

As Johnny had described, smoke rose from the stone chimney stack, disintegrating into wisps as the breeze caught it. The fragrance of wood smoke lingered. The fireplace appeared to draw well. January smiled, fueled by a rush of pride regarding her workmanship. In fact, the house looked good. Not too big, not too small. The ell where the bathroom was going to be when she found an able plumber was only visible at certain angles, which did not include where she waited now. The house sat on a carefully built rock foundation. She thought when it was complete, she'd paint the walls white with some contrasting trim. Dark blue maybe, or wine red, or perhaps black. In the spring when the weather warmed up.

Before she could think more, motion caught her eye. Eli had arrived at his destination. Clucking to Hoot, she rode up the lane toward the front door, pulling her .38 from the holster and hiding it between her body and the pommel of her saddle.

Wasted effort. At where the porch would soon be, she drew rein. Stiff with the ride and cold from a combination of nerves and weather, she dismounted, dropping to the ground with Hoot's bulk shielding her from anyone looking out the house windows.

Her eye caught movement from her right. Eli had already made his way around the house and, silent as grass growing, stood only a few feet away, ready to follow her in.

Firming her mouth, she stepped around Hoot and ran on tip-toe to the door. Looking toward Eli, she saw him nod. Drawing a breath, she turned the door latch, disgusted the new lock Johnny had applied yesterday now hung from a broken hasp.

Her anger renewed, she flung open the door.

# CHAPTER 14

JANUARY'S .38 LED HER RUSH INTO THE HOUSE. THOUGH the sun shone outside, the room was dim, the north-facing windows obscured by a lacy coating of frost. Still, she had no trouble spotting the man in the chair. He sat in front of a dwindling fire and he wasn't moving. Not one bit. Not even when she commanded him, in a voice just short of a shout, to put up his hands.

He didn't move then, either. Or lift his head. Or speak.

Through the silence, a steady drip pattered to the floor, sounding as if icicles were melting from the roof. But, it struck her, there were no icicles. Anyway, icicles didn't smell of blood.

January couldn't have said how, but she felt empti-ness in the rest of the house. This man was the only one here. And he posed no danger. If he wasn't dead, he soon would be. Even at this distance she saw his skin was ashen and already taking on a bluish tinge.

"Eli," she called. "Come on in."

The room dimmed further as he filled the doorway.

Stepping inside, he paused, surveyed the room at a glance, then moved toward the man in the chair.

"There's a single horse out back, and tack laid out in the shed. His, I expect." He touched a finger to the side of the man's neck and shook his head. "Signs say others were here earlier. Two men, at least. There's tracks coming down from behind the hill, same as the route you told me to take. Three, maybe four horses."

January stood as if rooted to the spot. After a moment, she blinked and holstered her gun. "Is he alive?"

Eli met her eyes. "Barely. Doesn't look like he will be for long. Are you all right?"

She nodded, though that may've been a lie.

"See the way he's tied to the chair?" Slowly, he circled the man. "My guess is he's meant to be a warning —or maybe a lesson—from someone to someone."

"Who?" She figured she knew, but what was his take on this?

"I suspect from Holzer. Or Peel. Must be connected to them and whatever plans they have. Who else could it be? As to who they mean it for, you'd know better than I."

Bewildered by his logic, she shook her head. "Why would either of them kill his own man?"

"Hard telling, right off." Eli shrugged and bent over the man. "Come here and help me with him. We'll lay him out on that bedroll. I suppose it belongs to him."

She hadn't paid attention until Eli spoke of it, but a tarp and a blanket were spread in front of the fire. It struck her as obvious the man had been shot as he slept, and only tied into the chair afterward. A copious amount of blood had pooled there, as well as under the chair.

Another bedroll had been rolled and set aside. Two tin plates sat on the raised hearth. Gathering strength, she forced herself into motion. Dear Lord! Hadn't she had enough in these last couple years of handling wounded or dead men? Even if her intentions were good, it didn't come easy.

"He wasn't alone here," Eli said.

"No. I see. He had a partner."

Eli's gaze searched the room for answers. "Wonder if the partner killed him?"

"But why? And what is the point of tying him in the chair when he's already incapacitated? It doesn't make sense." A chair she regretted bringing here before the house was finished. One thing for certain. She'd never sit in it again.

Meanwhile, Eli had an answer. "Kind of intensifies the lesson, doesn't it?"

They got him to the floor without dropping him, which would've been easy to do as he was a weighty fellow. Eli held his shoulders, January his feet. The man's belly hung over his belt buckle and he sagged in the middle as they moved him. January held her breath until he was safely down.

Someone had stacked freshly split wood beside the fireplace. Eli grabbed a chunk and pitched it into the embers before poking around with a charred stick. He blew on the pile until the fresh wood burst into flame.

With the fire, the light improved enough to see the man's features. A stranger, or at least someone she'd overlooked, provided she'd ever seen him in the first place. The blond hair, sand-colored beard, closely set eyes, and rather large ears made no living picture for her.

"Do you know him?" she asked Eli.

"No."

"Neither do I. I don't think he's been in town."

"Maybe just on his way to join the gang."

A short exploration showed he hadn't been shot, after all. His killer had taken a more personal approach. When Eli turned him to check the wound, they found a large gash between his ribs, the strained cloth of his shirt slashed and soaked with blood. Only a knife like a Bowie, or maybe a bayonet, could've done so much damage, the penetration deep into his body. Blood no longer pulsed from the wound, nor even seeped. He'd been tied to the chair for too long. Long enough to bleed out.

Kneeling beside him, January started to unbutton his shirt to get a better look, only to stop when a breath gurgled from his mouth on a foamy wash of blood. His last breath. She felt the life go out of him. So, they'd learn nothing from him.

Her hands dropped to her side.

"He's dead," she said to Eli. He prowled the room, stopping to search through the saddlebags dropped by the side of the hearth. He drew out a paper and gave it a wave.

She stood up.

"Maybe this will give some answers," he said, unfolding the paper.

"What does it say?" She had an almost over-whelming urge to clean her bloody hands on her canvas riding skirt. Halting the inclination, she found a rag she'd been using to wipe sanded surfaces free of dust and used it instead.

Wordless, he handed her the paper. Hunkering beside the body, he began a search while she read.

She gasped. "Deputy U.S. Marshal Benedict Frear? What in the world? A marshal? Do you suppose he's the one who broke the lock to get in the house?"

"Couldn't say." Eli finished his search and showed her the badge he'd found, and a wallet. He looked through it. "Another letter of introduction. Money. More than you might think. Whoever did this didn't rob him. I wonder why."

January thought for a moment, remembering what Johnny had said when he told them about her house being broken into. About what he'd seen on his way to town this morning. The two horses, the seeming secrecy of keeping them out of sight from the road. Two horses, but Eli reported only the one in the shed now. And tracks from other. A second bedroll laid out by the fireplace, as if its owner might be back. Signs of more than one person eating. So where was the other man?

"According to Johnny, there should be two men. Does that mean two marshals?" she said. "Or do you suppose he had a prisoner who managed to kill him?"

"Maybe." Eli glanced around the room. "But why wasn't he robbed? If he had a prisoner, why would they have stopped here? I'd say there's a partner. But where the other man is, I don't know."

January's heart gave a thump at a sudden, overwhelming thought. "I do. At least, I think I do."

His mouth quirked. "Where?"

"At my house. My old house, I mean." She spared a glance at the dead man. "He's a deputy U.S. marshal. Well, I know another deputy marshal fairly well. I suppose it's possible he told this one about me. About where I live. What if the marshals intended to combine forces with the sheriff's office on the sly?"

"Why?"

"I have no idea. Because of Holzer and Peel?" *Not to mention Ruby Pasco.*

She considered further, her senses stirring. Apprehension? Anticipation? She wasn't sure. "It's possible the missing deputy is the one I know. That might explain why two marshals chose this house to hole up in."

Eli eyed the dead man. "Then I'd say your marshal is lucky he didn't end up like this one. Provided he's not laid out somewhere between here and the ranch."

He skirted the idea of a dead man at each house, January realized with a shudder. "If it's who I think it is, taking him by surprise might not be so easy. Or overpowering him, either."

"I expect that's what this one would've said. Mount up, Deputy Billings. We'd best go see what's doing."

As if she needed this pointed out.

She spun around. Then spun back. "What about him?" She gestured toward Frear's body.

Eli shook his head. "He'll keep. He's not going anywhere."

The ride between her two pieces of property had never seemed so long. On the other hand, neither had it ever seemed so short. Hoot, anxious to be in his own stall, moved at a brisk pace. As for her, rising dread kept January silent. Eli, too, remained quiet. They'd have answers when they got there. Or not. No use, she thought, in borrowing trouble ahead of time.

And yet, she couldn't help wondering—and

worrying—about what was happening in town. As for Eli, she noticed the way his dark eyes scanned restlessly across the horizon and into the periphery, and how he frequently turned to look back, watching for trouble. Unless he had keener eyesight than she, the only things moving in the landscape were geese in the sky, their wings like a synchronized pulse overhead as they headed south, a lone coyote in the meadow searching for rodents, and a few head of her beeves on their way to water at the stream, running loud even at a distance.

When they came to the lane leading down to the house, a single set of fresh hoofprints showed in the muddy road. None led away. Whoever had made the tracks must still there.

"Looks like you're right," Eli observed. "You've got a visitor. Let's hope he's alive."

January didn't answer.

They stopped on the rise, Hoot shaking his head as if anxious to go on. January soothed him with a word and a pat on the neck.

"We should split up," Eli said. "I'll go first, you can either take the long way around or wait until I draw whoever is there out." He spoke as though very sure the visitor was no neighbor come to chat about the weather.

Well, so was she.

But this time, January shook her head no. "I'm through pussyfooting around. This is my home. I won't slink in like a little girl afraid of her welcome."

A half-smile quirked Eli's lips. "What if we're met with a bullet?"

She'd thought of that. "Then I'll trust he's shooting at you, you being the bigger target and easiest to hit."

He laughed, surprising her.

As it turned out, nobody shot at them.

Except for the set of hoofprints indicating other-wise, the place might've been deserted. It certainly appeared deserted. No smoke rose from the chimney, no strange horse stood at the rail. Her chickens pecked undisturbed in their pen, clucking contentedly.

Hoot's brother, another silvery gray, came to meet them, nickering a welcome, hanging his head over the fence and shaking his black mane.

"Johnny left everything ship-shape when he headed out this morning. And he has Pen with him." January didn't stop at the front of the house. She rode around, approaching from the rear. Dismounting, she slapped Hoot on the rump to send him off to the barn. Silently, Eli following close behind, she opened the back door and peered inside, leaving the way open.

The kitchen area was empty, the stove cold, she saw. Everything just as she'd left it when Sam came for her. It seemed like days ago now. Had it really been less than twenty-four hours? Time enough to kill a man. Time enough to see two more men die.

She slid her .38 from the holster and, lips clamped in determination, entered the house on a rush.

A man rose slowly from the rocking chair sitting next to the cold stove. The dimmest part of the house ordinarily, but now a glint of sunlight shone through the front window, catching in amber-colored eyes so light they were almost gold. An eagle's eye.

"So it is you," she said, unsurprised at his identity.

"Yes. Me." He took a step toward her. "Where the dickens have you been? I expected you to be here."

"I've been in town." She took a breath. "I was called in to apply a little law and order to a situation. Then I...

we...stopped at the bridge house. Why are you here?" She decided not to mention Frear at the moment. Not unless he did.

He didn't seem to hear her question. "We?" he demanded.

"Mrs. Billings is including me." Eli's voice came cool and precise, almost as plummy as a British duke's.

Ford Tervo's unfriendly stare poked at Eli, who'd come in behind her. "Yeah? And who are you?"

Eli's dark gaze caught January's. "Do you know this man?"

She nodded. "Yes. He's not an enemy." Then, suddenly unsure, she stared harder at Tervo. "At least I don't think he is. He's Ford Tervo, the deputy U.S. marshal I mentioned." She paused. "Ford, this is Eli Pasco. He moved to The Falls since you were here last."

Ford looked thinner than the last time she'd seen him. Harder. Deadlier. His dark hair had grown long and he wore it clubbed back. New lines creased around his mouth and those golden eyes. They'd been able to laugh together a year ago. He didn't look as if he'd laughed much lately and she felt sorry for that.

Warily, the two men shook hands.

Ford, she noticed, had a funny look on his face. "You rushed in like you expected trouble, January. Why is that? You said you stopped at the other house. Didn't Frear tell you I was here?" He peered around her. "Didn't he come with you?"

She and Eli exchanged glances. She nodded.

"Deputy Marshal Frear is dead," Eli said. "Murdered. Stabbed as he slept, from the look of things, and bled out."

"Dead?" Ford repeated, his voice a snarl. "Stabbed

and bled out?" He looked to January as if he didn't believe Eli.

She nodded. "Were you friends?"

"We were partners on this job. I can't say as I knew him well." He gave the rocking chair a shove, sending it skittering into the stove. "But he had a wife and a couple boys back in Nebraska. Damn it." The last came out explosive.

January felt about ready to explode right now, too. She eyed Ford, one eyebrow arching. "Ford," she said, "this is not a time to keep secrets or dodge answers. What are you doing here? Who killed Deputy Frear? And don't tell me you don't know. I'd bet all I have you do."

# CHAPTER 15

INSTEAD OF ANSWERING JANUARY'S QUESTIONS, FORD stared long and hard at Eli, his gaze focusing on the Mauser Broomhandle rig snugged across Eli's chest. "Pasco, huh? If my memory serves me right, I believe I've heard of you. You're the bounty hunter known to carry a semi-automatic weapon. You like handling the high-priority cases with the biggest rewards."

He didn't, January thought, sound particularly approving.

Eli knew it, too. He flushed and his eyes narrowed to slits, but he didn't flinch. He knew his reputation.

"I expect that'd be me, all right," he said, agreement with frost clinging to it. "As for the biggest rewards, why go for some penny-ante crook when either kind can kill you just as dead?"

It was the most January had ever heard him say about his former method of making a living.

"Yeah," Ford said. "Makes sense, I suppose." With this grudging admission, he shifted his attention back to her. "Got any coffee around here? I could do with something hot."

He made his familiarity with her and her house clear and Eli...well, his narrowed eyes showed he took close notice.

January sighed. "Maybe you should have started a fire in the stove seeing you've made yourself at home."

Eli blinked a little at her caustic tone but Ford, evidently taking this as an invitation, moved toward the woodbox in back of the stove and picked out a few sticks of kindling.

"Didn't suppose you'd be gone all day," he grumbled. "I figured to catch you alone when I saw the Johnson kid head off towards town this morning. Glad to see he still works for you, by the way."

"He's a good hand and a good friend. But you already know that." She studied him a moment. "You didn't answer my question, Ford. What are you doing here? Not only in The Falls, but here, in my house?" She glared. "Not to mention breaking into the house at the bridge and destroying two new padlocks."

He turned toward her. "Sorry. I'll buy you new locks."

"Yes," she said. "You will."

At least he had the decency to *act* regretful over breaking into not one, but both her houses. Not that this one had been locked. Still, there'd been no invitation to simply walk in, either. Not that January believed his contrite look. From the first time they met, he'd been adept at playing a part. He'd been pretending to work for a scoundrel while acquiring evidence against him back then, carrying off his part to perfection.

The anger flooding through her now came as a

surprise. It wasn't the destroyed padlocks that bothered her. The botheration was caused by how little he had to say about his partner being killed. Murdered. In *her* house. Let alone his silence for the past year. He could've written.

"We found the dead man, your partner, tied to a chair in January's new house. Looked like he may have been tortured." Eli was watching Ford closely.

She wasn't alone, January realized. Eli had spotted his lack of reaction, too.

"Frear was tied to a chair, you say?" Ford blinked.

Eli had passed beyond patience. "It's Deputy Billings' job to keep the peace in this county, Tervo. You owe her your best help." He snorted. "And honest answers upon asking."

"The hell." Ford went on with his fire-building, crumbling a handful of cedar shavings over the kindling and striking a match. "I'm the law here. I don't answer to you. I don't even answer to January, though I'm sorry she's been discommoded."

She couldn't stop her gasp. "*Discommoded*! Is that what you call it?"

Eli shook his head. "The law here? Are we to take your word for that? Because last I heard U.S. Marshals work on federal crimes. Is there a federal crime we need to worry about?"

Ford turned his back and set the match to the shavings. "You don't need to worry about a thing, bounty hunter."

"My town, my friends. I'd say I do."

"You…" Ford started.

January stopped whatever he meant to say by slamming a tin cup down on the table with a clatter loud enough to rattle the salt shaker into tipping over. Salt spilled out, and both men jumped. "Enough! That will do, Ford." Her voice rose. "No more cat and mouse games. We, those of us who live here, believe a theft—a major theft—is about to take place. We think the bank is the target. We know a gang of outlaws has moved in, and they seem to be waiting on something or someone to carry out the job. A store was robbed. The town marshal has been attacked, and a ranch hand who simply happened to be in the wrong place at the wrong time has been killed. This morning a man shot at me." Gritting her teeth, she finished her roster of criminal activity. "Only he's the one who ended up dead. And now there's another dead man. Frear. This...this reign of terror needs to end *now*."

Ford heard her out. After a minute, he seemed to come to a decision and nodded. "I don't know anything about the marshal or the ranch hand or the robbery. Nor, I'm sorry to say, about whoever shot at you. Just happy to see he missed. This local business passes me by. But the theft part. Yeah. Still, that isn't the main reason I'm here."

"Then why are you?" Impatient now, January brushed past him and grabbed the coffee pot out of his hands. Taking it to the sink, she pumped in water and in seconds, ground a handful of coffee beans to throw in the pot. Setting it on the stove, she faced him, glaring. "Well?"

"January asks a good question, Tervo." Eli straightened from where he half-sat on the edge of the table where he could watch the other man. "Whatever the reason, it has to be why Frear ended up dead."

Ford sent him an unfriendly glance. "How'd a bounty hunter come to get involved in the first place?"

"Because I asked him to," January said. Although, it struck her, until Ruby played her tricks on him, Eli hadn't really said yes or no. Still, he'd insisted on coming with her to the ranch and she assumed—

She turned to him, her lips forming the word *please*. She didn't mention Ruby to Ford.

A nod so slight as to be almost invisible indicated agreement. Surprised relief washed over her. There was something about Ford. Something that made her uneasy. The pot of hot coffee when it finally finished boiling may have eased their innards but did nothing to warm the atmosphere between them.

Afterward, with the sun shining on the road ahead, the three of them had started back to the bridge before Ford finally got around to putting answers to January's questions. Some of them, at least. She thought there might be information missing. How much? The critical point?

With the road too narrow to ride three abreast, January led the way on Hoot. Eli followed at the back with Ford sandwiched in-between. She turned in the saddle, the better to watch Ford when he cleared his throat to talk.

"Frear and me, we'd been appointed to go after and apprehend a man on our wanted list. Word came to the marshal service about someone putting together a gang with the intention of robbing a mail train and spilling fresh blood along the way. This matches up with the methods favored by the gang's leader, so here we are." Ford nodded at Eli, who pulled up beside him as the road widened. "A mail train. Federal. Make sense, bounty hunter?"

Saying nothing, Eli met Ford's hard gaze with one of his own.

"Why here?" January demanded. "And who is this man? More importantly, who do they plan to kill?"

"Nelson Peel is the felon." One side of Ford's mouth lifted in a half-grin. "Ever heard the name?"

In trying to stifle a gasp, January coughed. She slid a quick glance at Eli and caught his surprised look before he wiped all expression from his face.

She made an attempt to match his composure. Apparently, she didn't succeed because Ford said, "Oh, ho. You have. So the rumors I heard are true."

"What rumors?" Unwilling to miss anything she might read from Ford's expression, she slowed Hoot to match his horse, even though it meant riding halfway into a ditch.

"News that filtered in on the monthly reports." He shrugged. "About a woman deputy here in eastern Washington who arrested a man named Frank Peel. Got him sentenced to prison for the next twenty years or so. The woman deputy wasn't specifically named, but I figure I know. That would be you, January, wouldn't it?"

January's cheeks heated. Her shrug equaled his for nonchalance.

"Thought so. Anyhow," he went on, "some of us recognized Frank Peel's name from the time we captured Nelson Peel and put him away. They're brothers in the trade of selling women, liquor, and whatever else they can make a profit on between here and Canada. Nelson had a good sideline in mail trains until he got caught and started serving time. I guess you know Frank preferred dealing in women. Or girls. Now, with his brother in prison, Nelson's had to find new partners and that's where he went wrong."

She could tell by Ford's face he got a kick out of relating the story.

"They should've hanged him," Eli said.

"Well, I don't dispute that but they didn't just let him go. He escaped. First thing he did was kill the federal judge who sentenced him, then run off to Canada. The marshals got called in. He got tracked to The Falls, which is why me and Frear got sent here. We planned to stop him before he gets to his next intended target."

Sudden suspicion hit January like a lead pipe. "Who is his next target, Ford?"

"Oh," he said, sort of offhandedly. "I figure it might just be you, January." He made a kind of bow, bending over his saddle horn.

Though she'd suspected it, she still went cold, feeling it all the way down to her toes.

Eli muttered something under his breath. "Seems to be only one cure for this man, Tervo, and I think you know what it is. I've got one suggestion for you."

Ford cocked an eyebrow.

"Don't get in my way," Eli finished.

January realized immediately what he meant to do.

No fool, so did Ford. "Works both ways, bounty hunter."

But Ford had more information, and he grinned as he shared it. "To all accounts, the Peel brothers are close. Or maybe just birds of a feather. Nelson didn't much care for Frank being taken down by a woman." He speared Eli with a hard stare before urging his horse ahead "Or for anybody who helped her. So it could be you're a star player on his list, Pasco. We've had word of an informant giving him all the details, along with something about twin nephews. Any idea who that informant could be?"

January shuddered. Therein lay a tale fit to equal a story from Edgar Allen Poe. One for which she needed no reminders.

She reined Hoot to a stop, barring the path and forcing them to stop. Her cool gaze leveled on both men, longest on Ford Tervo.

"So what," she said, maybe a touch overly loud, "are you going to do now?"

"Take care of business. Nobody kills my partner and gets away with it."

Eli said nothing.

Satisfied, she spun Hoot and heeled him into a gentle lope. It was time—past time—to get back to town.

* * *

INFORMANT. Tervo's brash declaration echoed in Eli's head. He'd seen January's involuntary reaction, as if a goose walked over her grave. Only which part of Tervo's story was she reacting to? The Peel nephews she'd killed? Or the comment about the informant?

He figured only one person in this trouble stood in that position, and January knew as well as he. Ruby Pasco back in her usual role, out to settle old grudges in a permanent fashion—as long as she could make a profit.

Tervo peeled off when they got to the bridge. "I have a crime in need of investigation, and time's a wasting."

He swallowed as if his throat was filled with dry corn-meal. "I'll be along with Frear's body when I finish up here. As I remember, there was an undertaker in town. Is he still there?"

January answered. "Yes. And Doc Le Bret will need to take a look at the body."

"I'll need his report right away. Notify him first thing, will you? Tell him to get a move on?"

Apparently, January was none too pleased at Ford's assumption of being first in line, or her role as his lackey. "He's already gotten two bodies to deal with today, but I don't imagine he'll delay. If you're willing to wait, I can send Hannon out to get the body. Save you having to tote it through town, scaring children and angering parents."

Tervo cocked an eyebrow. "Just make sure you hurry him along, will you? I've got to get moving on this business."

"He's dependable. He'll work you in when he can." She shot him a cool look. "And don't forget to lock up when you're done. I'm getting new locks and sending them out with Hannon. Thurston at the mercantile will see you get the bill."

Eli held back a laugh when Tervo opened his mouth to say something, then abruptly closed it again. Wise of him. January clearly hadn't been joking.

Leaving the Deputy U.S. Marshal to gather what information he could from his partner's body and the room where he'd been murdered, Eli and January continued toward town. They made good time as the road had dried fairly well and the day had turned clear.

On the way out, Eli had been puzzled by the cautious way January approached a certain intersection along the road. A narrow trail broke off from the main section, winding through what, for all he knew, might have been thousands of acres of forest. A short-cut, she'd told him.

Returning, they took the trail, her caution growing. Eli watched as she scanned this way and that, her head cocked, obviously listening for any sounds that didn't belong in the woods.

She raised a finger to her lips, indicating he should remain quiet as they neared the road again. Eli heard nothing out of place.

"What..." he began quietly, intending to ask what there was about this place that put her on edge, when a deer burst from cover only a few yards away. Startled, his horse shied.

Balance recovered, he glanced over at January, surprised to see her standing in her stirrups, gaze fixed on a cluster of boulders. Judging by the bushes grown up around them, they'd been left by the road-building crew some years in the past.

An unintelligible scream—if January Billings could be said to actually scream—and the way she sent Hoot lunging deep into the woods bordering the intersection, alarmed him. Eli's horse followed Hoot of its own accord. A flurry of gunfire chased them.

"Get down," she yelled. "Down, down." Bullets ranged close. Foliage rattled, lead thudded into tree trunks. Miraculously, neither human nor horse were touched.

He didn't have to be warned twice. Eli flung himself from his horse, reaching for January at the same time and hauling her down with him. Roughly, as it happened, and straight into his arms. Another bullet pinged into the bark of a large fir, scattering wood chips into his face. He felt the wet of blood, but no real pain. Only relief. Until he'd grabbed her, she'd been directly in the bullet's path.

Neither of them hit, then. Only the victims of a bark shower. They hit the ground together, sheltered in part by a drainage ditch left during road construction.

January pushed away, her hand against his chest. "He was waiting for us."

"Yes. And you were looking for him. For someone. How did you know?" Eli had his Mauser out, ready to fire if he got a target. Just for luck, he sent a single shot into the bushes where he thought the shooter was hiding.

The attacker shot back, which gave him a better idea of where to aim.

"Tell you later." So saying, January rolled two full body turns, taking her deeper into the ditch. She made a hand gesture indicating what she meant to do, crawled a few more yards, and after a quick glance around, rose onto her knees behind a fallen log all of three feet high, with a foot or more buried in the ground.

A hail of bullets continued to splatter around him, showing the shooter either carried a gun like his own, or more than one piece. When next he raised his head, Eli saw January had her .38 in hand. She nodded at him.

Clearly, the bushwhacker had no compunction about shooting a woman. Most of his bullets were expended firing at January—or where he apparently thought she was. If she'd stayed in the bushes where they'd come to earth, Eli figured she'd be dead by now. The fallen log provided much better protection.

But only if she remained prone behind the log. Which the stubborn woman wasn't doing. Eli shook his head violently as she crawled toward the narrow top end of the fallen tree. He knew she saw him, too, but ignoring his signal, wriggled into position.

Another flurry of shots cut divots in the wood, echoing through the woods as the man fired repeatedly. A waste of ammunition, as Eli realized the shooter couldn't have seen January at all. He was still aiming where she'd first landed. And, most unwise of him, he was ignoring Eli.

The gunfire stopped. After a period of no movement from either of his targets, the bushwhacker, lulled into thinking he had the upper hand, cautiously rose his head above the boulder.

*A little more*, Eli thought. *Just another couple inches.*

In the silence, January's mahogany-colored hair blended quite well with the bark of the log as she stirred to peer around the log's jagged end. She'd taken off the silly, though strangely charming cap she'd been wearing, Eli noticed, being wise enough to realize a glimpse of its vivid colors would show her position.

One thing certain, the bandito didn't expect her to pop up like a jack in a box firing live bullets. Nor expect to face the roar of Eli's Mauser when he, too, clambered to his feet and pumped three shots toward the bandit.

The man rose up as if drawn by ropes. He staggered, two separate blood spots marking his coat front. Still not done, he lifted his gun another time.

The noise ended with a pop of January's .38.

# CHAPTER 16

"WHO IS HE, DO YOU KNOW?" JANUARY GAZED DOWN AT the dead man. He lay where he'd fallen, sprawled on his back. Retrieving her Norwegian cap, she put it on, covering cheeks that felt icy cold, and looked up at Eli. "How would he even know where to find us? I suppose he's one of Holzer's men."

As a matter of rote, she extracted cartridges from her gun belt and reloaded the .38.

"And yet," Eli said, "you seemed to be expecting him. Or someone." He shrugged, his face grim. "I've never seen him before. Regardless of what you might think, January, I don't know every criminal in the territory. As to the rest...I have a hunch."

"Ruby," she said.

He gave a sort of half-nod in a resigned kind of way.

She blinked. "Well, too late to do anything about *her* right now, but I plan to arrest her first chance I get. Stuff her in a jail cell and maybe prevent more trouble. Or cause more. It's hard to tell."

Eli didn't speak.

Sighing, she glanced around. "I wish Pen was with us. I don't see this man's horse. She'd sniff it out and save us from having to look through the timber." Turning a circle, she peered through the trees before giving a sudden little grunt. "Well, pish-posh. I'm an idiot."

On that note, she gave a piercing whistle through her teeth, startling Eli and causing him to stare at her.

He stared even harder when Hoot, reins dangling from when January bailed off him, trotted from behind some bushes, a sprig of green clinging to his bit, and came over to nose her. "Good fella," she whispered to him. Then, standing right up in front of him, she blew into his nostrils and said, "Hello."

The gray horse shook his head, his black mane bouncing over his neck as if he might be laughing.

"Yes," she said. "I hear you. Say it again." At which, after another puff into his nostrils, Hoot lifted his head and emitted a loud neigh.

"Good boy." Smiling, January gave him a pat, then cocked her head. Within a second or two, from somewhere off to the west, another horse answered. Another horse, but not Eli's. The horse he'd been riding wandered toward them from the same direction as Hoot.

January pointed and grinned into Eli's bug-eyed wonder. "Over there. Not too far, I don't think. I'll go fetch him."

"How did..." He blinked. "Where did..."

January sobered. "My husband trained him. Shay encouraged Hoot to talk to him but I'd forgotten this trick, until just now. Truth to tell, I'm surprised Hoot remembers."

"And horses talk to each other." Eli still appeared thunderstruck. "Your husband must've been a fine horseman to teach him that trick. Very fine."

"Shay Billings was the best. The very best horse trainer in the whole state." Her answer slipped out even as her eyes filled with sudden tears. Shay Billings might just have been the best husband in the state, too. Maybe in the whole world. Before she lost him. And this, right here on this spot, was where he'd died. Been murdered, his blood soaking into the ground.

"I believe it." Eli turned away, giving her a private moment.

"I'll go fetch the horse while you see if you can find anything revealing on him." Her gesture indicated the dead man. Gathering the reins, she climbed aboard Hoot and headed in the direction of the other horse's call. Eli, she saw from the corner of her eye, hunkered down beside the dead man and began a systematic search through his pockets.

January only appeared stoic outwardly, going about the business of deputy duty as if this was all in a day's work. But it wasn't. To end up here, where Shay had died, and have another life gone gave her goose bumps. Worse, by far, than what she'd showed to Eli. He'd turned away when she spoke of Shay. Because of what he'd read in her expression, or because he didn't want to know?

Glad to be alone for a few minutes, she patted Hoot on the neck as they crossed a small stream, one that soon ran into the larger stream, which in its turn, joined the river. What a day. Dead men showing up like fleas on a dog.

Not that her Pen had ever had fleas.

All credit to Hoot, she found the outlaw's horse tied to the leafless branch of a bush with peeling bark. The bay mare, her coat already long and thick in preparation of the upcoming winter, nickered a welcome at sight of them. She trotted alongside Hoot on the way back to where Eli waited. He'd had time to wrap the dead man's body in the tarp he carried on the back of his saddle. The one he generally used to cover Henry when leaving the horse outside in inclement weather.

January, grateful to be spared having to look at the outlaw again, forced what she knew was a rather crooked smile. "Did you find out who he is?"

"A certain Edward Zimmer, late of Walla Walla state prison." Eli shrugged. "He has release papers, so I reckon he served his time."

The name drew a blank for January.

Helping Eli load the body onto a mare unsettled by the smell of death allowed January to recover her equilibrium—until Eli asked the question she'd been dreading.

"You sensed this was about to happen, didn't you?" His dark eyes surveyed her, noting, she was certain, the way she flinched at his next question. "Coming and going, you were on edge. What is it about this place?"

She swallowed, trying to dislodge the knot in her throat. But Eli deserved to know the truth. "This is where Elvira Hammell murdered my husband. He was found here, lying dead in the road. I hate riding past here. Every time I have to go to town, I hate it just as much as the first time." She stopped short of confessing the place haunted her.

January watched Eli, looking for his reaction. She

was almost able to see wheels turning in his mind. But what he said surprised her.

"Maybe you should give up on finishing your house at the bridge." He kept his voice level, thoughtful although she saw his jaw muscles tighten. "With all the trouble you've had there, I'd say it's not worth it. Your place is the end of the line on the other side of the creek. Tear it all down, house and bridge, and build another bridge closer to town from the other side. One where you never have to take this road again."

She opened her mouth to speak, then closed it.

His idea gave her something to chew on as they rode back to town. Had he, in a kind of roundabout way, suggested something different, something deeper than the import of his actual words? Not that she let her guard drop as they covered the distance as quickly as the bay mare would move. Nor did Eli, his head turning, his eyes searching.

They stopped at the edge of town.

"Where's this Hannon's Mortuary I've been hearing about?" Eli asked.

January's lips compressed. "All the way down Main Street to the other end of town. Last place on the right."

"Last place," he repeated. "Figures. You want to take the long way around?"

"Nope. We're going right down the middle of the road." She straightened in the saddle, knees griping Hoot's sides tightly enough to make him toss his head and prance. "I know I told Ford to not parade through town, but maybe I was wrong. Scared children or not, I'm through pussyfooting, waiting for Holzer and Peel to decide the action. It's time to stir the pot."

His grin quirked. Unbuttoning his coat, the

Broomhandle lay revealed across his chest. He'd been wearing gloves, but took them off and flexed his fingers. "Ready? Then let's go."

Not wishing to dwell on her decision, January led off, setting Hoot to a business-like walk. Close behind, Eli led the bay mare bearing the man-shaped burden. The dead outlaw hung crosswise over his saddle, and though Eli had tied him down with a rope looped under the horse's belly, as the body stiffened, he'd slid a little. Just as they crossed in front of the hotel, one of his arms came loose and trailed down, fingers dusting the road surface. Macabre. She knew it and now, so did everyone who turned to look.

She was certain every person on the street stopped what he—or she—was doing to stare. Children's eyes grew wide. Mothers gasped and tried to block their view. January didn't suppose this, well, *parade* would make her any more popular in town, but if an invasion of outlaws was to be stopped, she had to learn just who —and how many—she had to fight.

Squirt and Sam came to stand in the livery door and watch their little procession pass in front of the hotel. Once, when he knew he'd caught her eye, Squirt made a point of looking up at a small balcony off a second-story room. Without moving her head, she followed his gaze.

A man stood there. A man who caused her skin to pucker. His cold eyes followed her every move, leaving a feeling like ice melting on her skin.

She'd heard the man she and Eli had brought to justice, Frank Peel, had a twin brother. But as with the set of twin nephews she'd battled, she hadn't known Nelson Peel would be identical. When she saw him at the train station, he'd worn a hat and coat. Now he didn't and the resemblance was stronger. She hesitated to admit it, but the identical factor made them even more frightening, as if they could keep multiplying at will. She'd heard things like twins ran in families. Seeing it must be true didn't make her feel any better. It only made her wonder how many more of the lineage might be around.

"Above us," she said, shaking away the sudden wobbles like a wet dog shakes off water. She spoke only just loud enough for Eli to hear.

"I see him. Nelson Peel. Him and his brother Frank —uncanny in likeness." Even as the words passed Eli's lips, another man joined the first. "Ah. And Arden Holzer, come to join the fun."

"Fun," she repeated, her lip curling in derision.

January passed beneath the balcony's shadow in a blink of the eye. Riding out the other side, she kept expecting a bullet in the back, muscles tense against the piercing of her body. Or maybe they'd aim at Eli. They might shoot him first, figuring him more dangerous than she. She knew Peel wanted to savor her death. Draw it out. Sense her fear. It was almost a letdown when nothing happened.

Nothing but laughter. One of them said, "Bang. Got her dead center," and the other laughed again and replied, "Save it until later."

They meant her to hear. They meant her to be afraid.

*Damn them.*

"Don't turn around." Eli's voice was so quiet she might've imagined him speaking.

He didn't have to tell her. She knew.

Then they were beyond the balcony. Other horses

and their riders, wagons and teams, folks striding along with purpose provided a foil to the outlaw's implications.

Yet January felt no real relief.

Hannon met them at the wide back way into the mortuary, a large room in the basement of the house where he worked and lived. A ramp led down from the outside where his well-trained horses could back a wagon, easing the transport of coffins and bodies. He showed no particular pleasure in greeting them and the burden they delivered.

"Another one?" Hannon's eyebrows rose in double arcs. "Good God, woman, what are you doing today?" The undertaker's usually dignified demeanor soured for the moment.

Although not attired in the formal black suit he wore for funerals, Hannon wore good pants, a snowy shirt and collar, and a subdued paisley-print vest. The chain to a gold watch looped from belt to vest pocket. He appeared prosperous—and overworked.

January knew all about the overworked part and had no particular sympathy. "And another in need of a pick-up," she said. "He's out at the house I'm building at Kindred Crossing bridge. Deputy U.S. Marshal Tervo is there, investigating the circumstances of his death."

"You didn't..." he said.

"No. My house was broken into and the man murdered there. When you, or whoever drives the ambulance, goes out, I'll send new locks along. Marshal Tervo has said he'll lock up."

At mention of Tervo's name and title, the undertaker took on a less frazzled appearance. "I'll send Jed. Give me a half-hour to take care of this one." He pointed toward the body on the horse. "Who is he, by the way?"

January took a breath. "Mr. Pasco can fill you in. I'll get the locks at Thurston's Mercantile and have them delivered here." Which would give her the opportunity to talk with T.T. She trusted he'd been able to gather more information about the situation in town by now.

She wasn't mistaken. No real surprise. T.T. had a finger in every pie and, if she'd occasionally had cause to regret it, in this case she did not.

Detouring to the store's hardware area, she selected two more locks and brought them to the front counter. This, happily enough, was a slack time for shoppers. She and Thurston had the store almost to themselves, even Edna, T.T. told her, having gone home to start a cut of beef roasting for supper.

T.T. stared down at the locks as if he didn't recognize them and slowly swiped the back of his hand across his face. "Didn't you...didn't that kid who works for you...?" He stopped, worry lines etching his face.

"Yes. Johnny Johnson had two identical locks put on my bill yesterday." She had to smile. T.T. clearly thought he might've dreamed the sale and now wondered if he'd become clairvoyant. Or else that he might be losing his mind. "This time you can charge Ford Tervo at the U.S. Marshal Service. He'll be in to pay."

T. T., who'd leaned forward to hear better, chuckled. "I remember him. He helped after your husband..." He paused delicately. "After Mr. Billings passed on."

"Yes." January's voice came out desert dry. At least she'd have no argument over the billing.

"Seen you riding down the street a bit ago, heading

toward Hannon's with another body. You and Mr. Pasco." He stared at her. "Anybody I know?"

"Doubtful. Johnny reported the locks he just installed were already broken and someone had taken up residence in my house, so Mr. Pasco rode with me to investigate. On our way back, the man attempted to dry gulch us. As you see, he didn't succeed." She mouthed the information carefully, the better for him to understand. She didn't mention the marshal's murder. Best if that news didn't spread just yet. The townsfolk wouldn't take the news well.

"Glad for that," Thurston said, adding grimly, "Bad doings all around." He shook his head, the bandage Dr. LeBret had wound around it yesterday beginning to unravel. As if to underscore the disarray, he thrust a finger under the bandage's loosened edge and scratched, grunting a little as he probed a painful spot.

"Have you heard or seen anything out of the ordinary going on at the bank, Mr. Thurston?" January persisted. "Spotted anything to report?"

T.T. stared around the store. Unless someone hid behind a stack of boxes they were alone, but still he motioned her closer.

Complying, she breathed, "What is it?"

"Look across the street at the bank."

January did.

"See those men standing one at each corner?"

She nodded, recognizing them as Holzer's men once again playing bodyguard.

"I seen three men go inside the bank a few minutes ago. Strangers, and Missus Billings, I know most folks around here. They're well-dressed, like gentlemen, but two of them are as hard-faced as any criminal you ever saw. They had Len Pearson escorting them—in theory. Looked to me more like they was escorting him, maybe at gunpoint. None of them has come out yet. Those men you see waiting outside are guards, only they aren't working for the bank."

January's breath drew in. Well-dressed, but hard-faced. He had to be describing Holzer and Peel. The third most likely was the man from the train. They must've headed for the bank the moment she and Eli passed under them on the hotel balcony. Was the robbery going down right now? If so, where was the rest of the gang? What, for instance, about Ruby Pasco?

She managed a little chuckle. "Why do you suppose they need guards? Do you suppose they're scared some other gang is gonna beat 'em to the money?"

"Looks as if, don't it?"

"At any rate," she said. "it's the move we've been expecting. I'll just amble over and see what's happening. Thank you for the warning, Mr. Thurston."

She spun, ignoring his startled yelp.

"No, ma'am. Don't you go over there alone. Missus Billings!"

It was as if she were the deaf one, the way she appeared not to hear as she walked away.

# CHAPTER 17

Scanning the street outside before she left the store, January eyed the men standing at either corner of the bank. They were strangers. Each bore the appearance of someone just out of jail, their constantly shifting eyes, hard mouths, and overly casual stances giving them away.

T.T.'s estimation had been right on the mark. Holzer or Peel had set men to guard their backs. Not to be deterred, she couldn't let herself be intimidated.

Stuffing her bright knit cap in a pocket, she unbuttoned her coat, allowing it to flop open and reveal her .38 was available if the need arose. The badge under the coat lapel became visible. Her bright mahogany hair flowed free. Pushing it behind her ear, the S-shaped scar showed clear. She drew her boot-gun, a small, but lethal .25 caliber, and placed it in the coat pocket.

Every sense on alert, head held high, she crossed the street. Time seemed to tick with the thuds of her heart as she dodged wagons, horses, and people. And then, before she could change her mind, she opened the bank's glass-fronted door and darted inside. One of the men moved as if to stop her an instant too late.

The silence inside struck January first. Aware that banks and other places of business were rarely noisy what with everyone wanting their finances kept private, this quiet struck at her sensibilities. As if the bank itself was aware of violence waiting just around the corner.

A tremble shook her when every eye in the place turned her way. Even those of a child holding her mother's hand.

"Mama?" the child said, then, "Ow."

January imagined the mother must've squeezed the little hand a bit too hard.

The two stood behind a male customer, second in line at the teller's cage. The man ahead of them stood at the counter, golden-oak affair with wrought irons bars ending a few inches above the surface. Money and some papers were passing back and forth between him and the teller. A lumpy bag of coins sat open below the bars. Besides the teller, who was busy counting the coins, the male customer and the woman and her fidgeting child, only one other person was present. A female secretary sat at a desk outside an inner door. A brass plate with Leonard Pearson's name picked out in black letters hung at eye level.

January had met the woman before, last year during her battle with Marvin Hammel and Albert Sims after Shay died. Mrs. Filmore had wanted to help her then, but had feared losing her job and means of support. In the end, January's involvement allowed the woman to keep working when Pearson took over the bank. If she were gracious enough to credit January with the opportunity, perhaps she'd be of help.

Pearson, Holzer, and Peel were conspicuous by their absence, no doubt shut behind the door with its brass plate.

Nodding at the teller's wary look as he spotted her badge, January strode over to stand in front of Mrs. Filmore's desk.

Mrs. Filmore looked up, a quick smile flashing as she recognized her visitor.

"Good afternoon." January smiled back at the woman, certain that friendly served better than threatening. "Is Mr. Pearson available for me to speak with? I have some important information for him."

Mrs. Filmore, her plain black dress crackling with starch as she stood, cast a worried look over her shoulder at the closed door. "I'm sorry, Mrs. Billings. He's with other customers right now."

January didn't try to keep her voice down. She spoke loudly and clearly. "I'm not plain Mrs. Billings today, Mrs. Filmore. Today, I'm Sheriff's Deputy January Billings and I need to speak with Mr. Pearson immediately. I'm here to warn him that his bank may be in danger of being robbed."

"Robbed?" Mrs. Filmore's voice wobbled. "Oh, dear."

"Yes." January wanted to see inside the office. With the opportunity, she'd be able to tell more about the situation by gauging the interaction among the men. Whether Pearson was a victim with no way out, or a willing partner in whatever scheme Holzer and Peel had going. Those two and someone else. Someone she didn't yet know.

It appeared her wish to see inside the office was about to be granted. Voices sounded beyond the door, loud enough both she and Mrs. Filmore turned. January reached into her coat pocket and gripped the butt of the little .25-calibre pistol. She didn't take it out, figuring to shoot through the coat if it became necessary. A hole in a coat could always be mended. One in her body might not.

"I won't do it," Pearson was saying as he flung open the door. "The deal is off. Get out."

That may have answered one of January's questions.

"No, no. That wasn't our agreement." Holzer spoke smoothly and much more quietly. He shot his cuffs and winked at Mrs. Filmore who stared at him. "Reneging on our agreement will have repercussions, Pearson. Severe repercussions. I'm sure you don't want to find out what they are."

For a moment January's presence didn't seem to register. Then it did. His eyes flickered, but it was Peel who chuffed a surprised-sounding noise through his nose as he stared at her. He reached into his jacket, then slowly withdrew his hand.

"You…" With a visible effort, his facing turning a peculiar purplish color, he took hold of his animosity. "Mrs. Billings, I presume? I've heard of you." If he'd been a wolf, it would've been a growl.

Inside her coat pocket, January's hand tightened around the pistol butt. She managed a short chuckle. "Yes. I rather imagine you have. Just as I've heard of you. I'm surprised to see you've been released from prison. Or have you?"

An axe would've been necessary to chop through the resulting heavy silence.

The bespectacled man from the train twitched as if swatted with a whip made of thistles.

"Prison?" he repeated. His eyes blinked rapidly

behind the spectacle lenses, and far from the brisk man he'd been earlier, he seemed suddenly to shrink and sag. His face took on a grayish pallor. "Prison? Holzer, what's going on here?"

"Oh, yes." January assured him. "Prison. Both Mr. Holzer and Mr. Peel."

His complexion turned almost gray upon hearing January's announcement. It took only a moment before she decided he was another like Pearson, duped and coerced by Holzer and Peel into doing something this news caused him to regret.

"What's past is past. That's all behind me." Peel nodded at Pearson with a meaningful glance toward the gray man as he did so. "I'm a businessman now, isn't that right, Pearson?"

"Everything completely on the up and up," Holzer added smoothly, and smiled.

Pearson swallowed. "Yes," he muttered. "Of course."

He hadn't been particularly convincing. The gray man shot him an appalled look.

"Glad to hear it." Everyone ignored the insincerity of her reply. She turned to Pearson. "Mr. Pearson, I have reliable word your bank may be comprised. In danger of being robbed. I need to discuss this situation with you."

Pearson looked, she thought, like a rat caught in a maze, frantic with panic.

"I...I..." He couldn't bring forth words, his gaze going from Holzer to Peel and back.

"Now, sir," she said firmly. Stepping forward, she took his arm with her free hand. "It appears your present business is concluded. I'm sure these gentlemen will excuse us."

Holzer stopped Peel's move toward her with a

glance. "Of course. Our business is settled. We'll speak later, Pearson."

With that, he gathered Peel and the gray man and swept them out of the bank ahead of him, striding across the floor like he owned it.

An unquiet thought struck January. Perhaps he did.

As for Pearson, she felt him tremble under her hand. Sweat ran down his face.

Mrs. Filmore's fingers twisted together. "Mr. Pearson, are you unwell? Can I get you anything? Some water?"

"No," he said faintly, then more strongly, "No, Mrs. Filmore. Just see that no one interrupts us. This won't take long." He took a breath and turned toward his office. "This way, Mrs. Billings."

"Deputy Billings." January smiled wryly as she corrected his assumption. "This is an official visit, sir." One where she might have to push hard to learn anything since Holzer appeared to have the banker thoroughly cowed. Would he even tell her the truth? The way Holzer's warning had shaken him indicated he might consider her to be the lesser threat.

Or so he believed now. If he had a lick of sense he'd better rethink that.

Once inside the office, he sank into his chair without inviting her to sit. "A robbery?" he asked. "Are you serious?"

"I'm absolutely serious."

"Them?"

She nodded. "Them. Tell me about it, Mr. Pearson."

A bottle of what she recognized as expensive imported Scotch whiskey sat open on his desk with four used glasses. Shaking, the bottleneck clacking on the rim of one of the glasses, he poured himself a generous tot. He didn't offer the bottle although January might've appreciated a sip. She had to admit meeting Peel head-on had shaken her.

"And you're part of the plot. A mistake." January sank onto the nearest chair and leaned back into the soft leather. Ritzy. Maybe too ritzy, showing a man with ambition beyond his grasp in this particular place. "What are they...you...waiting for?" she asked when his silence went on for too long. "Or who? Your best bet is to tell me all, Mr. Pearson."

He stared at her. "Money. They've been waiting for more money. And whoever brings it." He poured another shot into his glass and drank. "How did you know? Who told you?"

She eyed him dispassionately. The man was a bigger fool than she'd thought. "When men easily recognizable as outlaws and convicted felons begin permeating a town, it's simple to guess something of an unlawful nature is on the docket. My personal knowledge began when three people broke into Thurston's Mercantile and not only stole a valuable pistol, but caused T.T. bodily harm. I happen to know someone else became suspicious before that, when a visitor arrived after dark and was secretly admitted to this bank."

"What? Who told you about—" He stopped, face ashen with guilt.

"My sources are protected."

Elbows on desk, head in hands, Pearson moaned. "He told me they'd leave me be if I allowed this transaction to pass and didn't say anything. He said they'd even cut me in for a small share. Alternatively, he said if I didn't do as ordered they'd kill me, my family, and set this town on fire."

"He? He who?"

"Holzer." Pearson's voice didn't rise above a whisper. "But not at first. Why, the first thing he did was deposit a wad of money. Five thousand dollars. How was I supposed to guess? He said that was only the beginning. He didn't lie. The next week he deposited more. But then..."

"How much money altogether?" Aware of how harsh she sounded, January made an effort to soften her voice. "What's its source?"

Southbrook had mentioned a bank robbery, one she'd read about, which had taken place in Ellensburg last month. Yeggmen had cracked into a vault using blasting powder. And then later, she'd heard of a train robbery near Walla Walla. A large party of masked men had burst into a mail car stopped on a siding. A man had been shot. Were these the source of Pearson's windfall? Perhaps it could be checked.

"Was Holzer your only contact?" If so, it was odd no one had mentioned seeing him around before.

At this, a wave of hot blood rose in Pearson's face, turning him a bright crimson.

"Ah. I see. A woman is involved." January took a leap, not one too farfetched, considering. She eyed Pearson, finding it impossible to keep all her disgust contained. "A woman named Ruby."

His reaction told her all she needed to know. Learning the rest, given the amount of scotch Pearson had consumed, became quite straightforward and undemanding. The story spilled out, surprising her with its scope. So much more than a mere bank robbery and investment scam. They intended to take a whole town.

Leaving the bank, conscious of eyes watching and a feeling of danger surrounding her like a cold wet blanket, she figured it was the only simple thing. What to do about it had a different word. *Impossible.*

* * *

SQUIRT, taking a little rest, pulled his works out of a pocket and built a quirly. Leaning against the livery's outside wall, he smoked, watching folks on the street. Now and then, as relaxed as though he had nothing else to do, he'd wave at someone. Or so it appeared. But then, appearances aren't always what they seem.

"Here she comes," he said, apparently into the air on a cloud of smoke.

Eli, standing just inside the barn, relaxed a cramp in his jaw. "About time." Then, "Is she all right?"

"Steppin' lively so she must be fine." Squirt's jacket rubbed on the outer wall with a scraping noise "She's walkin' on past. Ah. Gave me the high sign, just now. Looks like she's headed for the marshal's office."

"Means she's got news." A great weight fell off and lightened the load on Eli's shoulders. "She stayed in the bank so long I figured..." He didn't finish the sentence.

"Yeah." Squirt dropped the quirly and ground it under his boot. "Me, too. Expect we would've heard the shootin', howsomever if that's what they was up to."

Eli managed a grim reply. "There's always more than one way to kill a person."

Squirt's boot ground harder, until tobacco shreds and paper disappeared. "Truth. Some of them silent." After a moment, he added, "She's gone into the jailhouse. Time for you to follow. I'll be along in a bit."

Eli had his doubts about anybody actually being fooled by spacing out their arrivals at the jail, but it probably didn't matter. Apart from the covertness of their actions allowing Squirt to feel a thrill, he figured it all wasted effort, anyway.

He dodged out the rear of the livery, tromped through the corral, and finally slipped into the jail. His gaze sought January first of all, and found her standing by the stove where a fire roared. She looked drained.

"I can't seem to get warm," she said. Plaintive. Not like her usual self at all.

Southbrook was leaning back in his chair, eyes closed, face pale, the gauze around his head smeared with a little blood. He looked as if he needed a dose of the doc's morphine. Or at the least a bed, warm blankets, and maybe a tumbler full of whiskey. The smooth stuff, not any of the cheap hooch Knowles sold to cowboys over at the Barefoot on a Saturday night.

Eli, while not unsympathetic, figured the marshal might as well do just that. Take to his bed, that is. He wouldn't be any good if it came down to shooting, and might even get in the way.

A minute later Squirt, breathing hard, darted inside. "Hot damn," he said. "My roan mare just brought herself home. No sign of the man who rented her."

Eli exchanged a telling glance with January. "Good thing you charged the fellow in advance, Squirt," he said. Since he wasn't a mind reader, he couldn't have said for sure, but something about January's expression just then—for instance, the slight flinching of eyelids over those dark forest-colored eyes of hers—told him she had a good idea. Well, so did he. Marshal Ford Tervo hadn't pulled any punches when he talked about taking down these outlaws. This likely was his first step. One to go along with the bushwhacker who'd tried to kill January and himself.

And, he admitted, even though he didn't much care for Tervo, in this case, good for him. One fewer to worry about. Eli planned on taking down more of the gang himself.

The idea shook him, thinking about it. Looked like he wasn't out of the bounty hunting business after all.

Which probably had something to do with what he said next. Or, not what, so much, but how he said it.

"Don't keep us waiting, January. We're all here. This is no time for theatrics."

# CHAPTER 18

*THEATRICS?*

The anger that rose in January at Eli's unthinking remark burned like a steam scald. When in her entire life had she ever indulged in, or even been allowed theatrics? She knew herself to be the most prosaic of women. A childhood spent with her grandfather and the insanity that led him to carve the letter S on her cheek—not to mention the other things he intended to do—had taught a valuable lesson. Whether too many tears or too much laughter, out-of-control emotions were dangerous and unreliable. She'd grown up fast.

For Eli to even think of theatrics in connection with her—she was no Ruby Pasco.

"I beg your pardon?" she said coldly, squared her shoulders and stared unblinking into Eli's dark eyes.

The temperature in the jail chilled enough for Squirt and Southbrook to exchange puzzled glances.

"Uh." Southbrook, after a frozen moment, said, "Squirt, if you'd close the door between us and jail, please. I don't figure Oldham needs to hear what we're saying."

Squirt hustled to comply, shutting off yet another muffled complaint from the prisoner. "Though it ain't as if he's gonna be telling anybody."

"I trust not, but just in case." Southbrook took a breath, and began. "Everybody find a chair and sit. We've got to figure out what's going on and make it pretty dang fast. You first, Mrs. Billings. You were at the bank. What did Pearson have to say?"

January, ignoring the offer of a chair and made aware of the other men's discomfort, broke eye contact with Eli and turned her back on him. "He had plenty to say, once he figured out I knew parts of it already." Her mouth twitched. "Or at least, he thought I did. A few generalities served me well."

"For instance?" Eli braved her ire by asking. He, too, refused a chair, instead perching on the corner of Southbrook's battered oak desk.

"For instance, when I told him I knew he'd met with these same outlaws in secret, he admitted to accidentally falling in with their plan to take over a whole town. An out-of-the-way place, where they can do what they like. He says prospectors have located what appears to be a high-grade silver mine up north near the town, and investors are clamoring for a piece of it. But first, they had to compel the owner of the land to sell. To the investor's good fortune, he died this spring and the deal with his heir is in the final stages. They've been negotiating in secret so the price doesn't get driven up. That's why the money is being held here, in Pearson's bank instead of a bigger one in Spokane. They want to keep the funds handy so they can close the deal the moment the heir says yes."

Eli was frowning, as if he had deep thoughts. "Hmm. Don't make sense unless the money is in cash. Is it cash?"

"Apparently. Most of it, anyway, according to his account of deposits."

"Deposits?" Squirt repeated, as if the word was foreign.

"What town? Do they mean to somehow take over The Falls? Where is this mine?" Southbrook's anxious questions showed his worry all too plainly.

At this, January looked at Eli and flashed a brief quirk of her lips. "You'll never guess." Then, after a brief pause, said it herself. "Claremont."

A clamor arose between Southbrook and Squirt, somewhat along the lines of Squirt saying, "What? I ain't never heard of any silver mines up there. No mines a'tall, in fact." And Southbrook agreeing with, "Nope, no mining prospects found there. Not ever. And not because there were no prospectors. There were, back in the 80s about the same time they found silver in the Idaho mountains." And Squirt again, pointing at her and asking, "How much money has been collected, Mrs. Deputy? Did Pearson say?"

"Over $75,000," she replied. "With another large deposit set to take place this afternoon."

Squirt's whistle pierced their eardrums, harsh as a hawk's cry. "I'll be a monkey's uncle."

"More than enough money to make all this trouble worthwhile," Southbrook said.

January scowled. "Worth murder and investors' broken dreams?"

"More than enough for them. This landowner..." Eli hesitated. "I don't suppose he happened to live in a little ramshackle cabin up north, did he?"

January's mouth tightened. They, Eli and she, had discovered a gruesomely tortured dead man near Claremont in the spring. He'd been part of what led them to Frank Peel and his scheme to sell kidnapped girls. "He did, as a matter of fact." At least the knowledge put to rest one thing that had puzzled them both. Hank Schlinger, who'd still been sheriff then, had never solved the mystery of why the man had been tortured and killed. This could explain it. The new surprise was of how long this particular venture had been in the works.

Eli had yet another question. "Did Pearson say when the deal is supposed to close?"

She nodded. "Tomorrow. Supposedly, anyway." She paused, "So I expect the bank robbery will take place tonight."

"Tonight! Holy sh...moke." Squirt struggled to talk over his excitement. "That soon. Uh, how many men does this gang have on hand? Does Pearson know we'll have to fight?"

"Or did you think to ask?" Southbrook added.

Southbrook and Squirt gazed upon her as if thinking she should be an expert strategist, which made January real nervous. The time she'd spent reading a manual regarding a sheriff's department rules and duties provided valuable knowledge, but a skinny little book was no substitute for experience. Experience she didn't have. "No. Sorry," she admitted.

"We can make a guess," Eli said. "And while we're at it, we'd better think how many of us can get together to stop them. Squirt, you've been in on this from the beginning. I take it you'll see us through."

Squirt nodded. "Hell, yes. I ain't been in a good fight for a long time. And Sam. He'll want to take a hand as well."

"Tervo?" Eli looked to January.

"I would expect so. If he gets here in time."

"How about the kid who works for you, Mrs. Billings? Johnny Johnson?" Southbrook acted ready to pin a badge on him—or anybody else who happened along—man, woman, or child.

"I sent Johnny back to the ranch with my dog." She straightened her shoulders, willing to fight for the exclusion. "I told him to stay there. I'll not have him shot on my account again." He'd almost died once already while in her employ, as Southbrook knew. Her fault.

The marshal's lips lifted in the slightest of smiles. "Aside from Johnson making the decision for himself, this isn't on your account, Mrs. Billings. This is for the town, the county, and lord only knows how many innocent folk about to be bilked out of their hard earned money."

January, not especially sympathetic at this reasoning, blew a raspberry. "Maybe they should've been wiser in their investments."

Eli laughed. A moment or two later, Southbrook joined him. "I reckon that's one way of looking at it. And you could be right, Mrs. Billings. But maybe you're not."

Squirt clumped over and tossed another chunk of wood in the fire as if he, too, felt the chill. "So," he said. "What should we do first?"

Drawing a deep breath, January took stock. The

situation struck her as not much different than running a ranch. You did this, then you did that, allowing the next step to feed off the one before until you reached the ultimate objective. In this case, chasing down and incarcerating an unknown—at this point—number of armed and dangerous outlaws.

She sighed. "First thing, arrest every stranger in town. If you don't know someone, Marshal Southbrook, and Squirt or Sam don't know him, haul him in. I imagine Eli can identify half these people already."

Eli raised his eyebrows, but didn't deny her claim.

Southbrook frowned. "What are we gonna charge them with? We can't just..."

January had no patience left. She interrupted without a second thought. "I expect half of them have warrants pending. No excuse needed. If they're carrying guns, tell them we have a law against guns in town. Or charge them with vagrancy. The men I've seen are just standing around ogling every female they see."

Southbrook nodded and, pondering, fingered his long mustache as he thought. "Thing is, this jail won't hold more than three or four men. Where are we going to put the prisoners? I figure Holzer still has more than that, even with the ones you've already..." He broke off, looked at her a moment, then finished his sentence. "Got out of the way."

For a moment, January blanked. *Got out of the way?* One way to put it, she supposed.

It was Squirt who came through with a solution to the problem. "Barlow, the old goat who owned the livery before me. He built himself a dugout to live in, before he had money for a regular house. It's a good size, and is mostly underground with a ramp down to a good, stout door. I store extra tack and feed down there sometimes. Shove the prisoners in there. Shouldn't take more than one good man to guard it."

Southbrook snapped his fingers. "Out of the way, too. Not many folks around who'd remember the old place. The outlaws wouldn't know where to find it."

"I know you're not well, Marshal Southbrook, but if you could, maybe you could take guard duty on."

After a moment, he nodded. "I'll do it."

Relieved, January spun around and eyed Eli. "With your experience, I doubt I need suggest anything to you."

His leg, which had been swinging free, stopped. "No, ma'am. You don't. I'll suggest something to you, though."

"What?"

"You should have a partner. I know you're tough, January, but you're not weighty enough to take down somebody like Arden Holzer."

She didn't want to admit it, but he was right. "But I'm good enough to take down Ruby Pasco." Her expression dared him to think, let alone say, anything different.

He didn't.

More ideas and instructions came to her. They'd make every effort to keep the arrests quiet. Use the alleys, always in the shadows. Watch the rooms over at the brothel, which to her knowledge had proved popular with Peel and his men. Let 'em go in the front and catch them coming out the back. See if T.T. and his son could keep a watch and keep them informed of where Holzer's men were stationed. Maybe January could entice a man or two into following her to where Eli could make an easy capture.

And when they'd done what they could to thin out the enemy, they'd filter into the bank and wait for the final reckoning.

Glancing at Eli, January realized he hated the plan. Hated it, but unable to find a better alternative, couldn't disagree.

Calls from the street outside jarred the four of them into silence. Until Southbrook said, "What the hammered hell is going on now? More trouble?" Looking as if lifting himself out of the tilting chair he sat in was just about beyond him, he heaved himself to his feet and went to the jailhouse door. Opening it a crack, he peered outside. "Who..." he started, eyes bugging as he took in the pair of horses stopped at the rail in front of the building. A body was bound over one horse. Ford Tervo sat the other, the same dun he'd been riding the last time he'd been in town. Stiff-legged, he dismounted.

Southbrook stepped outside. "Who're you?" he demanded, hand hovering over his holstered gun. "And who's this?"

Ford, his eagle's gaze already spotting January standing behind the marshal, nodded to her. "January, you want to introduce us?"

January, surprised the two hadn't met last year, hastened to comply. But she had the same questions as the marshal. "Is that Deputy Marshal Frear? Didn't Hannon make it to the ranch to pick him up?"

"He made it." Ford nodded. "This ain't Frear. This is the sonuvabitch who murdered him."

Southbrook frowned. "Deputy Tervo, I've been

hearing about you." His approval seemed a little cloudy. "Hannon's ambulance will carry more than one," he went on, "and I suppose this feller will end up at his mortuary, too. Why'd you bring him here?"

"He's dead because he tried to draw on me. Reluctant to come under arrest, I reckon." Walking over to the horse, Ford drew his skinning knife—habitually carried razor-sharp—and cut the rope holding the body, allowing it to flop to the ground with a leaden thud. "He wasn't fast enough. I figure to use the body as a deterrent, his last, and probably only service to humanity. Prop him up here in front of the jail for everyone to see. Show the outlaws what happens to their kind when it comes to robbery and murder. Might make one or two think twice about hanging around. A man who's just got out of prison probably isn't too eager to go back in."

Eli, who remained out of sight inside the jail, snorted. "So you'd think. But more than a few think of state prison as their second home."

Surprisingly, Ford Tervo laughed and agreed.

As for January, she wondered how any part of prison time was even tolerable. More, she wondered what Ruby Pasco's impression would be when she finally ended up there. Although it wasn't as if she cared what Ruby thought.

Squirt, at Southbrook's instigation, sprinted over to Hannon's mortuary to beg the use of a cheap pine coffin in which to display the corpse. Eli helped lay the man in it as soon as Squirt returned wheeling a coffin on a cart. A note got pinned below two bullet holes burned in the dead man's blood-stained shirt where his heart had beat its last.

*Here lies Mort Post, the third outlaw killed in The Falls*

*today. A smart man will take his death as a warning to get out of town,* it said in January's finest, boldest penmanship.

The men propped the filled coffin against the side of the building where it soon drew a crowd. Men and women, plus a few children and several curious dogs, came to take a gander and murmur shocked comments. But by that time, the four had gone off on the hunt.

Squirt and Southbrook left first, aiming to close down the livery and collect Sam to join their undertaking—outnumbered though they might be. Then, accompanied by Marshal Southbrook, Squirt's most pressing intention was to hasten on over to Barlow's cellar with its windowless rock walls and hard-packed earthen floor and see it opened up to receive prisoners.

Eli took his leave, drifting past the gathering outside the jail almost unseen. His destination was the alley behind the saloon, and thence on to the hotel where Holzer and Peel were staying. Fertile ground, they figured, headquarters of the leaders who were sure to be collecting information and giving orders to their followers.

This left January to Ford's tender mercies. Or maybe, she thought, smirking a little as he elbowed his way through yet another a pod of men exclaiming over Mort Post's carcass, it was she with the tender mercies.

Fully assured, she led the way on foot toward the river, Ford puffing along beside her. He'd gained weight since she'd last seen him, she noticed, while his face acquired a certain hardness. His lack of wind proved his athleticism had faded in the past year. He didn't seem the same to her any more. Not in the physical sense, and not as they talked.

Oh, he still flirted, in a desultory sort of way, but she didn't believe there was anything intentional behind it. With so much on her mind, she barely paid attention, answering his banter in like fashion. When he'd helped her avenge Shay's murder, she thought there'd been a rapport between them. But now, whether because of her or because of him, whatever it was had gone missing. She didn't know whether to be glad or sorry.

*Glad.*

The realization struck. Along with relief and an unexpected—and unwanted—vision of Eli Pasco toiling over the mountains carrying her old dog on his horse.

*Fickle.* The perfect descriptive word for her. She'd loved Shay, even though she hadn't known him long when they married. Then, later, she'd considered Ford Tervo. And now Eli Pasco. She didn't understand herself.

Ford evidently didn't notice the wayward thoughts coursing through her. And thank God for that. Their conversation died without pain as they made their way to where Fat Mary's brothel had been doing a booming business with a sudden influx of customers this afternoon. According to Squirt's report, at least, who had a coterie of friends to keep him informed of such things. A fine spot, she figured, to bag their first prey.

And that was Ford's—and her—only real consideration.

If they were lucky, the outlaw's friends would think anyone who went missing had fallen in the nearby river and drowned. All in all, not a bad solution.

"This way," she told Ford, cutting off his last teasing remark and pushing through a cluster of thorny bushes. She named their objective.

"What?" His amber-colored eyes opened wide in pretended shock. "Mrs. Billings, what does a respectable lady like you know about a place like this?"

Her elbow slammed into his ribs, ungentle and not by accident. "Oh, shut up, Tervo. This place is hardly a secret. Ask any resident in town, from the very young to the very old. Male or female."

He laughed, the sound dying as they approached the building via a hard-packed trail that followed the river. The house, seen at the end of the lane, rose in two stories. A wide porch faced the front. Small windows, barely large enough for a full-grown man to crawl out of, should he find it necessary, showed the layout of rooms. Outside, a steep stairway led to the ground at one end of the house.

The wood siding had been painted during the summer. A bright yellow in color, with vivid red trim and brown shutters, it looked, in January's opinion, like a fairy tale house. Maybe the one belonging to the wicked witch. Tall evergreens thickly planted surrounded the place ensuring privacy should someone important need to remain unseen.

Four horses, cinches loosened, stood in front, reins flipped over a rough wooden rail set between a couple iron posts.

"How many girls work here?" Ford asked, eyeing the horses.

She shrugged. "I don't know. Three or four probably. Maybe more during harvest or roundup when the itinerant workers come through the area. The Falls is a family town, for the most part."

"You recognize any of the horses?"

"What? Oh." She frowned, then squinted knowledgeably at the animals tied up in front. "I know the pinto belongs to Squirt. So a hire, probably one of the outlaws who came in on the train. I see two from the Polson ranch. The other I don't know. Not everybody brands their horses..." Shay hadn't. Not ever. "...but somehow I doubt—"

A gunshot cut her off. A woman started screeching like a cat with its tail caught in a door. A man shouted, then another voice joined the fray.

"Get out! Get out of here, I say, before I club you down and smash you into blood butter." The speaker, man or woman, from this distance it was hard to tell which, seemed angry enough to follow through on the threat.

January, with her experience at churning her little Guernsey cow's cream into butter, had a sudden, jarring vision derived from the description.

Another shot, another scream. An agonized yelp, half-scream, half-growl, this time definitely from a man.

As January and Ford watched, the red-painted front door slammed open and a man, a pistol in one hand, a single boot in the other, dashed outside and headed for Squirt's livery horse. The woman chasing him carried a club fully five-feet long. It looked as if it had been forged of iron, with a knob on the end.

Another man trotted behind the battling pair. This one was slighter, fully dressed though rather disheveled, his face, under a falsely black handlebar mustache, oddly pale. His hands waved in the air, a sort of bull-snort bellow wailing something about she'd be sorry if she touched another hair on his head.

January wasn't sure if he meant his own head or the other's fellow's.

"Get out," the woman said again, almost quietly this time, considering. Although those two words were peppered with graphic expletives. "And don't come back. You'll regret it if you do. Both of you."

"Blood butter," January murmured, still more shocked over the threat than the cuss words, not that she would ever have confessed to it. Beside her, Ford choked back a laugh.

The woman with the club was one she'd seen at the bakery this morning, although right now she looked more like a she-devil than someone who enjoyed pastries. Blood spotted her dress, one which appeared to be the bright and fanciful creation of an Arabian tent-maker.

The fellow in the lead tried to leap aboard one of the horses but, possibly because of the blood running into his eyes from the cut on his forehead, he must've forgotten the loosened cinch. The saddle turned under him, spilling him to the ground.

Casting a wary glance at the woman, the other fellow did a better job with his mount, pausing just long enough to give the cinch a quick yank.

The woman, Fat Mary in the flesh, stood with her club cocked threateningly over her shoulder. She was howling like a hunting coyote and waving what January assumed was the fellow's other boot. Cocking back her arm, Fat Mary flung the boot at the escapee, hitting him in the chest.

The pitch, in January's opinion, proved as effective as any hurled by a Boston Beaneaters ace. Staggered, he thumped onto his rear, landing in the horse manure liberally coating the ground.

Even from where they stood, January could see the force of the throw almost knocked the wind out of him.

The little man shook his head, pointed his own horse in the direction of town, dug in his heels and abandoned his companion without a second look.

Fat Mary had words for him, too. "Don't you show that ugly face here ever again. Hear me?" An exceedingly thorough chastisement of the man's antecedents accompanied her command. And then the door banged shut.

A wide grin flashed across Ford's hard face. "If you ask me, they ought to be begging us to take them in. Did you see the size of that head-banger she's carrying?"

January's grin stretched to match his. "Pretty hard to miss. The woman has an arm on her. The Spokane baseball club ought to think about hiring her on."

# CHAPTER 19

THEY WAITED, IMPATIENCE GROWING, UNTIL THE FELLOW Fat Mary had unceremoniously driven from her house got his boots on and his saddle straightened. Though wobbly, he mounted and, head hanging, began his slow way back into town.

"What do you suppose he did in there?" Half-laughing, Ford glanced at her from the corner of his eye. His main attention remained on the road, his well-learned caution always present. On foot, him leading the way, they cut across a wooded corner to reach the road before their quarry arrived, planning to waylay him where no one could view the arrest.

"Beyond the obvious, you mean?" January asked dryly.

Ford laughed. "Mrs. Billings. Are you being indelicate? I'm shocked."

She knew he was no such thing.

"Why the gunshots? Do you suppose he plugged somebody?" He seemed to be thinking out loud.

Another thought struck him. "Or maybe somebody shot at him."

"If so, he—or she—wasn't a good enough shot. I'll go back and check later."

"Better watch your reputation concerning who you associate with, Deputy." Ford's dancing eyes belied the words. "That's one tough madame. Knew how to handle her club just fine too. She'd make a good match for you. You suppose, if she don't want a job pitching, she'd like to hire on as another deputy?"

"Maybe she'd rather run for sheriff," January said dryly. They were almost to the road by now. The clop of the horse's hooves on the hard dirt road gave warning of the outlaw's approach. Then it stopped and they heard the sound of retching. January made a face. Ford just grinned.

After a few moments, the clopping began again. With perfect timing, January stepped out into the outlaw's path.

"Stop right there." She waved her hand in the horse's face.

The horse snorted, shaking its head as Ford took hold of the closest rein.

Thanks to her good fortune—or maybe due to Fat Mary and her club—the outlaw was still three-quarters drunk and showing the effects. Also, he was suffering, aside from the gash in his head, from a badly bruised chest. Swaying in the saddle, he gazed blankly down at her.

"Get outa the way." His words slurred, maybe from the hooch, maybe from the pain. "I got business elsewhere."

She smiled. "Why yes, I believe you do. I'm placing

you under arrest and you'll be going to jail. Drop your gun on the ground."

"Wha...? You? Hah." Spurring the horse, he yanked the rein out of Ford's hand and tried to run her over.

She simply caught the reins under the horse's chin and turn it in a circle. "None of that," she said. Ford stepped up, his hand on his undrawn gun, the U.S. Deputy Marshal badge gleaming on his chest.

"Ah, hell," the outlaw said, finally spotting the badge. His hands raised and he moaned.

The arrest went smoothly from there.

"Good work, Deputy Billings." Ford's mood seemed to pick up. He winked, as cheerful now as a robin in spring. "One less of them buggers to fight. What say we go find us a half dozen more?"

Minutes later, they delivered the man into Squirt's less than tender care. Upon commenting on the prisoner's bloody condition, Squirt laughed wholeheartedly when Ford regaled him with how the outlaw came to be so battered.

"Wait 'til your boss sees you." The hostler chortled, shoving the protesting man down the ramp into the cellar with due ceremony. "That Peel, he ain't gonna be pleased. Holzer neither."

Not, January knew, that he had any idea what either would say. He just liked ribbing the guy.

Reminded of Holzer and Peel, January didn't find any part of it amusing. Ford evidently did. He grinned along with Squirt.

Did Ford believe capturing criminals would be this easy all the time? As if all they had to do was flash a badge and the bad guys would give up? His attitude said so although she suspected his experience said otherwise. She had a different impression, for sure. She thought it more likely every single one would put up a fight first chance he got.

But, as it turned out, Ford was right and she was wrong.

Not, however, because the gang was reluctant to fight, but because they were nowhere to be seen. The drunken brothel patron had been the only one unwise enough to show his face in the hours following Ford's gruesome display of the dead man. No more prisoners turned up.

January had taken over the sheriff's office, by now, bringing in drinking water and wood for the stove as if preparing for a siege. Working in tandem, Eli and Ford shifted Oldham, the shooter from the morning, over to the cellar.

When they got back, Eli looked tense with new worry. "Business all over town has come to a stop. The streets are quiet with folks sticking close to home. The locals are keeping their heads down. They all know something is up."

"Probably good, don't you think? They're safer inside," January said.

"Maybe." He shook his head. "But I didn't see any strangers, either. They're evidently holed up inside, too. Unless they all left town."

"I can only wish, but I think we'd have heard if they had." She sighed and dipped water into a dented enamel coffee pot. "I doubt we've scared them off. What's more, I can't imagine Nelson Peel, who's apparently a lot like his brother, being unduly concerned if something happens to some of the men he's got here. They're expendable."

Eli nodded. "I expect you're right. I'd say they're waiting to make a big move."

"Waiting for what, though?" January slammed the coffee pot onto the stove, already impatient for it to boil.

"Time. Money. A person. January, I don't know. But there has to be a reason." Seating himself at the desk, he took his Broomhandle Mauser apart and cleaned until it gleamed. The smell of his gun oil filled the place, the pungent odor making January sneeze.

They were alone for the moment, Southbrook's concussion having caught up with him. January had sent him off to a cot in Dr. LeBret's surgery. Sam wandered back to the livery saying he needed to clean stalls and check on the horses. Squirt got bored and stomped out to chop more wood in the woodshed at the back of the jail. As for Ford, he went to check around town and see what he could see.

"I'll be back soon. Don't wait for me if anything happens," he said. "I'll find you."

As for January, her stomach turned somersaults, clenching into knots as she paced round and around the sheriff's office. The quarrel she and Eli almost had forgotten.

The afternoon drew on towards dark; the streets as empty as a ghost town's. After the excitement of seeing a dead outlaw—a murderer at that—put on display outside the sheriff's office, the townsfolk had grown cautious. Men finished their business, gathering briefly to talk before hurrying away. A few women slipped into Thurston's store for last minute supper supplies, then slipped out again without pausing to gossip. Children were called inside. Even the dogs disappeared. More importantly, none of the strangers showed his face.

"They're meeting somewhere, getting ready for the robbery tonight." Ford, having returned from his foray around town, sounded very sure of himself. No surprise. He usually did. January, for one, found herself resenting his attitude.

But this time Eli, his lips tight, nodded agreement and turned to her. "They must be meeting at the hotel while staying out of sight. I figure Holzer and Peel are holed up calling the men to them, giving out orders. I'd like to know what they're saying. Do you know anybody who works in the hotel, January? We need somebody who can listen in and tell us what's going on."

"Best not take the chance," Ford said. "Good way to get somebody killed if he was spotted."

"I know," Eli conceded, growling frustration. "And we don't have anyone to spare. But it's still information we need."

January agreed with both—in part. Eli, because they did need to know what the outlaws were planning, and Ford, because the danger it posed to whoever did it was certain.

"I'll go," she blurted, unable to bear the tension another moment. "I don't know anybody but I can flaunt my badge and ask questions." She sucked in a big gulp of air. "I'll arrest Ruby while I'm there. Cause a commotion. Give Holzer and Peel something to think about instead of the robbery."

"You will not." Eli, who'd been lounging in the tilting chair, jumped to his feet, half-shouting.

And Ford, though it seemed as obvious as the nose on his face he'd just been going to say the same thing, chose to disagree.

"Nah, she's right. January's our best bet. If she does

get caught, Holzer ain't likely to take her serious. If I remember correctly, he don't have much of an opinion of women. Thinks they're weak and stupid." He eyed January, grinning at the quick way she took offense. "But he don't know our Mrs. Deputy Billings. She ain't weak and she ain't stupid."

Eli scowled. "No, she isn't. But she's reckless."

"That she is." Ford nodded. "Set in her ways, too."

* * *

JANUARY HAD one important item on her agenda to accomplish before showing up at the hotel. An item—or did she mean an idea?—she'd conceived while waiting for full dark. As it turned out, her timing worked to her advantage. This shadowy betwixt and between was even better at hiding her movements.

Oh, she started off toward the hotel openly enough. Where she went astray was at the first deep side street leading to the service areas behind the hotel—among other places. She was careful, too, once she entered the side street. After all, she wanted to hide her movements over the next quarter hour not only from outlaws, but from her own people.

The side street brought her to the edge of the woods along the river. A path allowed hotel visitors a fine vista of the river and its namesake falls, plus the rolling hills beyond, where they reached for the forested mountains. The trees here, a mixture of evergreen and cottonwood and a few bushy maples, allowed tourists to believe they were in the wilderness. The whisper of rustling leaves and rubbing branches welcomed the chittering of birds preparing to roost for the night. Stars were beginning to show in the ever darkening sky. January relished being alone, her footsteps silent on the soft earth.

The path went all the way to the brothel, a convenience for certain hotel patrons. Convenient also for January, an almost pleasant walk with the river chuckling along beside her. Yellow light shone through Fat Mary's back windows, throwing the women gathered around a table in the kitchen into silhouette. Laughter rose above the sound of the river. A large black man wearing an apron and a pouffy hat wielded a ladle as he filled bowls with what January imagined was stew. She caught the scent as someone threw open the door, and tossed a cat outside. Rosemary, thyme, onions, and beef. It smelled delicious, she discovered. It had been hours and hours since she and Eli had eaten at the café. Her stomach growled.

Someone called for the door to be closed just as she stepped onto a porch. Lumbering footsteps headed her way as she raised a hand to knock and Fat Mary's round face appeared in the opening.

The madame blinked. "Well, well, if it ain't Deputy Sheriff Mrs. Billings."

She spoke quietly, the girls around the table never noticing.

"You know me?" The woman's recognition surprised January. She didn't know how to address the woman. Fat Mary didn't seem appropriate, though it was the moniker by which she was universally known.

"'Course I do. What do you want?" Fat Mary's thinly plucked brows drew together as if she were not only put off by January's visit, but worried. She stepped onto the porch.

"I came to thank you for the way you dealt with that

man today. The one you thumped with your club. It allowed Deputy U. S. Marshal Tervo and me an easy capture." January spoke quickly and quietly. "And I also wanted to ask about the gunshots we heard. Was anyone hurt? Is there anything I can do for you?"

The woman shook her head, setting earrings heavy enough to stretch the lobes practically halfway down her neck to jangling. January wondered if they were real gold.

"Nah," Fat Mary said. "I took care of him before he could do any damage to speak of. Shot a couple holes through a bedroom wall is all. Easy enough to patch. Came near to scaring my girl Thelma into a heart attack, howsomever."

January let out a breath of one part relief, one part amusement. "I'm glad you're all unharmed. Please, let me know if more like this one shows up and makes trouble for you. I intend to make sure all citizens of The Falls are safe." She made it a request, not a demand. Although, as she knew very well, it would probably take at least a murder before Fat Mary called in the law.

"You got it," the madame said, just as if she'd actually comply. "Some of them fellers have been—" Mary stopped suddenly, as if remembering who she was talking to. "If they do," she went on, "I'll take care of them and you can pick 'em up later."

From inside, the black man's deep voice rumbled a question and Fat Mary turned her head to answer before turning back to January.

"You go on now, Mrs. Billings," she said. "And be careful. I heard them talking. One of the leaders of this hellbound bunch is out for your blood. You in particular. He's an evil man. I got a guard on the door of whatever girl he chooses."

She had to mean Peel.

January barely had time to tell Mary thanks for the warning before the door snicked shut. She retreated as she'd come. If word got around about where she'd been, she felt sure the county would not approve of their female deputy indulging in a friendly talk with the madame of a busy brothel.

\* \* \*

IN ONE WAY, January thought as, making her way to the hotel by slinking closely against the buildings where she'd melt into the background, the deserted streets were a relief. At least she didn't have to worry about innocent bystanders getting shot. But in another, the silence and emptiness made her every move more obvious and easy to spot. She felt certain Holzer, Peel, and their men were tracking her every movement. It was as if eyes were fixed on her right now, beady eyes, like a circle of rats. Unsettling, to say the least.

By the simple act of displaying the dead outlaw lying in a cheap coffin, Ford Tervo had declared war on the gang. Rather than the deterrent Ford said he was aiming for, January feared his action had been interpreted as an invitation to a fight. Specifically, a gunfight. The gang had many men in their corner. She and the town had only the few.

The odds were not in their favor.

She dared not allow the thought to take hold, even as it looped through her mind like a train on a circle track. God only knew how many more people might die before this day ended. Sometimes she wondered if it would be better to allow the robbery to proceed without hindrance and catch up with members of the gang afterward. If possible.

But she just couldn't do it. That way gave lawlessness free rein. She had to take a stand. Stop the gang here and now.

And Ruby. What about her? If Ruby thought her vendetta against January justified, it was nothing compared to what January felt toward her.

# CHAPTER 20

JANUARY PUSHED OPEN THE HOTEL'S HEAVY GLASS DOOR and stepped immediately to the left, entering into a dark-paneled lobby. But as it turned out, no one was waiting to shoot her. Or even to see her. Quite spacious, the room contained a couple couches and a few chairs with small tables beside them. A fire blazed in a massive fireplace made of stones from the river. A lone man, his eyes shut, sat basking in the warmth. Otherwise, the room was empty. Although she froze in apprehension, the man didn't move. He was, she discovered a moment later, snoring like a buzz saw.

Across from the fireplace, a long counter with a fancy brass-bound cash register sitting on one end and a leather-bound ledger on the other, indicated the business area. She let out a relieved breath.

No one stood at the desk at the moment. A piece of luck. Probably, January thought, because beyond the open double-wide doorway on her right, the hotel dining room was abuzz. Waitresses rushed about, turning sideways to get around crowded tables. Three roughly dressed men stood just inside as if looking for a place to sit. There were no spare seats. The normal clatter of eating utensils being plied combined with raucous laughter and talk louder than politeness dictated.

The three men, she saw, were looming over an elderly man. He was the clerk who, she supposed, under normal circumstances would be at the lobby desk. His absence was good for her mission, perhaps. Not so good for him as one of the men rammed a tight fist against his chest and pushed. The clerk staggered.

Regretting the necessity, since her natural inclination was to confront the wrongdoer, she whipped over to the counter and drew the ledger to her. Ruby had, she recalled, arrived in The Falls yesterday. Turning back a page, she ran her finger down the column of signatures.

There. Bold as brass. *Ruby Pasco*. The room number indicated the woman—Eli's erstwhile stepmother, January reminded herself—was not lodged in the best room. Briefly, she wondered how Ruby felt about that. According to the number, her room was just at the top of the stairs. The noise would be at its peak there, carried up the stairwell. Feet would tromp past her door at all hours of the day and night. Odor would be directed toward her room as a natural outlet.

She couldn't help but smile.

In a matter of moments, she'd found the master key to Ruby's room and mounted the stairs. Her heart thumped. Apprehension? Anger? Anticipation? She didn't quite know. Lips pressed into a straight line, she knocked.

She had a plan for if Ruby was inside. If she wasn't, well, January had a plan for that, as well. Hence the theft of the key.

After a few seconds, she knocked again. In another moment, she'd unlocked the door and slipped inside.

Eyes opening wide, she became aware of her mouth dropping open. The place looked as if one of those tornadoes she'd read about had whirled through it. And it would, if January wasn't mistaken, have appeared even worse if the room hadn't been so dark. A little light came from the single window, plus a kerosene lamp had been left burning. By its glow, she saw clothing strewn over every surface, including the floor. The riding outfit Ruby had worn in the morning had been trampled underfoot and kicked into a corner. A pair of lacy drawers was tossed dangerously close to the lamp, actually touching the hot chimney. Looking closer, January saw a spot of scorch on the lace.

Her nose wrinkled. Then wrinkled again as she noticed a corner of the bed had slipped from the slats and drooped to the floor. Blankets flung aside; stained and rumpled sheets—she figured she knew what that meant. Ruby had been enjoying an afternoon fling.

Unless she'd been fighting someone off. Not, she decided, anything for her to worry about. Ruby had made her bed. Or not.

One thing certain, January doubted any room in Fat Mary's bordello could possibly look any worse. Or, as she caught the odor of male sweat, smell any worse.

But to sit in judgment of Ruby's untidiness or of her morals—or lack thereof—wasn't why she was here. Darting across the room, admittedly careless of where she set her feet, she began a search.

A hotel room didn't hold many good hiding places. She slid her hand as far as she could reach under the mattress on both sides. There was a packet of money, both gold and paper bills, but nothing to say where they'd come from. Payment for services rendered? Outright theft?

A small table with one drawer contained only a brand new Gideon bible. Unread, January figured. By Ruby, anyway. A rather large portmanteau proved more promising.

A promise fulfilled. Right on top was an envelope with a loose flap. Heart beating fast, she plucked two pages out of it.

The first document, a brief note, signified a package had been sent two days ago and introduced the dignitary delivering this important package to the bank. He —with the money—was most likely who'd arrived this afternoon on the train. The man Peel had met, she supposed, and whom she'd seen at the bank. Not only a dignitary, but the treasurer of the investment consortium himself.

The second document was an acknowledgment of deposit, delivered by hand from the Gregory Trust Investment Group into The Falls bank in the amount of $10,000. A list of investors was included on the receipt.

Pearson, January noted, had cross-signed the deposit slip. Nowhere did Ruby's name show up. Neither did Holzer's or Peel's. But it certainly explained why the group had gathered here and waited for a last deposit.

Pearson, she figured, was meant to be blamed when the funds disappeared in a robbery. Or, perhaps even more likely, the person who delivered the money would take the fall. Right now, January was probably looking at the only proof the sum of money had ever arrived in The Falls.

For this, men had been killed. More deaths, she was certain, would follow. The scheme made her blood boil, thundering so loudly through her veins that she didn't hear the footsteps approaching until it was too late to hide. Not that there was any place to hide.

A key was plugged into the door lock.

Cramming the papers back into the envelope, she flipped it back into the trunk, dropping the lid and skipping to the side as the door opened.

Ruby stepped through, turning to close the door behind her. She wore a low-cut teal blue gown that fit like a second skin in the spots where some folks—men—would appreciate it most. Her black hair was piled high, jewels glittered around her neck and on her fingers, and a dusting of make-up was artfully applied.

How she managed that elegance when the room was such a mess, January couldn't begin to imagine.

Voice shaking only slightly, she said, "There you are, Ruby. I've been waiting to talk to you."

Ruby, who hadn't been looking for a visitor, spun around, letting out a surprised shriek. It took a moment for her to recognize January. Or so she let on, anyway. January wasn't so sure the shriek and surprise weren't an act.

"You," Ruby said. "What are you doing in my room?" She glanced around, her narrowed gaze taking note of where January was standing, a slight flicker of her eyelids showing displeasure. "How did you get in."

January shrugged. "It's an old hotel. Not first class."

An answer that was no answer. She preferred being enigmatic.

A sudden rushed movement brought Ruby up close to her with only inches separating them. Ruby was the taller of two, a fact she made sure to emphasize before pushing January aside and opening the trunk. The envelope sat right on top of the other things there. Exactly as it had before January began her search.

Ruby let out a breath and let the trunk lid close. "How long have you been here? What were you doing? Snooping?"

January, who'd allowed the push, forced a laugh. "Why would I do that? Are you hiding something?"

"No. I..." Ruby's eyes narrowed. "We've got nothing to talk about, Mrs. Billings. Get out."

Shoving a stack of frothy underwear to the floor, January plunked herself down on the room's single chair. "Oh, I think we have a lot to say to one another. We have unfinished business from the first time I met you, but that can wait for a better time. This is an official visit, Ruby, in my capacity as deputy sheriff, dealing with crime in my town. It's right now I want to discuss. Tonight—and the robbery you and those men have planned."

Ruby flounced. "I don't know what you're talking about. What men? What robbery?"

"Oh, don't pretend, Ruby. You might as well admit it. Men like those two who robbed the mercantile the other day. Men like Holzer and Peel. Thieves and murderers, the lot of them." January's look of scorn spoke volumes. "How you can bring yourself to associate with men like that I'll never understand. Everything about them smells dirty." She made a show of lifting her head like a scent hound and sniffing. "I can smell them from here. Or is it just you?"

It was no surprise when Ruby hauled her arm back to slap her. But, as Oldham had learned earlier, January was no weakling. She caught Ruby's hand and flung it aside. "I see you know what I'm talking about."

"No. You're wrong." Ruby shook her hand as if to make sure it was still attached. "Anyway, what difference does it make to you? Ignore me and I'll go away. Come tomorrow morning, you'll never see me again. I guarantee it. I'll even leave you a going away gift." Eyeing January's outfit of split leather riding skirt, boots, and old barn coat, she snorted. "Enough for some new duds. You'd like that, I'm sure."

Was the offer supposed to be a bribe? January's stomach muscles tightened. "And Eli?"

Ruby smirked. "Eli is different. He's mine."

*Is he?* January didn't think so, but had no time, let alone any desire, to argue the question. She'd had enough of Ruby and her conceit. Besides, she'd learned what was important. If Ruby said she'd be gone by tomorrow, she meant the robbery was planned for tonight. Exactly what they'd suspected and now knew. But the thing was, now they'd met and spoken, Ruby had become more dangerous. Most certainly not anyone she wanted running loose behind her back.

January gathered herself and rose from the chair. "Ruby Pasco—" She made her voice quite sonorous. "You are under arrest for theft, assault, and attempted bribery of an officer. Get your coat and I'll see you over to the jail. Come quietly. It'll be better if no one sees what's happening."

Ruby laughed. "Better for who? Don't be stupid. I'm

not going anywhere with you. I doubt you even have the authority."

"Get your coat," January said again, a tiny piece of her mind taking notice that Ruby didn't even try to dispute the charge. "It's cold outside and that dress doesn't cover a whole lot."

Ruby wasn't listening. From somewhere within that too revealing gown, she produced a derringer and pointed it at January. "I've been wanting to do this since I first saw you," she said, and pulled the trigger.

If Ruby hadn't had to have the last word, she probably would've killed January right then and there. But those few words gave January a split second to gauge her intent and fling herself to the side. Ruby's gun followed, but not quite fast enough.

Without thinking, January lunged forward, catching Ruby's arm and thrusting it upward as Ruby shot a second time. A flurry of plaster flakes showered down on them.

Ruby screamed her rage, striking out with the emptied gun as if it were a knife. The short barrel came down hard on the tip of January's shoulder, making her whole arm and hand tingle violently, then go numb. The force of the blow knocked the gun from Ruby's grasp. It fell to the floor.

Her hand numb and her shoulder blazing with pain and seeming unable to do a thing to prevent it, January saw Ruby reaching for the derringer. Although, in retrospect, January didn't understand why the woman bothered since the pistol held only the two bullets and was empty.

But then, without thinking, she stepped forward and tried to block her.

Not her best move as it opened her stance and allowed Ruby to change direction. Teeth bared, the woman came up clawing at January's face, her feet, clad in high-heeled shoes, kicking at January's knee. It was as if the woman had undergone instant metamorphosis into a she-beast of some sort. One who fought dirty.

Pent up fury over Ruby's treatment of her, of young Zora Winkler, even of Eli Pasco, although she thought him quite capable of looking after himself, burst into being. Count her old horse Mollie, lost for months, into the mix as well. While her pain didn't disappear, January worked through it.

She kicked back. Advantage to her. She wore sturdy boots, tough enough to strike through the folds of Ruby's dress.

Ruby let out an eardrum piercing screech and came at her again. January turned sideways to shield her shoulder, and elbowed Ruby in the ribs with her good arm.

Gasping, Ruby toppled when January followed up with a kick behind the knee, collapsing her leg. The only problem being that she had a chunk of January's hair wrapped around her fist at the time and took her down as well.

They rolled, January coming up hard against one of the bed's legs, but she managed to fend Ruby off. With a quick twist, they changed places, January now on top, Ruby flat on the floor. By this time, Ruby's high-piled hairdo had tumbled, flying in black strands around her red and sweating face.

Convenient. January grabbed what was left of the top knot and raised Ruby's head up, then slammed it onto the floor.

Ruby did not fight silently. She'd been uttering a steady, if rather breathless string of epithets suitable for soldiers or sailors. But this time she cried out in pain. The sound did January's heart good, so she did it again, and when Ruby went slack, hammered a hefty blow with her good fist right into the outlaw woman's jaw for good measure.

Leaving Ruby lying on the floor, January rose. First onto her knees and only slowly, and with the aid of the broken bed, making it to her feet.

Realizing she hadn't come through unscathed, her wounds consisted of two bad hands and a badly bruised shoulder where the blow from the derringer had landed.

"Get up," she said to Ruby. "And put on your coat. I'll not have anybody saying I let you freeze on the way to jail." Although if she'd been thinking straight, she might have. For some reason she had this point of duty stuck in her head.

Ruby moaned and lay where she'd fallen. "I need a doctor."

"Yeah? If it's any consolation, I think I do, too."

But neither of them were apt to see Dr. LeBret in the next while. When January opened the room door and pushed Ruby out ahead of her, she expected to see folks gathered outside, drawn by the sound of those two shots. Not so. Noise rose from below even louder than before. The sounds, she discovered, of a fight having broken out in the hotel dining room.

She heard Southbrook's voice rising over the cacophony, calling for Doc to be fetched. A little surprised he'd roused himself to take this chance of being seen, January judged the outbreak an opportunity.

"Go." Nudging Ruby, she got the woman down the stairs in record time. They'd crossed the lobby and made it to the hotel doors when a commanding male voice rang out.

"Ruby," the voice called, mellifluous and suave. "Miss Pasco. Wait. Where are you going? I need a word with you."

*Miss* Pasco?

January turned to look, unsurprised when she saw it was the man from the train. The man from the bank who, she assumed, had delivered the $10,000.

"Where are you going?" he asked again, rushing to catch up with them. "You promised to join me for dinner—until this interruption. But the marshal is here. He'll soon have those ruffians straightened out." Apparently, he didn't notice January standing there with her hand on Ruby's arm.

Figuring she could've given the man advice, something to do with not being so needy, January kept Ruby moving. "Mrs. Pasco has important business to deal with at the moment, sir. Excuse us, please."

It took a second for what she'd said to sink in, but January caught the change in the man's expression when it did. He stepped back, only now apparently seeing the signs of dishevelment, of blood, of darkening bruises.

"*Mrs.* Pasco?"

"Damn you," Ruby, breathed the curse at January, her lips barely moving.

"But," the man said, "I distinctly heard...they called you miss—"

Ruby lifted her head. "Well, you heard wrong," she said, the words biting.

January smiled grimly. "Let's go."

This time Ruby got moving without complaint. Almost, to January's surprise, as if getting caught in a lie embarrassed her.

But no, that couldn't be.

# CHAPTER 21

"Why in the Sam Patch did you bring her here now? What are we supposed to do with her?"

"Lock her up, of course." January said. "That's what you do with criminals, isn't it? Even this one?" *No, all but this one*, she thought.

Eli's face was red as he took Ruby, protesting all the way, into the barred room at the back.

Though January didn't want to be cruel, she felt like laughing. Except for her own stupidity being at fault, she would have.

But Eli was right. Why *had* she brought Ruby here? Or why now? What *were* they to do with his father's former wife?

If her search of Ruby's room, meant to go undetected, had gone right, she would've been able to leave Ruby with the outlaws. With the aim of catching them all in the act, how much simpler, cleaner, the outcome.

But when Ruby caught her and they came to blows, she'd had no choice but to arrest her. Which led to the man at the hotel seeing them together. And that meant sooner or later, Holzer and Peel would hear of it. Their two and two would make four and they'd know something was up, all which might have the worrying result of the whole town being taken hostage. Of more killing. Those two might escape, even if they left the men in their gang to suffer the consequences. January didn't see how she could live with that.

All because she had to mix it up with Ruby in an untimely fashion.

Eli finally noticed she bore the earmarks of battle every bit as vivid as her opponent.

"Sit down," he said roughly as soon as he'd gotten Ruby locked away. "You look like you're about to fall down."

Felt like it, too, not but what she'd rather walk on nails than admit as much to Eli.

He shoved a chair under her legs and when she collapsed onto it, proceeded to collect some medical supplies. "What happened? Where'd you two meet up, anyhow? I see you're bleeding. Did she shoot you?" He glared down at her, waiting for her to say something.

"She tried. Missed. So she slugged me with the empty gun."

"You'd better pull your shirt aside so I can see the damage," he said.

Beyond them in the cell, Ruby had taken exception to the accommodations and was making her complaints clear. And loud.

Her refrain repeated over and over, addressed solely at Eli. "Eli Pasco, you let me out of here right now. This is wrong of you. I swear, I'll go away and never bother you again. Or your father. Truly. Just let me out. Remember what we meant to each other."

What had they meant to each other? January knew the question showed on her face.

Not for the first time, January wished for a door between the cell area and the office. A fine, thick door that shut out all sound. Judging by Eli's expression, he wished for it twice as much.

He looked at January; January looked back. They were sitting across from each other. Eli had drawn the shade over the jail window and the door was locked. Not because they were afraid, but because January's shirt was askew and Eli was checking her shoulder.

"This doesn't look too bad," he said. "Gonna be a bad bruise, I'd guess."

She could've told him that.

"Wouldn't have happened if you hadn't gone to the hotel."

Gone looking for Ruby, he meant. January flinched. "We needed information."

"What if you'd got yourself killed?"

"I didn't."

He sighed. "You could've just left, you know. I doubt Holzer or Peel paid much attention to her once her part was done. Unless I miss my guess, she just stayed to make sure she got her cut."

"Doesn't mean she's not part and parcel of the whole shebang." She meant to retrieve those documents in Ruby's trunk when there were witnesses present. And this time, make the charges hold.

Still, January agreed with him, in part, anyhow. Certainly with the staying to collect her cut part. She didn't know but what Ruby had more to her job than just leading the investors on. "Sorry. I didn't know what else to do. I couldn't take a chance on leaving her there to squeal to Peel about catching me in her room. I didn't want to give them warning."

Looking as if he wanted to shake her, Eli's mouth twisted. He'd gotten to the bandaging part of his first aid and his temper showed in the way he yanked the gauze tight around her arm, ignoring her heartfelt squeak of pain.

"He already knows we're on to him," he said. "Neither Holzer nor Peel is a fool. Killers and thieves, but they aren't stupid. They hire men to do the kind of stuff most likely to get 'em killed."

She had to agree with that.

"Tell me again why you went there in the first place."

He was persistent, for sure. She leaned closer to him, although in truth, Ruby was making so much noise in the back room that anything they said in here must be drowned out. The woman, she made note, was crying now. Great choking sobs.

*Balderdash.* Nobody wept that loudly and meant it.

"I wanted to see if she'd left anything lying around about their plans for the bank."

"And did she?"

"No...yes," she admitted. "Well, not exactly."

With a snap that made her yelp, Eli tied off the ends of the bandage. "What do you mean?"

"I mean I found a note that explained why they haven't robbed the place yet."

"Found a note?"

"Yes. They were waiting for a deposit. $10,000, to be exact."

He whistled. "$10,000?"

"Apparently so. I also found a bank deposit slip with today's date in that amount, and signed by Mr. Pearson."

"A copy?"

She shook her head. "Looked like the original to me." She had some experience with original versus altered documents and figured she knew whereof she spoke. "I think Ruby took it in an effort to hide their tracks. It will throw the blame onto Pearson. Or possibly the man who deposited it."

"No big surprise. It's the kind of thing she's noted for."

"Is she? I guess you should know." Ignoring his frown January pulled her shirt back over her shoulder. None of which was easy as her shoulder was throbbing fiercely at every beat of her heart. "So we'd better get on over to the bank and hide ourselves away. Sooner is better. The outlaws, aside from those rioting, were at supper when I left. Maybe they still are and we'll be in the clear."

"What about Southbrook? He got a message, and last I saw he was headed over to the hotel."

She'd forgotten the town marshal. "Yes. That's right. I saw him there attempting to put down the riot."

Eyes narrowing, Eli held up a cautioning finger. "I'd lay money on that being a trick to take him out of the game. He'll be lucky if they don't kill him."

"Which leaves just us, Squirt, and maybe Sam. Against a gang of professional thieves."

"I know." He sighed, and getting up, checked his Mauser and put on his coat. He left it unbuttoned, free to grasp the big pistol. "They'll have somebody on lookout at the bank. If you'll gather the men, I'll take care of him first thing."

Startled, she said, "Do you know who it is?"

"Got an idea. And January, you be careful. Wait until I signal the way is clear before you move on the bank."

Her be careful? He was the one taking the biggest risk. But January nodded anyway, wishing her head didn't hurt. Or her shoulder. Or her hand, still tingling from when she'd slugged Ruby and had yet to regain its flexibility.

Just for a second she had the idea she should give Eli a good luck kiss. The way he looked at her seemed to say he wouldn't find the gesture amiss. But then the corners of his mouth tweaked upward in a vestige of a smile. Unlocking the door, he slipped through the narrow opening into the night.

A couple minutes later she followed, pausing outside to listen. Either Ruby had realized nobody was coming to her aid and given up making noise, or the building was solid enough to bar sound because January didn't hear a thing. A good omen. At least she was taking it for one.

* * *

ELI, after studying the front of the bank building, eased around the street corner to the back. He waited there, eyes trying to pierce the dark, head cocked to better hear. As far as he could tell, nothing stirred. Not a single stray dog, feral cat, or wandering raccoon. No sound from the street reached back here.

And yet, it was as if he felt eyes on him.

Breathing deeply, he moved forward to the stoop and paused beside the split wood stacked there.

Nope. Nothing.

His hand on the door knob, he twisted. Not much to

his surprise, it turned, the click of the latch slipping from its notch loud in the utter silence.

So. The outlaws had arrived. The plan was in progress.

Drawing his Mauser, he pushed the door open into darkness and entered a room smelling of freshly chopped wood, musty paper, and...and unwashed flesh.

The last hit his consciousness a little late. Something, a gun barrel, or maybe a block of wood from the pile outside slammed into the side of his head, knocking his hat, and under it, his brains and balance askew. Another blow hit the top of his shoulder causing the Mauser to drop from his suddenly nerveless hand.

*Just like January. A matched pair.*

The thought flashed through his mind as a tackle by a heavier man took him down. His right knee twisted under the weight with a pop. The gunsight of a what he imagined to be a .45 dug into his throat. Only deep enough, he figured, to draw a little blood. A warning.

Gagging, he went still.

"Get up," a harsh voice said, as the pressure eased.

Dazed, he obeyed, struggling, his legs barely able to obey him, grateful when the knee held. Maybe better than the tackler thought, though no less painful.

He could see a little now. Able to recognize Desi Holloway's beaver teeth.

"Move." Holloway shoved him toward an almost invisible doorway.

As if he were still immobilized by the blow to his head, he allowed the push without resisting. Limping badly—all of that real—he staggered down a hall toward a faint light, entering the bank lobby where the shades were tightly drawn over the windows.

Behind the teller cages, Arden Holzer was working on the reinforced door of what appeared to be a closet, trying to open it. Eli figured it for the door to the vault.

Looking around with a snarl, Holzer stared at him. "Why didn't you kill him?" he said to Holloway. "He's no use to us."

Holloway shifted, his hold on Eli tightening. "Didn't figure you'd want folks hearing gunshots at the bank. Just in case somebody got curious and came to investigate."

"Huh. Who cares." Holzer stood up and gestured to another man who'd been standing at the front window watching the street outside.

Probably, Eli surmised, explaining how they knew he was coming.

"We're almost done here. Fetch Peel and Krakowski," he told the man. "Pearson, too." And to Holloway, "Shoot anybody you want. Or tie him up and stuff him in that room." He indicated a door Eli hadn't even noticed—maybe because his eyes were twitching in a strange sort of way. Probably because of the blow.

But then, when Holloway had him trussed up like beans in a Mexican tortilla, the outlaw finished the job with yet another blow and everything blanked out. Hearing, seeing, feeling. Everything.

\* \* \*

JANUARY WASN'T certain how long it had been since she and Ruby made their getaway from the hotel. Not quite long enough, from the look of things, for Holzer and Peel to set their plan in motion. Slipping out of the jail, she set out to follow Eli to the bank.

Over at the hotel, she could see the riot—if that's what it actually was—had yet to be put completely down. Those things were always harder to stop than to start. She wondered about Southbrook. Had the outlaws killed him? Taken him hostage?

*No time to worry now*, she told herself. Southbrook was the elected marshal. He'd have to take care of himself.

She chose to cross the street where a large fir tree cast a shadow all the way to the other side. In seconds, she reached the livery and knocked softly on the small entry door.

It opened a crack. "Who is it?" a hoarse whisper demanded.

Sam. It was Sam.

"It's me, January Billings."

"About durn time," he allowed, the door opening to admit her.

A hooded lantern stood off to the side, emitting just enough light to prevent tripping over one's own feet. Squirt came out of the tack room wearing crossed ammunition belts across his body like a Mexican bandito, plus a gun on each hip. He carried a sawed-off shotgun in one hand.

"About durn time you got here." He echoed Sam's greeting almost exactly.

"You'd better hope nobody shoots you in the chest," Sam said, blinking at the sight of his boss. "You'll blow up like a land mine."

"Mind your own business," Squirt replied. "Least-wise I won't run out of firepower. What you got? That dinky old shotgun?"

"Ain't dinky," Sam said. "You'll see."

In this light, it looked to January like a 12-gauge. Maybe even a 10.

"Where's Southbrook? And Pasco? Ain't they with you?" Squirt looked around as if expecting to see them.

"No, but Eli sent me to fetch you. He wants us to get set up at the bank right away We intend to catch the gang in the act."

Squirt frowned. "What's he doin'? Him and Southbrook?"

"Southbrook is at the hotel trying to quell a riot. Eli is scouting the bank as we speak. He plans to get rid of the lookout before we get there."

"A lookout?" Sam spat a stream of tobacco juice, wiping his chin for good measure. "What is this? The Indian wars?"

"Worse," January said. "Worse by far."

Squirt was still mulling over the news about Southbrook and a riot in the same sentence. "What riot?"

"The one I'm sure is meant to draw us away from the bank. They've got Southbrook, but the rest of us have our mission. A riot at the hotel is apt to help us as much —more—than it does them."

Squirt grinned. A huge grin. "You got that right, Mrs. Billings. Let's get movin'."

January reached behind her for the door handle. "Lead the way."

As she'd known he would, Squirt knew the sneakiest route to the bank. He led them around back off the street and took a confusing course toward the bank. Not being real conversant with the town's layout beyond the main thoroughfare, she wasn't sure where they were by the time he stopped and pointed into a small rear courtyard where a large woodpile with stacks of pre-split wood were lined up on the porch and against a shed.

Ollie's work, she surmised, eyeing an axe buried up to its head in a splitting block.

"This is it," he said.

Doing her best to breathe shallowly and keep condensation from rising over her head, she peeked over Squirt's shoulder. "See anybody?" she whispered.

"Nope." He held up a hand in a staying motion. "You and Sam wait here. I'll move on up to the door and when I give the word, you follow, one at a time."

Sam nodded.

"All right." January agreed, thinking the hostler was sure to be better at this sneaking part than she. Better than Sam, too, given the way he was panting right now, short puffs that sounded remarkably dog-like and anxious.

Then Squirt was gone, soundless as far as she could tell. A few seconds later she spotted him at the bank's back door. It opened and he scooted inside.

"We better get ready," Sam whispered.

"I am ready. We wait for Squirt's word."

His word was long coming. Too long. Had Eli been successful at subduing whoever was keeping watch on the bank? Was Squirt all right? There'd been no sound of shots. No shouts or suggestion of slugfests or other altercations. What did it mean?

January's heart drummed, the tension rising to almost unbearable heights at the delay. Then, just as she was about to make her own way into the bank regardless of Squirt's word, the door opened and she spotted the hat he customarily wore, distinctive because its total shapelessness. He was making a come-along gesture.

"It's Squirt," Sam said, eyes squinted against the black night.

Her withheld breath gusted out. "Go ahead," she told him and without waiting, he dashed for the bank, paused briefly, then went inside.

Minutes passed, then it was her turn. Without conscious thought, her .38 in hand, she proceeded more slowly, wide eyes searching the darkness beyond the door. Both men had disappeared from sight.

She knew something didn't bode well the moment she stepped into a little room, maybe an enclosed porch, that was bathed in murky darkness. This must be the room Ollie had spoken of, from which he'd been privy to the meeting of Pearson and Holzer. Coat hooks protruded from the wall as she found out after bumping into one with her already painful shoulder. A bench sitting against the wall and a bin holding more wood completed the room. Evidently banks were required to keep their customers warm.

But why hadn't one of them, Sam or Squirt, waited for her? She needed a guide to get her through to the room with the vault where Eli must've taken up station.

In fact, as she stood just over the threshold trying to get her bearings, she heard them. Or she heard somebody. Hurrying footsteps headed her way. Whoever it was wore spurs. She heard the tinkle of jingle bobs and long rowels scraping the floor.

Eli didn't wear spurs. Nor did Squirt or Sam.

Their plan wasn't supposed to work this way. She hadn't time to find a hiding place. Or even to retreat outside. Her only choice seemed to be pressing herself against the far inner wall beside the entry and hope whoever it was didn't notice her. Even better, she hunkered down, doing her best to look like a pile of detritus waiting to be hauled away. Her .38 held between her knees, it pointed up, ready to shoot.

The jingle bobs fell silent. Looking down, January saw the toes of boots standing in the doorway.

"Nobody else here, boss," he, whoever he was, called out.

"Throw the damn lock," a voice replied from down the hall. "We don't need anybody else barging in unannounced. Oldham has a key. He can let himself in when he gets here."

The spur man stepped forward and shut the outer door. A lock clicked and the darkness, if possible, grew even deeper.

"Yeah," he was saying as he fumbled his way back toward the boss. "But Oldham disappeared. Must've got drunk at that saloon this morning and went off somewhere to sleep it off."

January's lip curled. His surmise was close since Oldham was being held in Squirt's cellar right now.

The other man made a sound of disgust. "Hurry up and get back in here." There was a heavy grunt and he said, "I told Peel he was getting too many people involved. If he didn't have a vendetta against that woman—I forget her name—we'd be better off. This job would've been handled smoothly. But no. Add in Ruby Pasco, a troublesome *puta* if I ever met one, and between the two of them..."

The spur man passed January without seeing her, and the other man's complaints faded.

What he'd said was enough to scare the starch out of

her, though. The woman whose name he forgot could only be her. So evidently, she was the one to blame for this influx of criminals invading their little town.

But as she stood, a smile twitched her lips. Maybe she should be flattered if Peel thought it would take a gang of a dozen men to dispose of her. A dozen men and Ruby.

# CHAPTER 22

JANUARY HAD THINGS TO THINK ABOUT OTHER THAN HER popularity—or otherwise—with Holzer's gang. For instance, what had happened to Squirt and Sam just now? Where, and here her heart squeezed inside her chest, was Eli? How on earth had Holzer and his men moved quickly enough to capture all of her team but her?

An answer occurred to her. *He'd known they would be coming.*

A simple good guess? Maybe. Maybe they hadn't been captured. But if not, where were they?

Also, where the dickens had Ford Tervo gotten to? She hadn't heard from him since late afternoon, when they'd brought in Fat Mary's troublesome customer.

She didn't have time to ponder all the questions plaguing her now. She had to find Eli, Squirt and Sam. Best not to let herself wonder how, or in what condition, they'd be in.

Some consolation, she reminded herself. There'd been no shots, no outcries. They'd be all right. All she had to do is—remain undetected herself. Regaining her feet, January peeked through the opening into a short hall. Poorly lit, it was even darker than the little room she was in, but down at the end light glowed.

She followed the light. Staying close to the wall and on feet soft as a cat's, she crept in the light's direction.

If January recalled the layout of the bank correctly, when entered from the front it opened onto a commodious lobby. A long mahogany counter ran down the middle of the room. A couple straight-backed chairs and a small table were in a corner in case someone needed to sit. Although why anyone would want to sit in a bank lobby was beyond her.

To the left were two teller cages with half-barred glass windows tucked in behind a high counter. Just behind them a door led who knew where. January had always figured more offices, if she thought about it at all. Straight on was Mrs. Filmore's desk, which served as a barrier to Mr. Pearson's office.

So where, she wondered, was the vault.

Something it didn't take much longer to discover as the hall soon ended, stopping just behind the teller cages. The vault, she found, looked like nothing more than a closet with a strong door. Peeking around the hall doorway, she spotted a man kneeling in front of the open door, fiddling with the dial of a large safe that had been built into the closet.

He was muttering and shaking his head in disgust.

Aha. Leonard Holzer in the flesh. And although a renowned thief and murderer, it appeared safecracking was not one of his criminal skills.

He turned to glower at the fellow with spurs. "Holloway, what's taking them so long? We need Pearson here to do this."

"Eh, Peel got a little rough with him over at the hotel. Might take him a while to come around."

Raging, Holzer shot to his feet. "I should've known better than to bring Peel in on this. He's out of control since his brother got put away. It's no wonder half the town knows what's going on tonight. We'll end up having to shoot our way out this burg."

In January's opinion, Holzer sound a wee bit out of control himself. As if he might just enjoy shooting his way out of town.

Holloway shrugged. "Then we will. I got the guns for it." He plucked a couple guns out of his belt and waved then in a phony threatening manner.

The boss scowled and held up his lantern. "You even know how to use those things?"

"Course I do," Holloway said. Not much to January's surprise, he matched the description of T.T.'s attacker. The man he figured had stolen the Mauser.

The guns he held up, January saw, her eyes opening wide, were a matching pair of Mauser Broomhandles. That had to mean he'd somehow had gotten the better of Eli and managed to take his gun.

Her heart, already at a gallop, thudded even faster, the blood pulsing in her ears.

"Here," Holzer said to the beaver-toothed man, "take the lantern. Hold it a foot or so higher. I can't see squat." Hunkering again, Holzer made a show of listening as he spun the safe's dial while Holloway lifted the light.

Aimlessly spun, as far she could tell from the hall.

"This ain't working," he said at last. "You go get Pearson. Wake him up no matter what it takes. Grab him by the *cojones*. That'll do it. And make sure Krakowski is on his way. He ain't as good with safes as Oldham but he might do in a pinch. It's the only reason I brought him in."

Quick to follow orders, the man set down the lantern and headed right toward her.

She'd started to back away when it occurred to her there was nowhere to go. There were only two of them. She's take them by surprise. And her .38 was in her hand.

*Now*, she told herself. *Take them now.*

Being no kind of fool, January didn't bother to step into the light. She had excellent line of sight on both of them. Holzer was still on his knees in front of the safe.

"Stop where you are," she said. "Put up your hands. You're both under arrest."

Holloway, only a few feet away, came to an abrupt stop. His mouth gaped open.

She didn't expect either to obey, and she wasn't wrong. Holzer, quickest to react, popped to his feet reaching for his gun before the first directive was out of her mouth. Holloway, closer, fumbled one of the Broomhandles from his belt and brought it to bear.

No hesitation. She shot him point blank. Still, he jerked the Mauser's trigger as he fell backward, the bullet landing a scant inch above her head.

Close enough to scare her into flinching.

And Holzer, moving fast, rushed her, jumping over Holloway as if the dead man were no more than a fallen log.

Smiling. He was smiling.

So she shot him, too. Not a kill shot, though she aimed for one, but enough to stop him. A stricken look replaced the smile as his pistol, a short-barreled pocket gun, dropped from fingers splaying wide. His elbow, shattered by her bullet, made him scream. Rage. Agony.

And from somewhere, she heard a voice. Eli's voice.

Not dead. For a moment she felt dizzy.

"You," she said to Holzer, "on your knees." Stepping into the room, she kicked his gun out of reach, following it with the gun Holloway had dropped. The body lay on top of the second Mauser he'd stolen. Safe out of reach, she figured, for the moment.

"I can't, you stupid..." He called her a word beyond her vocabulary, probably a good thing.

In answer, she kicked him behind the knee. Kicked him hard. He screamed again as his shattered elbow jerked, but he dropped as readily as Ruby had earlier. Tears ran from the corners of his eyes. He didn't so much as glance at Holloway's body, but she paused to check.

Yes. Dead.

"January!" Eli's voice came again.

Able to determine the location now, she edged around Holzer. Spotting another door next to the vault closet, she pushed it open.

Two men lay on the floor. Squirt and Sam, trussed and gagged. Squirt appeared unconscious, while Sam's eyelids fluttered, although they stayed shut. Eli, though, was tied to a chair, his bonds eerily in the style of the dead Deputy U.S. Marshal from this morning. So. Either Holloway or Holzer had been part of the murder of the Federal officer.

If eyes could blaze, Eli's did.

Somehow, January saw, he'd managed to scrub the

rag tied around his mouth half-free and spit out the wad of whatever they'd crammed in to keep him quiet.

"You're not dead," he said, as if he couldn't believe what he was seeing.

"And neither are you." Holding up her forefinger, she said, "Can you wait just a minute? I need to make sure Holzer can't get away."

"You got Holzer?"

He needn't, she thought, have sounded so amazed. "Yes. Wounded. The other man is dead."

"Go then. I'll wait."

Not that he had a choice.

Holzer barely made it back to his feet. Careful prodding with the barrel of her .38—and the threat of shooting his other elbow if he so much as looked at her sideways—moved him into Pearson's office. From her earlier meeting with the banker, she remembered the heavy desk. If she anchored him to that, he'd never be able to get away.

A few minutes later, leaving him on the floor and tethered foot and unwounded arm, she closed the door on him. He passed out before she finished. Blood loss or pain, she didn't care which, would keep him silent for a while.

Back with Eli, she began working on the knotted rope wrapped around him like an Egyptian mummy's burial linens. "Were there just the two of them or am I missing someone?"

"He sent a man back to the hotel to bring the others." He flinched a little as her knife nicked the skin around his hands. "Hurry, January. It's been too long. They'll be here soon."

"I am hurrying." She was a little breathless, aware of

his dark eyes watching her. "I don't want to cut an artery."

He chuckled. "You won't."

The chuckle calmed her enough to work the knife blade under the rope and finally slice through the tough strands. His hands free, he rubbed vigorously to restore the feeling while she worked around his boots. Gaps there made it easier for her blade to get purchase.

He stood, only swaying a little. "Thank you." The words came just before he planted a kiss on her lips. Short and sweet. Then not so short, but still sweet.

January didn't recoil. Far from it. But after a while she did draw back and breathe.

As for Eli, he looked as gobsmacked as she felt.

"I..." he said, and stood looking down at her.

She swallowed.

And Squirt—even through a gag she knew his muffled grunts—drew attention to his plight with a drawn-out *mmmmmm* sound.

Sure her face had turned as pink as a Damascus rose, knife in hand, January hastened over to Squirt and ripped the gag from his mouth.

He, as cranky as a rusted pump handle, winced. "If you two are done nibbling on each other, you can get me out of these ropes. And take a look at Sam. He needs help."

"I'll see to Sam," Eli said, hunkering down to look at hostler. He, Eli, that is, to January's chagrin, didn't appear embarrassed in the least.

"You gonna stab me with that or cut me loose?" Squirt scowled up at her, but if she wasn't mistaken, his mouth grinned.

"I'm trying to decide," she replied.

Holloway or Holzer, whichever man had tied the two hostlers, hadn't done as thorough job on them. It took only seconds for her knife to slice through the bindings. Squirt got up and shook himself like a dog.

"What now?" he asked.

"Get Holloway's body out of the hall," January said. "Put him in Pearson's office along with Holzer. We don't want to tip whoever comes through the door first that the pool of blood belongs to one of them. Oh," she added to Squirt's back as he started off. "Eli's gun is there somewhere. And another Mauser is under the body. Don't miss either of them."

"Yes, ma'am, Mrs. Deputy." The respect in his tone was evident.

\* \* \*

THEY MADE quick work of clearing the place. January placed the lantern in such a way as to draw attention to the vault. A screwdriver lay on the floor beside the lantern. The rest of the bank was dark, helping to obscure the hiding places the three had chosen.

Sam lay in the room where they'd found him. Unbound now, and more comfortable with his head cushioned on a pillow from Pearson's office, he remained out of the fight.

Only a few minutes passed before they heard the creak of the outside door and feet traversing the hall. Even a few murmurs. Someone said, "That's blood." And a reply of, "If it ain't yours, it don't matter." Laughter followed, although January didn't see what made the concept funny.

Then, "Move along, Pearson. Sooner this is done,

the sooner we'll be out of your hair. Cooperation will be appreciated." The moan of a man in pain followed.

Pearson. And Peel.

"Arden?" Peel called out. Loudly, as if it didn't matter if anyone else heard. "Hi, Holzer. We're here. Where are you?"

January had chosen an excellent viewpoint, one allowing her to see how the would-be thieves spread out. They'd brought lanterns with them, making it easy for her to count heads and positions. Four besides Peel and Pearson. She didn't think Pearson would be a problem.

Peel pushed Pearson ahead of him toward the vault and waggled a come-along finger at a skinny fellow dressed all in black.

"Open it, Pearson," Peel said. "Now."

Pearson, his face a ghastly white, whined. "I told you. I don't know how. The head teller has always done that. I never have. He has the combination."

"Hogwash. I don't believe you. What bank president can't open the vault of his own bank?" Peel gave a short laugh.

"I'm sorry," Pearson said, barely audible.

"Yeah. Well, you ought to be." Peel turned to the skinny man. "Give it a whirl, Krak. If you don't have it open in five, we'll have to blow it."

Full of pride, the skinny man thrust back his shoulders. "I'll get 'er."

"You men, scatter around." Peel gave sharp instructions. "Keep your eyes open. Zehm, if anybody comes too close or gets too curious, take care of them."

"Sure thing, boss. Should I shoot 'em?" one of the minions said.

Peel's sneer was eerily identical to his brother's. "Well, I don't mean invite them in for a drink. But a knife is quieter," he said.

The man pointed at Pearson. "What about him?"

January's lips clamped tight. She hated knives. Could be Pearson did as well since his face nearly matched the white of his shirt.

Peel started to nod, then changed his mind. "Might need him yet. Sit him down over there and keep an eye on him." He motioned at one of the lobby chairs and glared at the banker. "I can always change my mind."

Pearson hastened to obey. He dropped into the chair and sat, head hanging.

There weren't so many outlaws remaining of those who'd ridden into The Falls. Relieved, January realized that between them, their small army had disposed of at least half of the Holzer and Peel men.

While Peel and the man he addressed as Krak were involved at the safe, the other three moved through the bank. One went to peer through the blinds over the front window. Another took up station where the hallway led from the main room to the rear. The last prowled, easing his way toward the teller's windows. A mistake. Eli was there. And he, she knew, was angry and if his expression earlier was anything to go by, feeling vengeful.

The outlaw standing sentry at the hallway spoke up suddenly. "Where's Holloway?" He was staring down at the dark blood staining the floor. "He oughta be here."

"He don't matter. I want to know where Holzer got to? If that safe is empty, I guess I'll know who to blame." Peel's face, even at a distance, caused the hair on January's neck to prickle. "Him and that woman. Ruby.

She's missing too, ever since supper. What do you know about her, Krak?"

Krak, his attention solely on the safe, didn't speak, but shrugged.

"You ought to know," Peel said, glaring down at the yeggman. "You traveled with her to get here."

Krak, with a faraway look on his face, ignored him.

For good or for bad, it looked to January as if there was some division in the ranks. Peel was angry, afraid he'd been double-crossed by his partner. Gathering herself as Krak concentrated on the safe with Peel hanging threateningly over his neck and the other three men cocky with confidence, January decided this might be the time for them to strike. Put an end to this.

Just as she was about to step into the open, a long groan stopped the men. Only Krak kept working.

Pool turned, his eyes flashing. "What was that?"

The man at the door shrugged. "It's all right. We bashed those livery fellers pretty hard. They've probably got a headache."

"Check on him. Check on them all. And kill that bounty hunter. I don't know why you left him alive anyhow. Zehm—"

The man prowling toward the teller cages stopped.

"You do it," Peel said. "Now. Cut his throat."

Zehm hesitated before saying, "Yes, boss." He stepped toward the room Eli and the others had been tied until the noise came again and he stopped. "Hey, that ain't where..."

Which is when the war began.

# CHAPTER 23

JANUARY ALWAYS THOUGHT, AFTERWARD, WHEN THE gunfire died down, that anyone with an ounce of brains would've flung up their hands and surrendered. Until she remembered every one of these men had been caught and jailed before at one time or another. None had any desire to go back to breaking rocks under the hot sun. Or shoveling snow berms. And yet, they were stupid enough, after being released, to have renewed their outlaw ways.

The game spiraled out of control the second the outlaw, Zehm, a puzzled expression on his face, realized the moans should've been coming from elsewhere.

"Hey," he said, drawing a sharp look from Peel. "That ain't where— That's the wrong room."

"What?" Peel, much annoyed, whipped around to at him.

Zehm may have been slow to spread the alarm, but spread it he did.

At that point, what could January do but rise up from where she'd been crouching under Mrs. Filmore's desk and point her .38 at the middle of *Peel's* chest? Right at heart level. Right, in fact, where his jacket lapels draped open to reveal a showy silk-embroidered vest of flowers done up in blues and greens.

"Hands up," she shouted. "You're all—"

Taking their cues, Squirt, still pale and tottering in his rundown, manure splattered boots, emerged from the shadows at the back of the lobby with his recovered shotgun aimed at the man in the hall.

As for Eli, he pushed away from the pillar at the end of the cages and stepped into the open. With Zehm in his sights, the outlaws were accounted for.

Except they forgot Krak, burrowed down with his head bent toward the safe. Which means they *all* forgot Krakowski. Including the men from his own side. So it came as a shock when, almost out of nowhere, a bullet zinged past January, clipping the side of her boot on the way, and taking with it a mixed strip of shoe leather, woolen stocking and dainty human skin.

January, who'd barely gotten the "hands up" part out of her mouth, clamped down on her tongue to shut off a cry of pain. She couldn't stop the clench of her trigger finger, which inadvertently loosed a shot of her own. Her bullet came closer to Eli than it did to Peel, causing him to flinch.

Peel, without hesitating, dived over the top of Krakowski, leaving the yeggman behind as he raced down the back hall.

Eli sent a shot after him, a waste of ammunition.

Anyway, Zehm was quick on the draw. The second Eli switched his aim to Peel, Zehm got his gun out and started shooting. Two quick shots at Eli, both of which missed, but forced a retreat behind the pillar. One at

Squirt, also a miss although it went right through the plate glass window at the front of the bank. And another at January.

Sadly for him, not so sad for her, the bullet plowed into Mrs. Filmore's desk, passing first through the bank of side drawers, pinging on a metal trash basket, and completing its journey through the wall into Pearson's office.

January dropped to the floor again, aiming from under the desk in a cockeyed fashion at Zehm. Squirt beat her to it. The thunder of his shotgun about deafened her and put a stop to the shooting.

A man screamed, "Don't shoot. Don't shoot," and she had an impression of a man fleeing out the front door. Pearson, making a break.

Then Zehm fell at her feet, his dead face turned toward her, and she forgot about the banker.

"Ugh." The next thing she knew, Eli had lifted her off the floor and she, perforce, was hanging onto him. He felt solid. Steady.

"Thanks," she said, although she would rather have stayed down. Her stomach roiled. Reeling, she pulled away, bracing herself against the desk.

"Are you all right? Are you hurt?" Anxious dark eyes swept over her.

She gulped. "I'm fine. Just—I'm fine." A lie. "You?"

"I'll live, but Peel got away," Eli said. "I'm going after him."

She nodded. "Go."

He ran, following Peel down the hall. Her ears still ringing, as if from far away she heard more gunshots. Not from Eli's Broomhandle, she thought, cocking her head. But with a sound different from the six-shooters.

Maybe Southbrook had joined the fray. Or Dabney. But no. It wouldn't be Dabney. Right now, looking down at Zehm, his chest half blown away by Squirt's shotgun, she didn't even care.

But she still had things to do. Straightening, she stared around the bank's interior where the single lantern still provided the only light. Squirt had stumped over to where the man who'd been guarding the back still stood with his hands in the air. He was the only one who'd obeyed her command.

As for Krakowski, he lay, eyes closed, in front of the safe. She didn't know if Peel had done something when he made his escape, or if Eli had deliberately knocked him out. Relieved not to consider him, she didn't much care.

Squirt grinned at her. "We saved the bank," he said, his pride obvious.

"I guess we did." More gunfire from outside made her think again. "At least for now."

Her foot burned like it'd been branded, but she could walk on it. It didn't seem too bad, except for the sticky wetness of blood in her boot—her ruined boot. Walking over to the front window, a test the foot managed to pass, she peered through a crack in the blinds. In the street, someone fired off a couple more shots, which meant the job wasn't yet done.

"I've got to get out there." She gestured vaguely. "Are you all right in here?"

Squirt nodded. "I'm good. Go get 'em, Deputy Billings."

"Keep your eye on Krakowski. He's a sneaky one and might be playing possum."

He chuckled, already busy hogtying his man. "I noticed. Don't worry. Go."

No denying the foot slowed her down, possibly owing as much to the missing boot heel as the wound.

A body sprawled across the bank's threshold. Pausing to check for a pulse, it was clear the man was dead. Across the street, in front of Thurston's Mercantile, another man lay on the ground. This body twitched, but from appearances, he wouldn't be a factor.

A shotgun poked out the mercantile's door, proving T.T. had joined the fight and guarded his own business. January waved and the shotgun returned the salute.

Though January peered all ways into the dark street, Peel and Eli had disappeared. She'd been too slow to catch them. Any other outlaws had scattered, already out of sight and, she hoped, on their way out of town. Cocking her head, she listened. Nothing. The night, feeling as though it listened with her, had gone silent, as if it were holding its breath.

Peel had gone off somewhere to regroup whoever of his men remained, she supposed, her innards beginning a queer jerk. And Eli had put himself in the open, seeking the leader by himself.

The door opened behind her. Startled, she jumped to the side, leveling her gun.

"Whoa!" Squirt threw up his hands. "It's just me, ma'am. I trussed them two up, tossed 'em in with Holzer and Holloway, and locked the door on them all. Sam is waking up, slow but sure. Says he's all right. He's got my shotgun and is gonna keep his eyes on the prisoners."

Relief surged over her. "Good," she said. The word meant more for Sam's recovery than the taking of prisoners. Now if she only knew where Eli had gone. Those shots gnawed at her mind like a squirrel at a nut. When Peel had run, Eli had followed. But where?

"Did you see which direction Eli went?" she asked Squirt.

He'd been grinning but that disappeared fast.

"No, ma'am. I didn't. I was a little occupied at the time. But—" a frown grew "—I did catch sight of Peel running off thataway." He pointed toward the river and echoed her previous thought. "I figure he intends on meeting up with the rest of the gang, what there are of them. Now we put an end to this here bank robbery, I figure he'll take a hostage or two and get out of town. There ain't nothing much the way he went. Nothin' but..."

"Fat Mary's..."

"Yes, ma'am. Fat Mary's."

"Let's go."

As usual, Squirt knew the best way.

Doggedly, every step a battle with her painful foot, January struggled to follow, hurrying after Squirt to the path running beside the rushing river, thence to the brothel. January counted seconds under her breath in a failing attempt to distract herself, aware that at the rate she managed, it would take too long to track Peel. With Eli on his heels, tense fear made her carry on.

"Forty-six, forty-seven, one hundred fifty." Aware she'd lost count, she barely heard Squirt's warning when he called out from ahead, "Catch that horse!"

A riderless horse trotted toward her. A roan she recognized as she caught at the dangling reins. "This is Ford Tervo's horse."

Squirt nodded grimly. "It is. Mrs. Billings, this don't look good."

Well, and didn't she know it? Without a second thought, she swung up into the saddle. "Climb on behind," she said and, turning the horse, set him into a lope as soon as the hostler was in place.

What about Ford Tervo? His absence preyed on her mind. He'd never just turn his horse loose to wander.

Minutes later, they came within sight of the brothel. The building loomed out of the dark, looking as empty and deserted as a ghost town derelict. Every window was shuttered. Only the faint gleam of a single upstairs light shone from within. Horses, however, were present, stirring a little in the night. Four were hitched at the rail.

"Yup," Squirt murmured. "They's congregating here, just like we figured."

"Keep a sharp eye out," January said. "There's bound to be men on watch. When the shooting starts, be careful what you aim at. We don't want to shoot any of the women."

"No, ma'am. We don't."

Was that fervent regard she heard in Squirt's answer?

"Plus," she added, "we have allies here." How could she ever forget Fat Mary's intent to make blood butter out of an outlaw earlier this afternoon?

They slid from Tervo's roan and tied him to a bush, then went ahead on foot. Squirt moved silently through the trees and shrubs surrounding the big house. January, though not perhaps as quiet, ignored her pain and matched him step for step.

They spotted a man left outside the kitchen entrance by the glow of his quirly when he drew strongly on the cigarette. He was standing slouched, his back toward them, apparently transfixed by the rustle and flow of the river. Squirt, separated from January by several feet, nodded to her and crept toward him like a permanent resident of the aforementioned ghost town.

The outlaw went down in a heap when Squirt clocked him alongside the head with the butt of his pistol. He dragged him into the shadows of the back stoop before motioning January forward.

"What next?" he said.

January's mind raced. "There's probably another at the front. You go see what's happening there. I'm going inside."

"By yourself?" Even in the dark she could see his eyes widening. "Ma'am, that don't seem like a good idea. Remember what happened at the bank."

"I've got to find Eli." Ford's loose horse nagged at her. "And Ford Tervo. If they're not out here, then they must be in there."

Squirt wasted no more breath arguing. "Watch your back." Then he was gone.

It took all January had to open the door and enter into utter darkness.

Ford's body lay just inside where one of the outlaws —Peel, she suspected—had caught him either coming or going. January realized it was Ford when she stumbled over a leg and landed with one knee on the dead man's chest. The other knee settled in his wet blood. He didn't move. And then her fingers, groping frantically, found the badge attached to the vest he wore. The five-pointed star of the U.S. Marshal's service.

Heart racing, she touched his face. Found the mustache he'd cultivated. Skin still warm. He'd hadn't been dead long. Minutes only, she suspected.

Choking on a ragged sob, she stood up. Why hadn't

he waited for her so they could come in together? Or for Eli or Squirt? Because he was impulsive, as she very well knew. Used to working as a lone wolf. Confident of his ability.

*Over-confident.*

If he'd waited, she could have told him about Peel. He may have thought he knew, but she was the one who'd come up against that family before. Their brutality. The joy they took in killing. Their penchant, once again, for knives.

Footsteps thudded nearby and she jerked away from the body.

The back door opened directly into the kitchen where she'd seen Fat Mary and her girls having dinner. As she remembered, there'd been a worktable with a heavy wooden top where the cook chopped vegetables and sliced meats. It had a couple tiers and was the best place of concealment in the room.

Floundering some, she crouched behind it a second before two men entered the kitchen. One carried a lamp, its wick flickering as if about out of fuel.

"Get rid of this body," one said, "before he starts stinking up the place."

"Where should I put him, boss?" the other wanted to know.

"I don't care. Just get him out of here. Throw him in the river."

*Boss. Which must mean this was Peel and one of his bootlickers.* January's heart thudded. She should rise up and shoot him. She knew it, yet fear held her hand.

Then it was too late as, having given his orders, he strode quickly away toward the front of the house. Left alone, the second man let out a breath punctuated by a curse.

January peered around the table to see a man squatting at Ford's side. He ran his hands through Ford's pockets, lifting a wallet and some coins, and stowing them in his own. Last of all, he emitted a short chuckle and unpinned the badge. Rising, he grabbed hold of one of Ford's feet and began dragging him toward the door, head bumping, a blood trail marking every lurch.

Incensed, January moved then. She leapt on the man's back as he hunched over Ford and, using a lesson from Squirt, clubbed the man hard behind the ear with her pistol. The outlaw might've had a soft skill. He went down, crashing on top of Ford's body.

She blew out the lamp before moving from the kitchen, thinking it best to leave the room dark. But when she followed the direction Peel had taken, into the front of the house, she discovered a few lights had been left burning. Enough to catch sight of Eli with one foot on the stairway's bottom step.

"E..." she started. He whirled, the big Mauser pointing at her heart. She threw up her hands for as long as it took him to realize her identity.

He strode toward her and, impervious to the fact they each held a gun, crushed her against him. After a moment while she heard his heart thumping—unless it was her own—he pushed her away. Eli glared down at her, his dark eyes hard, then drew her against him again. She wouldn't have minded staying like that for a while, but the respite lasted only seconds.

"What are you doing here?" he demanded, voice low.

"Catching a killer."

"Tervo," he murmured the name into her hair.

She swallowed. "I saw him."

He growled. There was no other word for it. January supposed he meant the wordless sound as regret her friend was dead and she had found his body, anger that Peel was still walking around killing people, and lastly, a vow to do something about it.

She nodded.

"There's two or three men somewhere down here. Peel just went upstairs." Eli bent his head until their foreheads touched. "I think those are all that's left. My guess is he's gone to grab one of the women as a hostage. The gang is broken, but he intends to get away. He'll use his men here to keep us occupied while he disappears. Best if you stay out of sight. He'll take you if he can."

"He can try." January felt her mouth tremble. "But he doesn't have three men. At least two are otherwise occupied, and I expect Squirt has dealt with the one out front by now."

Eli's face lit. "Then I'm going up."

January thought to protest, but he'd already let her go when they heard a shuffling noise at the top of the stairs. She took hold of his arm, stopping him from going farther. "Wait."

# CHAPTER 24

A MUFFLED SQUAWK SOUNDED OVERHEAD.

"Shut up, you fat cow. Wouldn't take much for you to tumble down these stairs. A little push. That's it."

January had no doubt Nelson Peel had somehow taken Fat Mary captive. A surprise. She'd thought the woman too stalwart and too smart to let herself be taken.

Motioning with her head, she indicated Eli should take a position on one side of the open stair. She would take the other. They would stand back. Let Mary and Peel make their way down and when they were past, attack from the rear.

Eli had no trouble figuring her strategy. Nodding, he stepped back and almost faded into the background.

Peel was halfway to the bottom, Fat Mary his reluctant companion, when Peel called out, "Elliot, where the hell are you?"

Receiving no answer displeased him. By this time January could see him well enough to know he expected his men to jump to his bidding. Saw, too, that he carried a knife with a long blade in one hand as he walked behind Fat Mary.

"Elliot," he yelled, louder this time. Then to Mary, "Hurry up."

But Fat Mary, smart enough to take care with her footing, was watching her feet since her hands were bound. She spotted Eli, who crouched beside the steps. He put a finger to his lips. She blinked acknowledgement.

Peel, some sixth sense warning him, let his impatience loose. Only four steps away from the bottom, he gave Mary a shove that sent her tumbling. She let herself fall, protecting her head by flinging up her arms. As soon as she stopped rolling it was apparent Peel had made a mistake.

A bad mistake. Mary impeded his exit and as he made to jump over her bulk, she reached up and grabbed a foot. He fell, sprawling on top of her. His knife dug into the floor beside her head and even in the dim light as January and Eli rushed forward, he grabbed it up and plunged it into Mary's stomach.

She let out a shriek fit to deafen her attacker. His eyes widened with the realization that far from killing her, he'd mostly made her angry. She grabbed at his head, bouncing it off the floor.

They fought, which gave January time to take pleasure in the sight of Peel taking a beating from Fat Mary.

But she, wounded, shaken from the fall and a shortage of breath, quickly began to fail. January stepped forward as Peel raised his knife again, and without thinking, kicked the blade out of his hand.

He rose upward as if to go for her then, but Mary, panting like a done in buffalo, grabbed his knife where it had fallen beside her, and flicked it across his throat as he reached across to grab January.

The knife, as it turned out, had been expertly sharpened.

\* \* \*

THERE WASN'T such an awful lot to do after that, except collect the bodies and hunker around in companionable discussion. They drank coffee fortified with generous splashes of bourbon. The body count seemed almost reasonable considering only two people on the side of law and order perished. That both had been Deputy U.S. Marshals didn't strike Southbrook as odd, a point he was quick to mention. It had been the marshals' job to wade into conflict.

Their job, maybe, which didn't stop January from mourning Ford Tervo's death.

For the rest, they were glad to be alive.

"Look at it thisaway, the gang outnumbered us two, maybe three, to one." Southbrook smiled wryly from a mouth swollen from its connection with an elbow during the ruckus earlier at the hotel. "We're lucky it ain't some of us laying in Hannon's funeral parlor about now."

"Or all of us," Squirt put in.

They'd gathered in the jailhouse, Southbrook sitting at his desk, January in the sheriff's chair.

"So many dead men," January said, hoping the shot of Old Crow in her coffee might help warm her. "If they'd come at us all at once, there'd have been a different outcome." She was still shaken by the day, her face cold and drawn. She couldn't forget she'd accounted for a few of those lives herself and it was catching up with her. The only death that gave satisfaction was that of Nelson Peel, and Fat Mary got credit for that. As well as the hefty reward.

After all was said and done, there'd be several windfalls from rewards. The railroad would be generous as it was notable in its dislike of train robbery.

There was only one more person to be accounted for, and she was raising Cain in the backroom jail cell.

Ruby Pasco. Crying and acting the injured party, with Southbrook and Sam becoming more and more uncomfortable with her confinement.

Squirt, on the other hand, didn't appear sorry for her at all. Doc LeBret, who'd come at last to check on Southbrook's wellbeing and January's injured foot, merely shrugged. The first thing January asked about was the wounded madame.

"I doubt her mother named her Fat Mary, but right now she can be glad she earned the name," he told January, carefully winding her foot in layers of gauze.

"She can?" January didn't see how, considering how exhausting it must be to shift three hundred pounds up and down those stairs.

"All that adipose tissue saved her." Doc grinned. "The knife didn't penetrate deeply enough to hit anything vital."

The men were still chuckling as he departed. Right up until Ruby let out another of those plaintive wails.

"Can't you do something about her?" Squirt glared toward the jail cells.

January, noticing the way Eli flinched, was of a mind to lock the woman up in Squirt's cellar with Holzer's men and throw away the key.

His reaction had January wondering. What did he think should be done with her?

"Is this town too poor to put up a door between this room and the cells?" Eli indicated something between scorn and anger. "Let alone a privacy wall for female prisoners."

"Not too poor," Southbrook answered. "It's just we ain't accustomed to such an influx of customers all at once. I don't remember as we've ever had a woman in jail here. Not in my time, anyhow. Even Elvira Hammell missed out. We're a group of law-abiding citizens for the most part. Even those gals at Fat Mary's."

Eli made a sound. "Yeah, well, I understand the Hammel woman got killed before anybody had a chance to lock her up. Are you suggesting Ruby ought to be executed?"

The inhalations of three men sucking air drew most of the oxygen from the room. After a moment, Squirt and Sam, without a word spoken between them, got up and walked out. Southbrook's mouth dropped open. His head turned as he looked first at January, then at Eli.

"Executed?" January spoke softly, aware her voice shook. "Is that what you think? Is that how you believe Elvira Hammel died?"

"Isn't it?"

She didn't even try to answer. "Tell me, Eli, what do you suppose we should do with Ruby? A thief, one complicit in robbery and murder. Not to mention luring men into committing crimes. Heinous crimes." Her voice was so tight it squeaked out the words. "Should we press charges here or turn her over to the U.S. Marshal's office? Or do you think maybe we should just deport her to South America? I hear that's popular among outlaws.

Or would you prefer I turn her loose? Those seem to be our choices. You choose."

"Missus Billings—" Southbrook started, then fell silent.

Eli's face turned red. "Damn it, January, she was married to my father. I can't—"

"Can't what?" Her lip curled. "Hold her responsible for her crimes? Why not? What kind of hold does she have over you? Or over your father? You told me once you hated her. Has something changed? Or was that the lie?" The questions tumbled one over the other. Her dark hazel eyes brimmed with tears and she blinked them away. "Choose."

"I can't choose." Eli almost shouted at her. "I'm not in charge here. It's not my decision. And I'm glad of it."

"You weren't in charge of the Elvira Hammel affair, either," she said then. "In plain fact, you weren't here and know nothing about it."

Sighing, she pushed herself up from the chair, holding onto the table for balance. Shoving her foot into the bloody boot, she pulled on her coat as she headed for the door.

"January!" Eli said, his right eyelid twitching.

She paused for a heartbeat, then went on without saying another word. Only closed the door on Ruby's wailing and left Eli staring after her.

A coldness settled over her. Anger, yes. But hurt, too. And a strange empty feeling, as if she'd lost her footing and was falling.

At the livery she saddled Hoot and rode out into the night. She needed her own bed, her dog, her home. Tomorrow was soon enough to deal with today's events. And with Eli Pasco.

# A LOOK AT: AULT'S HEIR

It's May, and the river is in flood. Mountain snow melt and torrential rain has plagued the area for a week. Knox Burdette witnesses a murderous attack on a neighbor and Anson Lowell can't let him escape. With no witness, the case falls apart. When one murder has been committed, a second comes at little cost, right? Especially when the witness is a no-account ranch hand. But William Ault lived long enough to press a letter onto Knox and beg him to deliver it to his attorney in Spokane. Knox, being an honest man, undertakes the task.

Knox is trying to escape the gang when a riverbank collapses under his horse. It is Tinker O'Keefe who discovers him clinging to a log. She effects a rescue of both man and horse and takes them in.

The gang, while searching for Knox, shows up at Tinker's house, making threats. The thing is, Tinker's home is a former brothel, and she is painted with the same brush. She hides Knox, and the next day they make their way to Spokane to meet with the attorney.

More surprises are in store, including to whom William Ault has bequeathed his ranch and the discovery of an independent witness to Ault's murder.

Even so, nothing will stop the murderer's urge to kill Knox and Tinker.

# ABOUT THE AUTHOR

C.K. Crigger was born and raised in North Idaho on the Coeur d'Alene Indian Reservation, and currently lives with her husband, three feisty little dogs and an uppity Persian cat in Spokane Valley, Washington.

Imbued with an abiding love of western traditions and wide-open spaces, Crigger writes of free-spirited people who break from their standard roles.

Her western novel, *The Woman Who Built a Bridge* was a 2019 Spur Award winner. Her short story, *Aldy Neal's Ghost*, was a 2007 Spur finalist. *Black Crossing* won the 2008 EPIC Award in the historical/western category. *Letter of the Law* was a 2009 Spur finalist in the audio category.